SECRETS OF THE PAST

JEAN WALKER

Enjoy the read
Jean Walker

© 2021 All rights reserved
Jean Walker

All people's names and some of the places used are purely fictitious, and the use of any person's name, living or dead, is purely coincidental.

Previous titles by this author:

Shattered Web of Lies
Echoes of Tragedy
Fortunes of Fate
Devious Dream Weaver
Red Kite Valley

PROLOGUE

Samuel Havers was in a foul mood that morning.

His horse, Sirius, had thrown him just over a week ago, and he'd hurt his leg badly. When the doctor had checked it, he said it was nothing more than a bad sprain and some bruising – a week or so of rest would soon have it back to normal – but Samuel didn't do rest! That seemed like a waste of time to him, and he'd carried on as normal.

His first visit to the stable two days later was to tell the groom to shoot the horse.

Davey, who'd tended Sirius since he first arrived, couldn't believe his ears when he heard the words. Sirius was only young and a bit high spirited. If his boss had wanted something quieter, he should have heeded his warning in the first place, and he protested vigorously.

'I'll take him out for a while and see if I can quieten him down for you if you like,' he implored.

Samuel glared at him.

'Did you not hear me?' his face suffusing with anger. 'I said shoot the bloody thing and get rid of it. I'll find a better horse!'

'But . . .,' he started to protest once again, but the look on Samuel's face and the drawing together of his brows warned him not to say anything further.

'**Do as I say, or get out!**' Samuel barked at him, as he turned on his heel and walked out.

He watched as Samuel limped away, before turning to look at the young and handsome horse. He went over and held a hand out towards him. Sirius tossed his head a couple of times and pranced around on his front feet, clearly unnerved by the altercation. As Davey murmured quietly and calmly to him, he began to settle down and came over to the groom, resting his silky muzzle into Davey's hand, and nuzzling with his soft lips to see if there might be some tasty morsel of food held there.

'Sorry boy,' he whispered quietly, gentling the horse and trying to keep him calm. 'You and me have something to do today – but I'm not going to be taking you out and shooting you – tha's for definite! I'll get you away from here and find you somewhere safe.'

He saw no further sign of Samuel that morning, and at lunchtime he took out his bike and cycled home to Millers farm, where he lived with his parents, four brothers and one sister.

'Dad,' he said after they'd eaten their lunch, 'can I ask a favour of you?'

'What is it lad?' Richard said, laying his newspaper to one side.

'I told you about Samuel Havers taking a tumble from his horse.'

'Yeh – I 'member,' his father said. 'I suppose thaa's made him more bad tempered than ever!'

Davey hung his head.

'He's told me to shoot the horse.'

'Wha'! A fine young animal like that! Din't he pay a lot of money for it?'

Davey nodded.

'Money doe'n' seem to matter to him – he's so puffed up with pride and self importance.'

Richard knew exactly what his son was talking about! His own land adjoined that of Samuel's and over the years he'd had several disputes with him over boundary issues. In the end, he'd installed a new track from the road to the farmhouse, putting in new hedges on his own side, making an indisputable boundary between his and Samuel's property. He'd also registered the track as being on his own land, and since then he'd heard nothing further from the man regarding boundaries; but knowing his nature, he was bound to find something else to make a dispute out of.

''ow can I help?' he asked of Davey.

'Can I bring Sirius up here? I been thinking, if we keep him in one of the fields on the far side of our land, i's in a bit of a hollow, and there's no way Samuel will ever know 'e's there. I can exercise him in the woods on the far side of the road where we won't be seen.'

'Le' me think on it,' his father said, lighting his pipe and puffing deeply.

'There isn' much time. I could do with getting him away today. Samuel's bound to come and make sure I've done it, and I'll ge' the sack if I 'aven't – then 'e'll probably shoot the horse himself and get it taken away by the knackers' yard.'

His father thought for a few seconds.

'Aye, we'll do it. Bring the 'orse here as soon as you can and we'll get him right over the far fields – right away from the man's prying eyes – but I only hope he doesn' find out. You do realise we could be accused of theft if 'e does?'

'I know,' he said, 'but you wouldn' want a beautiful animal like tha' to die, would you? He's only young. He'll calm right down in a couple of years, and he's already been gelded.'

'Yeh,' Richard replied. 'You go and get him and we'll 'ide him away before Samuel even knows he's gone.'

Luckily, when he got back, Samuel's car was missing, and there was no sign of anyone else around. His wife Mary rarely ventured out of the house. Everybody said she was going a bit funny these days, and she wasn't often seen.

Out of the six children they'd had, three had already died; two in infancy, and one at the age of 15. There were three still living at home, but Emily seemed to have disappeared recently, and nobody seemed to know where she'd gone. He'd heard she'd been seen around the village, but he wasn't sure if that was right or not.

Isaac, the youngest, was also absent a lot, and today his bike was missing from the lean-to alongside the stable where he always kept it. Good, that left Emma as the only person to worry about. She'd just finished school and she loved animals. At a loss with what to do in the future, she spent a lot of time in the grounds tending to the deer with their estate manager. If he bumped into her on his way and explained what was happening, he knew she'd say nothing. She often came down to the stables to see Sirius, bringing with her an apple or a carrot from the kitchen. Although she would have loved to ride

Sirius, Samuel forbade it. Davey thought that she was so gentle with the animal that she would have been the better person to tame him down rather than Samuel, and the horse liked her.

Sirius never seemed to cause him any problems either when he rode him. He thought that the problem was down to Samuel's pugnacious attitude, rather than to the horse's ill temper. The fall had probably been caused by the use of his crop, which he was prone to use quite harshly. Davey had often found wounds on Sirius that had been caused by that crop.

Saddling him up, he checked round quickly to make sure there was nobody watching before leading him out of the stable.

Samuel's car was still missing and Isaac's bike hadn't returned, so he quickly led the horse out and onto the track leading through the trees and down to the river. He mounted the horse when he was well away from the house, and turning to the left, he followed a well defined deer track through the trees and exited at the far side nearest the estate manager's cottage.

Urging the horse into a canter, he quickly cleared the open ground between there and the woodland at the farthest reaches of Samuel's land and entered the trees, slowing the horse to a walk when he was sure they could no longer be seen from the house.

At the far side of the wood was a gate, long disused, that opened directly onto the road, where he could reach his fathers' farm down the new track he'd created just a short way further on.

The only danger now was the road! If Samuel happened to arrive back while he was covering the short distance to reach the track, he'd be able to see them, and he'd know where Davey was taking Sirius. Then there'd be hell to pay!

Dismounting, he pulled the gate back on its rusty hinges, having to hack back the overgrowth of weeds and nettles surrounding it, before he could manage to open it enough for them to get through.

The road was quiet. Not a single vehicle in sight.

Quickly remounting, he urged the animal through the gate, and set him into a canter once more, managing to enter the track without seeing anybody. He'd left the gate open, but there was no way he was stopping to shut it! He'd go back and do that another day.

Tomorrow would be taken up with disturbing the earth somewhere in the wooded area he'd just left. Samuel would more than likely want to know where he'd buried the horse, and would undoubtedly go and check for himself; he was that sort of man!

Ultimately, Samuel never did buy another horse, and Davey, with no more horses to tend, was sacked and the stables left to their own devices.

With no horse to ride any more, Samuel had taken to walking his Neapolitan Mastiff, Jupiter, through the woods and round the grounds on the occasions when the weather was fine. He never went out in bad weather, except by car, and that usually only to work and back.

The very large animal spent most of his life in the open-fronted kennel Samuel had had built for him in the yard at the back of the house. He was never allowed inside the house, and the only person who tended to him was Davey, who'd taken the responsibility of feeding and cleaning the animals' quarters on himself.

It was a couple of days after Davey had been sacked that Emma realised nobody had been feeding the dog, and went to see to him herself.

It was a sorry sight that greeted her!

He slept on straw, and there wasn't much left of that – it was scattered all over the enclosure, and was foul with urine and excrement. Both his food and water bowls were totally empty and upside down.

Quickly she'd set to and cleaned the place up, before going to the stable and bringing back food and water for him, berating her father for his treatment of the dog when he returned from work that evening.

He said nothing, but she soon began to see that he was in no mood to hear her words. Suddenly, he reached forward, and with no word of warning, he side-swiped her across the face with the back of his hand.

'How dare you speak to me like that! I won't be spoken to like that in my own home!' he bellowed as she ran from the room.

From then on, she kept out of his way, and took the job of looking after the dog on herself, asking the housekeeper to order food for the animal with the weekly grocery order.

The dog was too large and boisterous for her to walk, but luckily Samuel usually took him out when he was home at the weekends, and he at least got some exercise.

She'd taken to keeping out of the house after that when he was home, and she'd found a willing ally in Denzil Farmer, the estate manager.

Part of his job was to look after the herd of deer that Samuel's father had introduced to the estate when he'd owned nearly 500 acres of land, most of which Samuel had sold off or rented out after his fathers' death.

He introduced her to the herd, some of which were very tame and would come to his call, where she was able to feed them by hand. He also showed her where the kingfisher nested, watching the flash of iridescent blue as it flashed across their line of vision and dived into the rippling water, and where the tawny owl nested. He showed her the red squirrels chasing round the upper branches of the trees and where he'd put up peanut feeders for them, and also the big badger sets under the old oaks.

She loved being out with him and learning how much wildlife there was on the estate. During the whole of her life, she'd never dreamt there was so much going on in the grounds: but then, she'd spent a lot of her time away from home at school, and hadn't had much of a chance to explore the grounds except in school holidays.

Today, striding through the woods with the dog, Samuel heard the sound of voices coming from somewhere up ahead and over towards the river bank.

As he came nearer, he heard the sound of female giggling, followed by the quiet and hushed sounds of a male voice. The giggling stopped and after a few moments, he heard the sound of quiet conversation between the two voices.

Reaching the spot where he thought they were, he made his way through the trees and out towards the riverbank, peering through the trees to see exactly where the voices were coming from.

Suddenly, they came into clear view and he recognised his daughter Emma, together with that of Denzil Farmer, his estate manager.

They were sitting side by side on the bank, heads close together, and talking in quiet and hushed tones.

Samuel, jumping to conclusions, was incensed!

Emma, barely seventeen years old was talking intimately with a man old enough to be her father. His immediate thoughts were that the man was grooming her! He wasn't thinking of her so much as his daughter, but as one of his personal possessions – something the man was trying to take from him and make a laughing stock out of him. He certainly wasn't going to tolerate that happening, and with a mere employee! It would be all around the village in no time.

Dropping the dog's lead, he strode out of the trees, brandishing the stout walking stick he was carrying.

'What the hell is going on here?' he shouted loudly. 'What the hell do you think you're doing?'

Emma jumped hurriedly to her feet.

'Dad,' she protested; real fear in her eyes, 'we were only examining some otter prints that Denzil's found on the river bank. He was showing me how to recognise their spraint.'

'Don't give me that! I could see for myself what was going on,' and with that he raised his stick to hit her a glancing blow across the top of her arm.

Denzil had already scrambled to his feet. He wasn't scared of Samuel, but he was scared of losing his job. He lived in a cottage owned by the man, with a wife and three children relying on him. If he was sacked, they'd have nowhere else to go, and no money to live on.

'Sir, please let me explain!' he protested. 'It's as Emma says – we were just looking for otter tracks.

Samuel gave him a withering look, and then turned back to the whimpering Emma, who was rubbing her arm where it was throbbing from the thump he'd just given it.

'Get back to the house!' he ordered her, his face red with fury.

As she turned away, he fetched her another heavy blow across the buttocks with the stick, and raised it once again to repeat the action – but it was never carried out.

Denzil couldn't see her take another blow. His own temper roused now – it was more than he was willing to stomach. He grabbed the stick while it was still in mid air and tried to wrestle it from Samuel.

He thought he'd succeeded for the moment, but then Samuel, still in a state of fury, seemed to gather up all his strength. Still holding the stick in his right hand, he put his left up to Denzil's chest and gave him a mighty push backwards.

Taken unawares, Denzil let go of the stick and staggered backwards. He was standing very near to the river bank, and his feet began to slip in the soft muddy ground. Arms flailing wildly, he toppled backwards and hit the water with an almighty splash, water cascading many feet up into the air.

By the time he managed to reach the bank and haul himself out, Samuel and Emma were almost out of sight; heading back towards the house, her father holding her arm in a vice-like grip.

Helpless to do anything more for her, he took himself off home to get changed and dried – their sandwiches left sitting on the bank and unfinished.

It was two days later that he received a formal letter from Samuel.

He'd been sacked; and he was to vacate the cottage within two weeks. The reason being given was his inappropriate association with the family's teenage daughter.

CHAPTER ONE

Riley Duncan heard the letters clatter through the letterbox and drop onto the mat as he passed the top of the stairs.

Leaning over the banisters and looking down, Connie, his wife was already picking them up.

'Anything interesting?' he called down.

'The usual junk mail,' she answered absentmindedly.

She seemed to be giving particular attention to a long white window envelope, turning it over and looking at the back.

'What is it?' he asked.

'It's for you,' she answered. 'It's from a solicitor.'

'A solicitor? Why would a solicitor be writing to me?'

'How should I know,' she answered. 'If you come down you can find out for yourself. Your breakfast's ready anyway.'

When he came down, the letter was alongside his plate of porridge, and he slit it open whilst waiting for it to cool.

Connie was already sitting opposite him and eating her toast; two slices with butter and marmalade every morning for as long as he could remember.

He read through the letter, re-reading it to make sure he'd got it right.

'Well?' she asked, standing up to pour the tea.

'Seems I've inherited something from somebody I've never even heard of. They want me to make an appointment to see them.'

She was showing an interest now.

'What is it?' she asked, just stopping herself from pouring tea on the table.

'Doesn't say,' he replied, turning the letter over to see if there was any further information on the other side before handing it across for her to read.

Reaching for the sugar to put on his porridge he said, 'Knowing my luck, it'll only be a few pounds, whoever it's from!'

'Isaac Havers,' she announced, rolling the name off her tongue as she read it through again, looking blank. 'I've never heard of him either!'

'Told you, didn't I? It's Saturday, so we won't be able to find out until Monday when the solicitor's open again. I'll ring them after I finish at lunchtime. I've no afternoon appointments.'

Anxious to find out what it was all about, he dropped off his last pupil of the day on Monday and rang the solicitor from a convenient pull-in along a quiet residential road.

Riley was a driving instructor, and, within reason, could be quite free and easy with his working hours.

A woman's friendly voice answered the 'phone after only two rings. She asked for the reference number on the letter, and then looked in her diary for a convenient date and time for his appointment.

'Mr. Mansell is free on Thursday morning at eleven o'clock,' she answered.

He quickly rifled through his appointments book and checked Thursday morning. He had one booking at 9a.m., but it was only for an hour. He could easily manage to make that time. It would still give him time to go home and change, and perhaps have a cup of coffee before going to see the solicitor.

His next appointment wasn't until 2p.m. That would give him plenty of time to hear what he had to say.

Connie was intrigued when he arrived home.

'Didn't you find out anything more?' she asked.

'No, I only spoke to the receptionist. She just made the appointment for Thursday. She probably didn't know anything more about the business than we do.'

He arrived at Mr. Mansell's office with plenty of time to spare. He was kept waiting for ten minutes, as the solicitor still had another client with him, watching the man leave as he passed the opaque glass in the waiting room door.

Several minutes later, the glass partition between him and the receptionist opened suddenly, and her head appeared.

'Mr Mansell will see you now. Just go straight up the stairs and he'll meet you at the top,' she announced, smiling.

'Thank you,' he said, standing up and making for the stairs, straightening his tie as he went. It was quite some time since he'd worn one, and he found it rather uncomfortable.

Mr Mansell was standing in the open doorway to his office and shook hands as they entered, pulling out a chair for Riley to sit on, and seating himself in the leather one on the opposite side of the desk.

'I expect you're wondering what this is all about,' he stated, as he pushed together the papers in front of him.

Riley nodded. He felt rather in awe of this tall, grey-haired man, with a very erect posture and serious manner.

'Do you know who Isaac Havers is, or should I say; was?' was the first question he asked.

'I've no idea!' Riley replied, perplexed by the strange name being thrown at him.

The man smiled.

'This must all be a complete surprise to you,' he continued.

'Yes, it is.'

'Firstly, I'll give you this,' he said, lifting a folded sheet of paper from those in front of him and sliding it across the desk. 'Once you get home, it'll make things clearer when you've had the chance to study it.'

Riley picked it up and unfolded it. It was a Family Tree, but before he had a chance to give it more than a cursory glance, the solicitor continued speaking, and he put it down on the desk in front of him for the time being.

'Isaac Havers was the younger brother of your grandmother on your fathers' side. He left England when he was in his 20's and moved to New Zealand, where I believe he owned property, a sheep station, in partnership with another man.

When he died last year, that property reverted entirely to his partner, under an agreement that was drawn up at the inception of the partnership. However, what Isaac seems to have overlooked is that there was another property in England: namely the property known as Havergill, where he was brought up as a child.

His father, Samuel, your great-great-grandfather, was the Chief Executive Officer of a bank in Liverpool, owned and founded by his father before him. When he died, Samuel, as the eldest son, inherited everything, including the house known as Havergill.

Samuel had already married, and he and your great great grandmother, Mary, moved into the house, where they had six children.

When Samuel died in 1977, his sons, Robert, Stanley and Bernard had already predeceased him; the first two in infancy, and the third at the age of fifteen.

That left Emma as the next in line to inherit, but no sign of her existence could be found after her christening at the age of 2. There appear to be no marriage or death records for her, even though an exhaustive search was carried out by his solicitors, which produced no results. Eventually they had her declared dead, and the ownership of the house reverted to your grandmother, Emily, but she too had died shortly after her father. That left Isaac as the sole beneficiary.

As this firm, under the auspices of my father at that time, had always been solicitors to Samuel, we were asked to manage the sale of the property, as Isaac didn't wish to return to England.

We put its management, and eventual sale, into the hands of an estate agent, and they've been taking care of it ever since.

Riley was amazed, hardly able to take it all in.

'And where do I come into all this?' he asked eventually.

'That family tree we've had made up should explain everything more clearly,' Mr. Mansell said, indicating the sheet of paper in front of him, 'but basically, you're the new owner of Havergill!'

Seeing his dazed expression, the solicitor gave him a few moments to take it all in, before going on to explain a little further.

'Isaac never married, and when he died, the property passed to his only living heir, your father, the son of his deceased sister Emily. Unfortunately, he too was deceased, so that leaves you as Isaac's only living direct descendant.'

He'd never known Emily, as she'd died before he was born, but he vaguely remembered his grandfather, Emily's husband. He'd died when Riley was only 10 and he'd only ever seen a rather grainy photograph of Emily taken many years before.

His own father had also died from a stroke when Riley was only 2. Fit and healthy when he went to work in the morning, in hospital by the afternoon, and dead before the night was over.

His mother, Anne, had never re-married. She'd had the odd date during his childhood, when his grandfather had come to look after him while she was out, but they'd never come to anything.

She also took a part-time job in a small general shop when he was young, and had gone back to work in the Telecommunications industry when he reached the age of 13. After her short foray with men and dating, she had now taken up almost completely with a small circle of unmarried or divorced women friends, and men didn't seem to enter her life very much at all nowadays.

His life had often been lonely, and he'd always longed to have brothers and sisters, as his friends always seemed to have. Even though they did squabble often, even that was better than being shut in his bedroom for hours on end reading or sitting watching television with his mother.

She was often clingy and her over-fussy ministrations made him irritable at times, when she would rant at him for being an ungrateful child, and leave the room in floods of tears. He didn't mean to be irritable, but he couldn't bear her constant fussing over him.

Even when he was outside playing with other children, she was always calling him in and stopping their game. It got so bad that he hid when he saw her coming out to look for him, and the other children swore blind they didn't know where he was; often giggling and calling him a mummy's boy afterwards.

'If you look through the family tree I've given you, you'll see how everything fits together,' Mansell's voice brought him back to the present as he withdrew a bulky envelope from the pile and pushed it across the desk.

'There are the keys to the property, together with the Title Deeds, and the rest of the papers we've received from his solicitors. All I need from you now is your signature on the necessary documents. You will, of course, need to re-register it on Land Registry; that's if it has ever **has** been registered before, but either way, that should present no problem. We can also handle that for you if you'd like us to, but there will be a small fee for our services.'

Riley signed the papers he handed over after he'd given them a cursory look through. His mind was still trying to get round it all, as the solicitor stood up to shake his hand, signalling that their time together was over.

'There will, of course, be little money, if any, left from Mr. Havers' personal estate, as most of that has been swallowed up by management fees of the property over the years, but there is enough left to cover ours and his own solicitors fees,' was his parting shot as Riley left the office.

He was in a daze as he drove home, and Connie was anxiously awaiting his return. He hadn't been with the solicitor for more than thirty minutes, so had plenty of time before his next lesson was due. Connie put a couple of meat pies in the oven while they spread the papers on the kitchen table before going through them.

There seemed to be quite a lot of old papers, going back many years, but little of interest for the time being, apart from the pamphlet from the estate agents' office. It gave details of the house and a rough hand drawn sketch of the grounds; the price being given merely as 'OFFERS'.

It also stated that the house was for sale with 20 acres of grounds, although tenancy agreements were in place for 10 of those acres, which would have to be honoured. The house itself comprised 2 acres, including the land the house stood on, and stating it was in need of complete renovation.

Most interesting of all was the Family Tree, which explained much of what they needed to know.

Starting from his great grandfather, Samuel, who had initially inherited the house named Havergill, and Mary, his wife, it followed down to their six children.

Riley pointed out their daughter Emma, explaining to Connie how she seemed to have mysteriously disappeared at some point after the age of 2, and nobody had been able to trace any sign of her since.

Calculating quickly in her head, Connie said, 'Surely she must be dead. She'll be nearly 80 now if she's still alive.'

'It would seem so, but they haven't been able to find any records for her either. No marriage or death certificate, and she doesn't feature on the 1939 census either. There are no other sorts of record either, so maybe she is still alive, although the solicitors have had her officially declared dead now. They've been searching for her since her father died in 1977.'

Then he pointed out his grandmother, Emily, showing how she'd died before he was born, and reminiscing about his kindly grandfather, George, Emily's husband.

He told her about trips to his allotment at the weekends when he was home from school and collecting manure on a handcart from a local stable, trundling it back through the streets and piling it onto the manure heap; sadly reminiscing how he'd died when Riley was only 10. He never knew how, or exactly when, he'd died. The first he'd heard was when his mother told him he was staying with her friend while she went to the funeral.

When they sorted through the documents, they found they contained a copy of the letter from Isaac's solicitors in New Zealand, and their own solicitor's reply, as well as the title deeds to the property, but no information relating to Isaac himself.

FAMILY TREE

Jacob Havers
1870-1928

/

Samuel - Mary
1895 –   1900 -
1977   1978

/

Robert	Stanley	Bernard	Emma	Emily	Isaac
1920-21	1922-24	1925-40	1930- ?	1933-76	1936-2008

/

David - Anne
1953-82   1956
        Still living

/

Riley - Constance
1980   1984
Still living Still living

They'd been married for a good few years now, and Connie had never known any of his relatives on his fathers' side; but then, apart from his grandfather, Riley had never known any of them either, since his father, David, had died when he was so young.

His grandfather had once told him that his father had a brother, but what had happened to him Riley never knew, and his mother had never kept in touch with his fathers' family. Once his grandfather had died, she'd never mentioned them – not that they'd ever shown any interest in him either.

He and his mother had lived in an annexe at the side of her parents' home, and he'd spent most of his time with them while she was at work. He'd only ever known that side of the family.

He and Connie ate their lunch before he had to leave to pick up his next pupil, still talking about their new possession.

'Did you notice where the property is?' she asked.

'No, I didn't think about that. All I know is that it's called Havergill, and the address is in Havergill Lane.'

She picked up the paper and scanned through it again.

'It's in Wales,' she declared, 'in a village called Ll . . . !! Ll . . .'

Her voice tailed off, unable to pronounce the word.

'I'll let you work that one out!' she finally said, tossing the letter across to him.

He tried several pronunciations himself, before he too gave up, and left her to it, still trying to get her head round the word.

As he climbed into his car, she popped her head round the front door.

'Why don't we have a day out at the weekend and go and find it? It might make a nice trip out and we can find a little pub for a meal.'

'Make it Saturday,' he called back. 'I have five driving lessons booked on Sunday.'

Saturday arrived as a misty and foggy morning, but as the day progressed, the mist began to lift and the sun broke through.

Riley only had one lesson that day, between 9.00 and 10a.m. Keen to go and visit his new property, he had deliberately cried off any new appointments, saying he was booked solid the whole day.

Connie was ready when he arrived back. After a quick change of clothes into a short sleeved shirt and jeans; he was ready to start their journey.

He programmed the navigator and they began the journey to find their new inheritance, as he liked to think of it, following the proscribed route into Wales.

They hadn't been going for more than ten miles before the navigator announced a road closure and advised an alternative route.

'Take the next turning left,' was the message it gave out.

Following the instruction, he found himself in a country lane with just enough room for two cars to pass comfortably.

On the left hand side, just as they rounded the corner, was the entrance to a farm track, where they could just make out buildings set far back off the road. On the right hand side was a set of green metal railings flanking a small embankment, on top of which was what looked like a disused railway track.

'I hope this is right,' Riley said, glancing quickly down at the small screen.

It wouldn't be the first time a navigator had put him on the wrong road, necessitating a long detour to get back to his original route.

Connie glanced across at the display.

'Yes, it is,' she answered, 'I can see where it joins back up with the road we've come off.'

He continued along the lane, open fields stretching to their left as far as the eye could see; the railway line still flanking them to the right.

After perhaps a mile or so, the lane began to dip downwards, and although the railway stayed to their right, the embankment began to rise higher above them until it was way above their heads.

At this point, the lane began a slow curve to the right, the embankment still following them, but beginning its own turn to the left, effectively cutting across their path.

'Looks like we're coming to a bridge,' Riley observed, as they rounded the bend, where one side of an arched stone bridge was just coming into sight.

Suddenly he applied his brakes sharply and they both lurched forward; their seat belts preventing them coming to any serious harm.

They'd nearly reached the bottom of the dip, and the bridge had now come into full view; a white van wedged firmly below the arched span. Even though he'd tried to go through at the highest point in the centre, the top of the vehicle had been peeled back like a tin can, and the driver was lying hunched over the steering wheel.

Connie, a trained nurse, was out of the car almost before it had stopped and was running towards him.

Riley, knowing how close he was to the bend, and knowing another driver following would be unsighted until the last minute, went round to the boot and lifted out a warning triangle, preparing to go back and erect it in the road behind them.

Before he was able to shut the boot lid, another vehicle appeared round the bend, swerving wildly to one side as he suddenly saw Riley's vehicle slewed across the middle of the road, and Riley standing behind it.

It was too little and far too late.

The lane was too narrow to permit any sort of evasive action, and as he swerved across to the left, his right front wing caught Riley's car a glancing blow on the left hand corner.

Riley's car was thrown towards the left, taking Riley with it, the boot lid coming down heavily on his head, and his body hitting the side of the still moving car, before being thrown backwards. His head hit his own car once again as he went down, his body skidding across the tarmac towards the embankment railings.

He came to rest in an untidy heap, the impact with the railings knocking the breath out of him.

Connie, hearing the sound of rending metal, was already running back.

It seemed the driver of the van was unhurt; his collapsed position over the steering wheel of the vehicle was more in despair than anything else. This was the third crash he'd had this year, and the company were bound to sack him this time. With a wife and three children at home, the situation looked bleak for the future.

The driver of the silver coupé was unhurt save for a few minor cuts and bruises, and was climbing out of his car when Connie reached him, but there was no sign of Riley.

She looked round in terror, fearing he might be underneath one of the vehicles.

'He's over there,' the other driver gasped, holding a rag against his bleeding head and pointing in Riley's direction.

'Is he dead?' he gasped, as Connie reached his side. 'Have I killed him?'

This was the first time she'd noticed Riley and she ran towards him, before carrying out all the necessary routine checks; trying to stay calm and collected. Difficult when it was your own husband!

His left leg was lying at an angle, and she realised immediately that the main bone in his leg, the femur, was broken just above the knee. His trouser leg was ripped and the bone was poking out through the flesh. His foot was also lying in the opposite direction to his leg, indicating that the ankle too was broken.

His left arm was hanging uselessly down onto the road, and she realised that had been almost torn off in the impact. Surgery would sew that together again if it wasn't too badly damaged, but whether he would regain full use of it would depend on how badly affected the nerves and tendons had been. When she examined the shoulder, it seemed to be dislocated rather than broken, but that too would need to be properly assessed in hospital.

There seemed every chance he might lose the arm.

But worst of all was his head!

The boot lid had hit him a glancing blow on the right hand side of his temple, with a deep indentation following towards the top of his head. Blood was pouring down his face and onto his chest; his right eye ballooned with blood and completely closed; the deep cut to the top and back of his head also oozing blood.

The prognosis wasn't good for his future! That's if he ever did recover from his horrific injuries! Most of them would mend, but it was the damage to his brain that was the most worrying. Would he survive that? And if he did, would he ever be the same again?

The other driver, at her shouted command, had come out of his state of torpor, and was already ringing for an ambulance, before slumping down by the side of his car and sitting staring across at the scene before him.

He'd been trying to eject the disc from his cd player, where it appeared to have become stuck, and failed to keep his eye on the road ahead of him; only catching sight of the stationary vehicle in front of him as he rounded the bend.

By then it was far too late to do anything about the situation!

CHAPTER TWO

'Riley . . . Mr. Duncan . . . Are you back with us? Open your eyes.'

He heard sounds all around him; the murmur of hushed voices; the rustle of clothing near at hand; something being moved near his right ear.

He tried to open his eyes, but they were immediately filled with bright light and he closed them quickly again. They felt sticky; as if they'd been closed for a long time.

'Mr. Duncan . . . Riley . . . Can you hear me? Open your eyes,' the woman's voice said from alongside him.

He tried again, and this time the light had been moved; it was no longer shining into his eyes.

'I see you've decided to come back to us, have you?' the voice said.

It was the face of a young woman, and she was leaning towards him, a smile on her face. She seemed to have some sort of an accent in her voice. Was it American? No, it was slightly different. When she spoke again, he realised it wasn't American, it was Canadian. Her tone was kindly and welcoming, as if she were glad to see he was awake once more.

'It's been a long time – I'm glad to see you back with us again. Are you feeling all right?'

He tried to speak, but the words wouldn't form, and all he heard was a weak croak.

He didn't know how he was feeling – he couldn't feel anything at the moment. He still wasn't properly back in the real world yet.

She leaned over and wiped his eyes and then his mouth with something moist and slightly scented.

'Does that feel better?' she asked.

He managed a slight nod as he savoured the wetness on his lips. They felt dry and cracked, and he desperately wanted a drink.

'Dr ... nk!' he managed, 'dr ...nk!'

She seemed to understand and proffered a sponge dipped in water, letting it trickle into his mouth. It wasn't enough – he desperately wanted more; but one more sponge was all she offered for the time being.

'You can have a proper drink later when you're more awake and the doctor's been to see you. In the meantime, get some rest,' and she left his side.

The water had refreshed him, however little it had been, and feeling better, he screwed up his eyes to look around.

He was in a hospital ward with other people all around him. Some were walking around; others were propped up in bed as he was; and some had their eyes closed as he had previously. All seemed to be in various stages of recovery.

After a few more minutes looking around, tiredness overwhelmed him and he slept once more. He was awoken by a deep male voice beside him.

'Mr. Duncan . . . are you awake?'

He opened his eyes and found himself looking into the face of a very dark skinned and thick set Indian doctor, sporting a bristling black moustache. The woman accompanying him was the same nurse he'd seen previously.

The doctor sat down on the edge of the bed, and looked through the notes he held on a clipboard, lifting it and holding it to his chest before he spoke again.

'You're very lucky to be alive after what you've been through, but I'm glad to see you're on the mend once more. It shouldn't be long before we can get you home again once you start getting out of bed and moving around.'

'My wife – is she okay?' he managed to croak, memories of their ordeal flooding back.

The doctor looked up at the nurse, not aware of the previous circumstances surrounding his patient. It was his job to mend, not to commiserate. She took her cue.

'Yes, she's fine. She's been in every day to see you while you've been in intensive care, but I'm afraid she's spent most of the time just holding your hand and talking to you. We've kept you sedated to allow your injuries to heal – but hopefully that's all behind you. You've been transferred to a normal ward now. You seem to be well on the mend and I'm sure she'll be glad to find you awake when she does arrive.'

While she was talking, the doctor had retreated to the bed of his next patient, where he was looking through his notes and waiting for her to join him.

'I'll be back with a drink for you when doctor's finished his rounds,' she said quietly, before hurrying over to join her colleague. She knew he could be an impatient man and didn't like to be kept waiting.

Riley lay back on the pillows and stared up at the ceiling, until he heard a voice near his side.

'Good to see you back with us again,' it said.

He looked across at the next bed.

A middle-aged man, clad in very gaudy tartan pyjamas sat on the edge of it, his head swathed in bandages.

'Wha' happened to you?' he said, and without waiting for a reply he continued, 'I fell off me ladder when I were painting the 'ouse. Bashed all the back of me 'ead. Been in 'ere a week now, but I'm goin' 'ome tomerra. 'E's just told me I can go. Gotta' ring the wife and get 'er to pick me up in the mornin',' and without saying anything further, he shrugged into his equally gaudy dressing gown of purple and yellow swirls before shuffling off down the ward.

Riley was glad of that. He wasn't in the mood for conversation, and he hadn't particularly taken to the man. He'd be glad not to have to spend time in his company any more than was necessary.

An hour later the tea lady arrived, a chatty soul in a wrap around apron who had time to chat to everyone she served.

''Ello love,' she said when she arrived at his bed. 'Glad to see you awake. Nurse said you can 'ave a drink today. Would you like a cuppa' tea?'

He nodded, and she poured one into a plastic beaker, putting a top on so that he could drink without spilling it.

'I've put plenty of milk in it to cool it down. I'll come back and 'elp you with it when I've served the others. It should be cool enough for you by then.'

She was true to her word, and although Riley usually liked his tea strong and hot, without much milk in it, he enjoyed it immensely, even though it **was** very milky and only tepid now. He was extremely glad of her help. He still felt very weak and didn't even think he'd have been able to lift the cup to his lips.

Connie arrived shortly after lunch, where he'd been allowed a small amount of soup and some stewed apple, which he'd enjoyed, although he wasn't able to manage very much.

She was overjoyed to find him awake; a grin spreading across his face as she walked towards the bed.

Kissing him lightly on the cheek, she pulled up the visitors' chair and sat alongside, taking his good hand in both of hers. The other arm, healing well now after several operations, was still bandaged from shoulder to elbow. They'd told him that it should function fairly normally after physiotherapy treatment, but only if he kept on exercising it after his discharge.

'How are you feeling?' Connie asked.

'Much better,' he answered. 'Have they said when I can go home yet?'

She laughed.

'Do you realise how long you've been here? Just look out of the window!'

For the first time he looked towards it and couldn't believe his eyes at what he saw; instead of the last warm days of summer they'd been enjoying, the trees in the hospital grounds were almost bare of leaves, with just a few withered and yellowed specimens remaining.

'What date is it?' he asked, incredulously. 'How long have I been here?'

'It's November, and we had the first frost of the winter last night. You've been here two months now.'

'What?!!!' he gasped, unable to believe it. 'What's happened to me? Why have I been here this long?'

'Well, amongst all the other cuts and grazes, you fractured your leg and ankle; and almost tore your arm off, as well as sustaining a fractured skull. They've had to insert metal plates to hold everything together.'

He remembered seeing a van stuck underneath a low bridge, and Connie going to help the driver whilst he'd gone to get out the warning triangles. There was a gap in his memory after that, but he remembered they'd finished their journey to Havergill and looked around the whole place – a large stone built house covered in Virginia Creeper. There'd been an old bridge over a river, and Connie had almost fallen in when the bridge broke up beneath them – and he remembered hearing the soft strains of a violin coming from somewhere near the house as they walked back.

The next memory was of finding a pub and having a delicious roast dinner before they returned home.

Had they had an accident after that? It must have been on their way home after the meal.

'Just when do you think I'll be able to go home?' he asked, anxious to return to normality once again.

She laughed.

'Have you tried getting out of bed yet?'

He shook his head.

'Not yet, but I'm ready to give it a go.'

Putting her hand on his arm, she became serious.

'It won't be easy. You've been in bed for so long you'll feel very weak and dizzy when you first try. They'll make you sit on the side of the bed first before you even try to stand. You'll be surprised at how weak you feel, and standing up for more than a few seconds will be difficult; besides which, you'll be on crutches for some time yet. You'll only be able to use one because of your arm, so that'll be even more difficult. You're going to have to be patient and take everything slowly at first.'

He looked across at her anxiously.

'What about you? Are you all right? The last thing I remember was a meal at a pub – I don't remember what happened after that.'

'Pub?' she said, wondering if she was the one who was confused.

'I mean after we'd visited Havergill. Don't you remember finding that pub and having lunch there? Did we have an accident on the way home?'

Now they were both confused.

'Riley,' she said finally after a few seconds pause; a resigned tone in her voice, 'we've never been to Havergill – we never got there. You had your accident, and you've been here ever since.'

He gazed at her; a frown crossing his face.

'Yes we did. We looked round the house and we explored the grounds. You almost fell in the river when the bridge collapsed. Don't you remember?'

'Riley, calm down,' she said. He was becoming agitated and starting to gabble as she realised that what he thought was reality had just been a dream during his long period of unconsciousness, 'I'm telling you the truth. We never did reach Havergill – we never ever made it! You had your accident on the way there and whatever you remember; you must have dreamt it all.'

He looked at her incredulously.

'You mean you didn't almost fall in the river?'

She shook her head.

'No, none of its real – you must have imagined it all in a dream.'

When she'd gone, he lay back on the pillows and thought about it. Could it really all have been a dream when it had seemed so real? He'd had dreams frequently in the past, but he'd never experienced anything that real or convincing in the whole of his life before. Could it have been down to the drugs they'd been pumping him full of?

If it had been a dream, how could he have known what Havergill looked like? There'd been no picture on the estate agents' brochure, and the sketch of the grounds had only been hand-drawn, not in any detail, and certainly not to scale.

Could he really have dreamt it all?

CHAPTER 3

The time finally arrived for him to leave hospital, and he 'phoned Connie to pick him up after the doctor had completed his rounds and declared him fit for discharge.

He'd made friends with another man of around his own age while he'd been in there, and they'd got on well together; finding an affinity of friendship that sometimes happens only once or twice in a lifetime.

Martin Jennings was a builder, with his own small company, and he'd fallen from some scaffolding whilst he'd been inspecting work done by a sub-contractor. One of his own men had informed him that he thought the work was rather shoddy, and he'd gone up to look for himself, stepping back rather too far to make the inspection. Luckily he'd landed on some bags of sand which had just been delivered and they'd broken his fall; but unluckily his leg had buckled under him on landing, and he'd broken it. It had been pinned, and he had a metal framework attached to it, leaving him unable to move from his bed.

He'd arrived while Riley had been in the process of getting back on his feet, and Riley had made it his business to fetch and carry for Martin; helping with his own rehabilitation and exercise at the same time.

They'd got on really well during Riley's final week there when Martin had been admitted, and had swapped 'phone numbers and addresses before Connie took him home.

'We'll go out for a drink together when I'm back on my feet again,' Martin said, shaking his hand vigorously as he prepared to leave.

'Yes, I'll look forward to that,' Riley grinned, as he made his way out of the ward.

He'd graduated from the crutch to a walking stick now, and was getting used to using just the one, as he had with the single crutch he'd only been able to manage previously.

Betty, their next door neighbour, was brushing her front path when they arrived and she stopped what she was doing to welcome him back.

'I've made a nice fruit cake. I'll pass some in for you to have with a cuppa' later,' she said, as Connie opened the front door.

'Come in and have some with us,' Riley said, 'I'll be glad of someone to talk to.'

'Right you are!' she agreed.

'Make it two thirty,' he said, looking to Connie for confirmation.

She nodded as they went inside. It wasn't what she'd envisaged after their long separation. She wanted some time to themselves – time to relax and chat quietly – time to savour the fact that she wouldn't have to drive to Wales every day after work and sit for two hours by his bedside while he was totally out of it, then endure the long drive back before she finally had the time to relax. She was feeling the strain herself, and just wanted some peace and quiet for the time being.

It was just after Christmas that Riley received a 'phone call from Martin.

'I got out in time to enjoy Christmas,' he told him, still seeming full of good cheer. 'We had a houseful with the kids and various friends and acquaintances calling. They all mucked in though, and didn't leave Kate to do everything herself, although I wasn't much good at helping out. I still had the metal framework attached, and was still using two sticks to get around, but they're all gone now. How did your Christmas go?'

This was the one time of the year when Riley always regretted that they'd never had children. It would have been so nice to have a crowd around them over the holiday, but instead, it had been just the two of them, as it was over four years since Connie's parents had died.

Connie had a sister, Tilda, but she lived in Scotland with her husband and four children. He worked on the oil rigs, and all that passed between them at the festive season was a card and a seasonal 'phone call on Boxing Day.

She also had an older brother. They never saw him either as he was a career soldier, unmarried, and mostly serving abroad.

His own mother, although still alive, always spent Christmas with her widowed sister; of which he was glad. Being as possessive of him as she'd always been, she'd never accepted Connie when she realised that they intended to marry, and had shunned any sort of association with her during the whole of their marriage. On the occasions when they did meet, she said very little to her, and kept as much distance between them as possible.

When he did pay his mother a visit, it was always alone and usually only on birthdays or Mother's Day; duty visits as he always called them. Instead of bringing them closer together, her possessiveness had only served to drive them further apart. Luckily, she was a devout churchgoer, and her church activities kept her busy most of the time, so she hardly ever bothered him these days.

He was surprised to find that Connie had taken a job while he was in hospital, but as she explained, without his wage coming in, she was worried about money becoming tight. They still had money in the bank, but she was beginning to eat into it while he was in hospital.

Today, Connie was back at work again, and he was alone until she returned at lunchtime. He was glad of the half hour chat with Martin.

Whilst in hospital, he'd told Martin about his inheritance of Havergill, and, being a builder, Martin had taken an interest at once. Now, he brought the subject up again.

'Have you been out to see your new property yet?' he asked.

'No, not yet,' Riley replied. 'When the weather improves we'll probably go and see it.'

He'd rather gone off the idea since his stay in hospital. It looked like it was going to be a white elephant now, and not the elegant country house he'd expected to find. He'd come to accept the fact that they'd never be able to afford to live there – and Connie was opposed to the idea anyway.

'I'll take a look if you like,' Martin volunteered now. 'I haven't been able to work yet, and the boys have been laid off over Christmas, but they're hoping to get back to it when the weather improves. We're building two new houses on a piece of ground we acquired from a farmer, and it's not too far from there. I want to go and have a look at them, so I could go and take a look at yours while I'm down that way if you want me to.'

'I still want to go myself,' he replied, 'but I'd be only too glad if you'd cast an expert eye over it as well; perhaps with an eye as to a rough idea of how much it would cost to renovate. The estate agents don't have a picture of it, so I can't be of any help there. I'll e-mail you the post code and directions.'

When he'd finished the call, he went straight to the computer and fired it up, but instead of e-mailing just the address and postcode, he scanned both pages of the estate agents' pamphlet and e-mailed them as well. At least it would give Martin a better idea of what he was dealing with than he could.

Within an hour, an answer landed in his inbox:-

Big place – big project! Depends on how bad it is though and how much work it needs. If we're to renovate it to the same specs, it'll probably cost a packet, but sounds too nice to lose any of the character.
Martin.

No details – just the bare facts; but then, the estate agents pamphlet only gave the barest of details anyway.

Perhaps they'd have more information if he paid them a visit in person. They might also have an idea of how much money was left to keep the maintenance going, and how much they were spending on it on a regular basis.

A week later, the day was fine and sunny, with that slight winter crispness in the air. Connie was working that morning, so he decided to make the visit straight after she left, that way they'd just be opening up when he arrived.

He found it easily enough in the High Street of the small Welsh town, although parking the car wasn't as easy as finding his destination had been. He eventually found a small Pay and Display car park at the back of the shops, and after a few minutes wait, he saw a parking space become vacant. He quickly pulled into it before somebody else spotted it.

Cutting through an alleyway onto the main street, he found the shop just three doors away and went in.

A young woman was sitting poring over a computer near the window and he went straight up to her as she looked up and smiled a greeting.

'Can I help you?' she asked.

She was small and petite, with wavy shoulder length brown hair and a small side swept fringe. He couldn't help noticing how attractive she was, and found his body responding appropriately.

Clearing his throat, and at the same time trying to clear his lascivious thoughts, he held the brochure out towards her.

'I've inherited this house just recently, and your firm is handling its maintenance and sale since the previous owner died.'

She took the brochure from him and keyed the reference number it bore into her computer before saying, 'Do you want to take it off the market then?'

Surprised at her reaction, he pulled himself together before answering.

'No, that's not why I'm here. I wondered if you might have any more information regarding the house. This is only a very preliminary outline – it doesn't give any proper details of the property.'

She placed the brochure on the desk and brought up several screens on her computer before frowning, and turning her attention to him once again.

'Maybe we don't have anything more detailed. Have you been to visit the property yourself?'

Without going into too much detail, he explained to her about his accident and how he'd spent weeks in hospital, only having been back on his feet a short while.

'Hold on a minute,' she said, lifting her 'phone. 'I'll ask the manager if he has any further details.'

A short conversation ensued, before she replaced the 'phone and asked him to take a seat. Picking the brochure up, she went through a door at the back of the shop.

After several minutes, during which he could hear muted conversation from within, she returned and sat down at her desk.

'Mr. Roberts will speak to you in a moment; he's just trying to find the relevant information for you,' and with that she continued poring over the computer screen once more.

After nearly another ten minutes had passed and he was beginning to get impatient, the door opened and a tall, smartly dressed man in a pin-striped suit and blue shirt appeared.

'Would you like to come into my office?' he said, standing back to allow him entry.

'I'm Alwyn Roberts,' he said once they were inside, 'please take a seat,' indicating a straight backed chair before a large desk; similarly seating himself opposite.

Several papers were littered across the desk, and a file lay open in front of him.

'You say the house is called 'Havergill?' he queried.

'That's right,' he answered. 'A relative in New Zealand died two years ago, and the solicitors handling his estate contacted a solicitor in this country, who gave me all the details. It seems I'm his sole beneficiary. I was told that my uncle owned a property in Wales that he'd inherited when his father died in 1977, and that your company have been handling the sale and maintenance of the property since then.'

'1977?' the manager was looking incredulous. 'Did you say '77?' He nodded.

'Well that explains a lot,' Alwyn stated, as if that had solved a problem he'd been having. He seemed to heave a huge sigh of relief.

'My company is a country wide estate agency, and we took over this small independent agency about five years ago. Unfortunately, I can find no record of this property in our files – even the dormant ones handed over from the previous owner – of which there were quite a number.'

'But you've been maintaining the property! Surely there must be some record of that!'

'I'm afraid not! There's no mention of any such property on our books, and certainly none of a company being paid to maintain it. I'm sure I would have found some record of invoices coming in, and certainly of any having been paid out.'

Grasping at straws, he finally said, 'Is there another estate agency in the town with a similar name to yours?'

'No,' the man shook his head. 'This brochure was definitely one handed out by our predecessors – we've still plenty of them kicking around the office for me to recognise one. We keep everything on file until they're either sold, or we're given definite proof in writing of the owners signing them out of our hands.'

'Can you just have another quick look before I go?' he asked.

Obligingly the manager opened screen after screen on his computer; still drawing a blank, and finally shaking his head in bafflement.

'I'm sorry, there's nothing under that name or reference number either. Could its name have been changed since this was issued?'

Thinking for a moment, something flashed into his mind. The stone gateposts had borne the name 'Havergill' and they certainly looked as if they'd been there since the house was built.

He was about to convey this to the man, but something stopped him while it was still on the tip of his tongue.

Was this memory fact – or was it part of the fantasy dream he'd had? Had they actually been within striking distance when he'd had his accident, and had he seen the gateposts before everything became a blank? It was hard to tell if what he was remembering was fact or fantasy.

He pondered on this all the way home, finally coming to the conclusion that the memory must all have been part of his fantasy.

He remembered the van stuck under the bridge, and Connie running to help the driver – and then the car was coming towards him, brakes squealing as it tried to stop. He even remembered the horrified look on the drivers face as he realised he wasn't going to be able to stop in time, and was desperately fighting with the wheel to try and avoid hitting him.

That was the reality! Nothing following that was real, or so he tried to tell himself, until he'd woken up in his hospital bed!

The next few weeks produced some very wet, cold and windy weather, and they hardly ventured from the house.

Bookings for driving lessons were dwindling. Nobody wanted to be out driving aimlessly round the streets in this weather, and if it hadn't been for the lack of income, Riley would have been only too happy to stay at home himself.

There was no word from Martin – but then there'd have been no way they could have carried on with any building work in this sort of weather, so he probably hadn't been down to make the visit yet.

At the beginning of April he received the 'phone call he'd been waiting for.

'Me and the lads went down to see the site yesterday – to see what sort of damage the winter's done to all the hard work we've put in – and I went to visit your house as well!'

His tone was half-mocking, half-laughing, as he finished off.

'And . . . ?' Riley prompted, hearing a chuckle from the other end. 'Was it that bad?'

'That bad . . . ? It was more than bad! You need to see it for yourself!'

Riley could hear the laughter in his voice now.

'Well, go on – tell me the worst,' Riley pressed, his heart sinking.

'There's nothing to tell really,' Martin said, becoming more serious now. 'It's nothing but a shell; practically derelict. There's been a massive fire there, probably many years ago, and there's nothing left standing except a few remains of the walls. It's hardly in need of restoration! It needs knocking down and rebuilding from scratch.'

That came as a shock. He'd had no pre-conceptions of what state the house would be in, accepting now that it wouldn't ultimately be as habitable as his dream had suggested – but this was something else! Something totally unexpected!

He waited for Martin to continue, but he didn't say anything more, obviously waiting for the information to sink in, and for Riley's reaction.

'What about the grounds?' he finally prompted. 'Has anybody been maintaining them?'

'What grounds?' Martin was laughing again. 'I saw no grounds, but there's plenty of jungle for you to hack your way through. It doesn't look as if anybody's been through there in years.'

Riley's spirits were dropping minute by minute.

'Then what the hell am I going to do with it? I can't sell it in that state? Nobody's going to buy it if it's as bad as you say.'

There was a pause before Martin continued.

'There's just a chance that a developer might buy it for the land, but it'll mean houses or some other type of development being built there. You could consider doing that?'

At that moment Riley's spirits were so low he'd have contemplated anything just to get it off his hands.

'There's a building of some sort near the river. Did you look at that as well?' he finally asked, remembering the sketch of something else at the far end of the woods.

He knew from the plan they had that it existed, and he wondered if that might be worth keeping and doing up to live in themselves. He didn't know whether Connie would consider the possibility, and if she didn't, they could rent it out as a holiday cottage and spend a few weeks there themselves every year. It was a long way from the house and couldn't possibly have been affected by the fire, but then, what sort of a state might that be in now. The plan didn't show what sort of a building, or what size it was either. It could have been anything from a small storage shed to a large barn – and then again, nearly 40 years was a long time to stand empty – that too could have fallen down by now.

Martin's voice interrupted his train of thought once more.

'No, didn't get that far. It might be worth taking a look at if you fancy a journey – but I warn you, you'll be very disappointed when you see the state of the place.'

His hopes had already been dashed, and he didn't hold out much hope for the building; cottage, barn, whatever it was, being in good shape either, but he knew he had to go and look for himself, even if they did have to hack their way through the bushes.

When Martin put the 'phone down, he poured himself a glass of bourbon and sat down to think about their conversation; lifting his leg onto a small stool to take the weight off it. Although healing well, he still used a stick to get around, and it ached badly if he spent too much time standing or walking around on it.

His two sons, the youngest still living with them, were both out on site with the rest of their small team, and working hard to finish the houses after the long winter layoff. He'd been cracking the whip just lately to get them finished and some money back in the bank. One of them was already sold, fifty percent of the purchase price already having been paid, and he'd already had interest shown in the second, hoping to sell that before or immediately after it was completed.

His wife, Kate, had gone into Chester to do some shopping with a mate, so she wouldn't be back for a good while yet.

Riley seemed to be very disappointed when he'd told him about the state of the property; eager to get rid of it, and at least make a little money out of it, even if it mightn't be as much as he'd hoped for in the beginning.

Perhaps, if the building did turn out to be a cottage or a barn, and was still standing, he might be able to persuade Riley to have it renovated, providing his firm with more work after the houses were completed. There was no further work on their books for the time being, and until he was back on his feet and with more money in the bank, he certainly couldn't look around for another viable proposition.

Then another thought struck him! If Riley wasn't able to sell the old house in its present condition, perhaps he might be open to doing a deal with him. What if he demolished the old place and applied for planning permission to build some large detached and expensive properties on the land. He wouldn't need to buy the land in question;

he could simply offer Riley a small percentage of the profit they made on the sale of the houses.

The land extended to twenty acres – that provided scope for a good few houses, even if they built and sold them with an acre or two of ground each. If they cleared some of the woodland, they could give most of them views of the river and the countryside beyond.

Refilling his glass, he went through to his study and retrieved the plan that Riley had given him from the drawer, sitting down at his desk and assessing how the properties could best be set out.

Perhaps they could obtain planning permission for up to ten houses on the land. With careful planning, an access road would easily reach the main road. There was a slightly wider and straighter stretch at one point, so there should be no argument from the highways department either, and four could be built directly fronting the road. They could each be provided with their own driveways leading straight onto it.

With this in mind, he fired up his computer and accessed an aerial view of the area in question. As Riley had already given him a postcode for the property, he had no trouble finding it, and he zoomed in to check the possibilities; his mind calculating and assessing for the next hour, as he pored over the map.

He almost jumped out of his skin when the 'phone on his desk suddenly started to give out the sound of an almost inaudible buzz – the sound that he'd allocated to Marianne's calls alone. Everything around him had been totally quiet until then, and it startled him.

He had two 'phones – one that he used for business calls, and the other for private calls. It helped to keep both sides of his life separate.

Marianne's, with its own special ring tone, he'd installed on the one used for business, the screen display merely showing the caller as 'M'.

There was the distinct possibility that Kate might answer the one for private calls if he wasn't around, but she never answered the one for business calls, and both 'phones were encased in different coloured cases.

Help! It was Marianne!

'Well, where are you then?' her voice demanded in his ear.

He looked at the clock. It was already twelve o'clock, and he'd said he'd be at her place by eleven.

'Sorry,' he stammered. 'I was working. I didn't realise how late it was getting.'

'Are you coming over or not then? '

She sounded annoyed now.

'Yes, I'll be right over,' he replied, shutting down the computer and getting up as he disconnected the call.

Kate had told him she'd be back from Chester around four, and he'd planned to spend the day with Marianne; covering his tracks by telling her he might not be at home if she called, but she'd catch him on his mobile. He'd told her he'd probably be following up a few inquiries and looking for more work to take on when they completed the new builds.

So far she hadn't called, and as he'd hoped, she'd probably be too busy shopping to bother about him.

He reached Marianne's home within twenty minutes; a small whitewashed cottage down a quiet country lane, well away from prying eyes. The only other property at the far end of the lane was a large country hotel. They used the lane only for deliveries and the staff entrance, so once Martin tucked his car away amongst the trees at the side of her cottage, it would probably go unnoticed until he was ready to leave again.

He looked up and down the lane to make sure there was nobody watching before making his way to the front door. She'd left it ajar, and he hurried inside, having another quick look round before closing it behind him.

Three hours later, he left the cottage, having another look up and down the lane before making for his car. All was quiet, save for a few squirrels racing up and down a large oak tree opposite, and the raucous calls of the crows and jackdaws in the trees surrounding his car.

He'd reversed into the trees so that he'd be able to take a good look round before driving out, and this time, still finding the lane empty and quiet, he turned out and headed for home. It would take him another twenty minutes to reach there, and it wasn't yet three thirty. That would give him plenty of time to have a shower and wash away the scent of Marianne's cloying perfume before Kate returned.

The one thing he forgot to do was check his rear view mirror before driving on.

There was a sharp right hand bend about 100 metres past Marianne's home, just beyond which was the rear entrance to the hotel. As he drove away, another car turned that bend and came into the lane behind him. Seeing his car, it stopped dead. The woman driver knew that car only too well. It belonged to her husband!

Quickly putting the car into reverse, she shot back in the direction from which she'd come, trying to get back round the bend before he saw her.

Unfortunately, she forgot to check her rear view mirror!

Suddenly, a horn blared loudly from behind, and glancing quickly into the mirror, she saw a large radiator grill, for which she was heading all too quickly. Even before she had time to realise what was happening, the inevitable loud 'crump' occurred, followed by the sound of shattering glass and the rending of torn metal as the car shuddered to a halt.

Stunned, she sat unmoving for the moment.

What had she done? Martin would have to know about the accident. She'd have to try and explain why she hadn't been in Chester as she'd said she'd be. How could she explain where she'd been, and why she'd just been leaving the hotel – and by the rear entrance?

It never occurred to her that Martin had been there on some nefarious business of his own. He often carried out building projects or maintenance work in people's homes, and he always paid visits to assess the work, so she didn't think this out of the ordinary. He'd already told her he'd be following up some inquiries while she was out.

Suddenly she heard an anxious tapping on her window.

'You all right lady?'

There was a man in a grubby khaki overall standing alongside her window. He was leaning down towards her, and she quickly put her finger on the switch to open it.

'I . . . I'm fine,' she stammered, unbidden tears springing to her eyes as she opened the door.

'Why did you run into me?' she asked, not realising for the moment that she was the one who'd been reversing.

'I think you'll find it was the other way round, lady!' he said, becoming indignant. 'It was you wot reversed into me! I'd already stopped when I saw your reversing lights come on. I didn't think you'd carry on when I sounded me 'orn!'

Looking up to where his vehicle had stopped, she saw a large white box van, with the logo of a meat suppliers painted on the front in green lettering. One wing was hanging off, his headlight on that same side was smashed, and she could already see that his radiator grill was crumpled.

She was scared to look what damage had been done to her own car.

She'd hoped it wouldn't be too bad and she could have had it quickly repaired before Martin noticed – but when she finally managed to take a look, it was far worse than she'd anticipated. This was going to be a job for their insurance company!

The other driver had already jumped into her car and pulled it forward away from the van and onto the grass verge as she gazed at it in horror. The tailgate was crumpled and the window broken, the rear lights were smashed; and as it moved forward, the rear panel below the tailgate fell to the ground.

'I don't think you're going home in that!' he said, joining her and looking at the vehicle.

And then, turning to look at his own van, he said, 'and neither am I going anywhere in that,' pointing to the trickle of water pouring from under the front end. 'Me radiators buggered! I'll have to call me firm to get it towed away. Good job that was me last delivery!'

For the moment, she didn't know what to do, as he jumped back into the van and drove it as far off the road as he could, leaving room for other vehicles to pass before calling his firm.

'Got any roadside assistance?' he asked as he joined her once again.

She nodded. 'Yes, I'll 'phone them now.'

He waited until she'd finished the call and then quickly wrote out a note, pinning it to her windscreen.

'What's that?' she asked as he came back.

'You and me are going back to the hotel to try and blag a cuppa' tea. That note tells the recovery where to find you.'

'I need to 'phone my husband first and tell him what's happened,' she said, already dialling the number as she spoke.

It rang for quite a while, even though she tried both the home and mobile numbers, but neither was answered, and she finally left him a brief voicemail before returning to the hotel with her companion.

'No reply,' she exclaimed as she walked alongside him. 'He was visiting prospective clients this afternoon, so he's probably still busy. I've left a voicemail.'

Little did she know that Martin had just entered the shower and was trying to rinse off any telltale traces of Marianne, following it up by putting his clothes, together with others he found in the wash basket, into the machine and starting up its cycle.

It probably wouldn't be finished before she got home, but at least all trace of Marianne would have been washed off by then, and she'd merely think he'd been a dutiful and helpful husband; never realising there'd been an ulterior motive.

When he returned to the living room, he saw the light winking on his mobile and accessed the message.

'I've had a bit of an accident with the car. Don't worry – I'm all right, but the car's not. Somebody ran into the back of me. I've called the recovery firm and I'm just waiting for them to tow me back. Shouldn't be long. Bye for now!'

Brief and concise, but her arrival wasn't!

It was almost seven o'clock before she arrived back! The recovery firm were having a busy day, and it took them almost two hours to reach her. By the time all the formalities had been gone through and the car towed away, three hours had slipped past.

She still hadn't had a chance to think up an excuse as to why she'd been where she was. For the time being she managed to skirt round it

– but it was only a matter of time. The inevitable questions wouldn't be long in coming, and a plausible excuse would be all too necessary!

Eventually she decided on saying that she and her friend hadn't had a very successful day's shopping, and had decided to console themselves with afternoon tea at the hotel.

It was probably a feasible enough excuse, as long as he didn't make any further enquiries at the hotel or mention it to her friend – but why should he? She thought she'd been discreet enough with her regular visits and she hadn't given him any grounds for suspicion.

CHAPTER 4

A few weeks later, Riley had a brief respite one morning between driving lessons. Connie was due home from work soon, and there should still be time for a quick bite to eat together before his next lesson.

He was just walking through to the kitchen to start making them both a sandwich when the 'phone started ringing.

Continuing on into the kitchen, he picked up the extension at the end of the work surface.

'Riley Duncan,' he answered, as an unfamiliar voice spoke at the other end of the line.

'Mr. Duncan, this is Alwyn Roberts from the estate agents. You visited us a few weeks ago with an inquiry about the property called Havergill?'

The voice seemed to be querying whether he remembered his visit.

'Oh, yes, of course I remember,' he answered, wondering if they'd at last found some record of it.

'If you remember, I told you we'd taken over the agency some five years ago?'

'Yes, I do remember,' he replied, anxious to hear why the man had rung.

'Well, I had another good root round after you'd left, delving back into the records left by our predecessors, and hoping to find some more information on the property. Unfortunately, I wasn't able to find anything relating to it in any of our, or their, old files.'

Then why the hell was the man ringing him? Had he rung just to tell him that? But the man was already continuing.

'I got to thinking that I couldn't just leave it at that. Even if the property may be derelict and uninhabitable after all this time, it is certainly still worth a great deal of money in land value alone. It would probably be of interest to a developer at least, and certainly a great deal more if planning permission could be obtained. Is that something you might be interested in pursuing?'

Wouldn't he just!! If the house was just a ruin, and the land all overgrown as Martin had already told him, he really didn't have much option but to offload it in any way he could.

'Of course I would,' he answered.

'I thought you might,' was the reply. 'We have certain contacts that we could get in touch with and see if they may be interested. There are always developers looking for available land, and I'm sure we'll be able to find someone who'd be interested, given a little time. Twenty acres is certainly not something they'll pass up on easily.'

'Thank you,' Riley said, ready to put down the 'phone.

'Just one more thing,' Alwyn Roberts continued. 'There's a lady working in the office. She's been here for many years now, and she still has the number of the previous owner, so I decided to give him a call and ask him if he remembers Havergill being on their books. Luckily he did. He told me he'd been the one to go and see it in the first place, and as it was in such a state, he hadn't been able to place any sort of value on it, which is why it was left open to offers.'

Here he paused.

'Is that it? Didn't he say why they'd stopped maintaining the property – or at least the grounds anyway?'

'Yes, that was one of the questions I asked,' Alwyn continued. 'It seems some sort of Trust had been set up by the original owner for the maintenance of the house and land after his death. He may not have realised that there was nobody to take it over after him; but we'll never ever know what his thinking was when he set it up. A certain amount of money was payable out of it every month for the maintenance costs. The previous agency continued administering the money and hired a local firm of gardening contractors to carry out the work when instructed.

Approximately fifteen years ago, money stopped coming in from the Trust, and when they inquired why, it was to be told that the money had completely run out. The Trust had written to the person in

New Zealand who now owned it, and he'd told them he wasn't prepared to put any more money into the place. He told them to just go on trying to sell it. Unfortunately, somewhere along the line, the property seems to have fallen off the radar and been forgotten about as it has been for sale for so long.'

Riley, already aware of how long it had been on the market, was now beginning to realise why it was left in such a state. Grand uncle Isaac wasn't interested in the property, even though it had once been his childhood home. He'd made a life for himself in New Zealand, and he had no intention of ever returning to England; but did he have no fond childhood memories of it? Had he cared so little about the place where his roots were? He just seemed to want rid of it as soon as possible – and had he even known about the fire?

Now Riley was growing interested in the previous history of the place. He needed to find out more about the family who'd lived there, and why so many of the children had died so early in their lives. Even more, he wanted to find out why the children who'd lived had wanted to get away as soon as they could – they were his own family when all was said and done!

He only wished that he'd known of Uncle Isaac's existence before he'd died – his input would have been invaluable for information about them all. He could probably have learned so much from him!

The first thing he needed to do was take a proper look at the place for himself!

Two days later, he was still thinking about Havergill and the family he'd never known anything about, when he had another call from Mr. Roberts.

'I've spoken with someone who has an interest in your property,' he said. 'He's a representative for a national firm of house builders and he's interested with the acreage on offer. He thinks it might be just up their street, but he isn't interested in restoring the house itself. That would have to be demolished as part of the building programme.'

But not up mine, Riley thought as they finished the conversation and put the 'phone down.

It was, after all, his ancestral home, and he hated the thought of it being lost forever, covered over by a housing estate. But what was he thinking? He hadn't even seen the place yet – although he felt as if he knew it inside out. He needed to go and see it straight away before events overtook him and he had to make a decision as to whether to sell to the developer or not. It would be money in the bank – and plenty of it – but was that all that mattered in life?

There were just the two of them; their mortgage almost paid off; and with enough money to live on from week to week. They both seemed happy and contented with their lives and their jobs, and they really didn't need a bigger house. Connie was a good homemaker, and this one was comfortable and homely – did they really need a stash of money sitting in a bank? They had no real need of it, and neither did they have anybody to pass it on to when they died. It would probably go to some long forgotten relative, who'd never even heard of him either – as Havergill had with him.

But then again – Havergill belonged to him – and with it the responsibility of owning such a place. It wasn't well fenced and children, or even adults venturing in, could be hurt, or even drown falling into the river. In the end he had to face up to the fact that he didn't have the resources to pay for its maintenance and its upkeep.

He'd have to sell it! He really had no choice – and to his knowledge, this was the first prospect there'd been of a sale – even if it were to be turned into a housing estate.

Taking the bull by the horns, he picked up the 'phone and called Martin.

'Look Martin,' he said when the 'phone was answered almost immediately. 'The agents have a prospective buyer for Havergill, a developer who thinks it could be large enough for a housing estate, and I haven't even seen it myself yet. Do you fancy going with me to see it on Saturday.'

Martin was taken aback. He'd still been considering his own proposal, and how he could put it to Riley. But whose idea would Riley find most acceptable?

Selling to a developer would mean money in the bank immediately, especially if planning permission was granted, and that would be a great deal more than he could ever contemplate paying him.

His own idea meant the building of only a few luxury dwellings – much more in keeping with the original property – but that would mean Riley receiving only a percentage of the profit on each house and little for the actual land they stood on.

On the other hand, if the building near the river did indeed turn out to be a cottage, or even a large barn, he could offer to restore or convert that at a good profit for himself. Riley had already intimated that he wouldn't mind living there, so that may sway the balance, and it was well away from where he envisaged the other houses being built.

The planners may even be more open to his ideas. They may not even allow a large estate served only by a small village.

The outcome would all depend on how Riley felt about the property.

Did he want to keep it as a small country house development – or did he not care about having it overrun with a cheap and soulless housing estate?

Which was more important to Riley: a development in keeping with the area; or money sitting in the bank?

He'd probably find out on Saturday.

CHAPTER 5

Robert Tanner – Bob to everyone who knew him – cycled home from his work at Groes Faen Farm.

He was hot and tired, and looking forward to his tea and escaping to the pub for a pint afterwards. With four children in a small cottage, and another on the way, he was glad to seek the peace and quiet of the pub until they were all in their beds, or just on their way up. Two boys and two girls were fine. They occupied the two larger bedrooms, and he and his wife squeezed their double bed into the smaller room – but what was going to happen when the new baby arrived? It was a tight enough squeeze now, and they'd have to try and rearrange things once again when it arrived.

Fliss had been at him for some time now to get the snip. He didn't fancy it one little bit. He felt it would emasculate him and make him less of a man, but now, with the fifth on its way, he knew he was going to have to make the decision. They were both hot blooded and ardent lovers, but all he seemed to have to do was to look sideways at her and she was pregnant again!

She'd become pregnant with their first child after only three months of marriage, and the others had come at regular intervals from then on. It was always a struggle to make ends meet on his meagre salary, but their cottage was owned by the farm and he couldn't afford to try and find something else. He only paid a peppercorn rent each month, and he'd never done anything but farm work since the day he'd finished school.

Both he, and his parents, had known he wasn't academically gifted, and hadn't passed many exams before leaving school, but growing things had always come easily to him. He'd always loved nature and watching things grow and develop; a gift he'd inherited from his grandfather, with whom he'd spent a lot of his childhood in the small nursery where he worked; learning to plant and nurture seedlings and cuttings.

Now, as he wheeled his bike up the path and propped it inside the little lean-to at the back of the house, his two youngest ran from their ball game in the garden to greet him.

'Have you brought anything today?' they clamoured.

He often brought home any overripe fruit or bruised apples and pears that the farm shop couldn't sell, but today all he'd brought were some badly misshapen carrots, a small cabbage that the caterpillars had been at, and some potatoes that were going a bit soft. These were all things that weren't acceptable for sale to the public, but all perfectly edible if the cabbages were checked carefully for more caterpillars and the chewed leaves removed – and all things that his wife welcomed.

'Sorry,' he said, 'there's no fruit today, only veggies,' as they turned away, disappointed, to resume their game.

Taking the carrier bag into the house, Fliss was already busy in the kitchen making their meal.

'Ullo luv',' he said, depositing the bag alongside the sink and giving her a peck on the cheek, but she brushed him off as if he was an annoying insect.

'Can't you see I'm busy cooking,' she said caustically. 'Go and ge' some of that muck off you in the outhouse. There's a kettle of hot water on the stove.'

He sighed. The pregnancy, although she was still only four months gone, seemed to be getting to her this time – but this time she was also well into her thirties and she didn't seem to find it as easy to cope with as she had when she was younger.

Thinking better of saying anything further, he picked up the kettle and went out to the outhouse, where he swilled himself down in the big stone sink and ran his dusty and muddy overalls under the outside tap before hanging them over the washing line to dry.

They tried not to use the washing machine any more than was necessary to save on the electric, and used it mainly for the kids clothes. They had to be kept presentable for school every day, but there were already three other pairs of his overalls in the plastic bath under the sink. He knew he'd have to use the machine for his own clothes very soon, or he was going to run out of things to wear. He only hoped it wouldn't rain overnight or he'd have nothing to wear tomorrow.

After they'd eaten, he and the two eldest helped her with the dishes before he prepared to go to the pub.

'Where do you think you're going?' she asked, as he came down the stairs in jeans and sweatshirt.

'I'm just going for a pint while you get the kids to bed,' he said, more in a tone of asking rather than telling.

It was on the tip of her tongue to tell him they couldn't afford for him to be drinking, but she thought better of it. He was a good husband, and he would have stayed to help if she'd asked, but after all, his job was hard and strenuous, and he deserved to have a relaxing pint after work, and he only did it once or twice a week.

Her mood softening she said, 'Don' 'ave more than one or two. We're a bit short this week.'

'I won't go if you don' want me to,' he said, suddenly feeling guilty.

'No, you go,' she countered. 'You deserve it after all the 'ard work you put in. You go an' I'll put the kids to bed. There's a programme on telly tha' I want to watch. It's not something you'd be interested in.'

Shrugging his shoulders, he gave her another peck on the cheek, and went back to the outhouse to get his bike, checking the lamp to make sure the battery was working for when he came home later that night.

As he was leaving, his eye caught sight of the old fishing rod that had once belonged to his father. If he could only afford one pint, he didn't want to get caught up with buying rounds in the pub when other regulars came in. He could just have the one and then go and do a bit of fishing in the river. It had been a warm day, and there'd been a full moon last night, just the right weather for the fish to be rising for flies, and he knew there were some good brown trout in that river. His wife would be only too pleased if he could help out by bringing some fish home for tomorrow's tea.

There were only one or two people in the bar when he reached it, and he joined in the conversation for a while, making just the one pint last; but he downed it quickly and made for the door when others began to arrive.

'Not staying Bob?' one of their neighbours asked as he met him leaving.

'Not tonight,' he answered. 'Goin' to do a bit of fishing. I 'eer there's some nice brown trout in the river.'

'Oh yer', there is,' the man replied. 'Old 'Etherington pulled out four smashers last Saturday night, and it's the right weather for them to be risin' t'night. 'E caught them down through the grounds of the old 'ouse, so I reckon that might be a good place to try.'

'Thanks, I'll give it a try,' he said, as he unlocked his bike and retrieved his rod from where he'd left it hidden behind a large shrub. It may be the country, but things still got stolen if you didn't keep your eye on them.

It took him ten minutes to reach the turnoff into the grounds of Havergill, and he cycled as far as possible up the driveway before it became impossible to make any further headway through the growth of weeds.

Pushing his bike between the branches of a large conifer and leaning it against the trunk, he moved back to the path and checked to make sure it couldn't be seen. The feathery branches had sprung back into position, where they swept right down to the ground once more. He could see no sign of it. Feeling sure it was safe, he hoisted the strap of the rod case across his back, and carried the keep net in his hand, before finding his way through the overgrown jungle that had once been a driveway.

Crossing the open space at the front of the house, he stopped and turned to look at it. The front, or what was left of it, was bathed in a golden glow from the setting sun, but the ruined and gaping window openings showed only a blackened and charred interior, dark and eerie in the half light of evening.

The whole roof had collapsed during the fire, as had the upstairs floors, and its interior was now open to the vagaries of the weather.

He and a mate had ventured inside once, when they were about 16, wondering what they'd find there, but they'd been so scared once inside that they'd exited rather quickly after just a few short minutes. There'd been a strange malevolent feeling about the place. Not something you could put your finger on, or give a name to, but they'd both felt it as soon as they'd stepped over the threshold. It felt as if someone had been watching and waiting. They couldn't get out quick enough, and he'd never been back since.

Continuing across the wide courtyard, he was just about to enter the path through the woods when he heard something. He stopped and listened, turning his head this way and that to pinpoint where the sound was coming from, eventually realising it was from the direction of the house. It was the faint strains of a violin being played, but even as he pinpointed the sound, it died away. The tune, what he'd managed to hear of it, was a soft haunting melody; strangely quiet and melancholy in the dying evening light. He didn't recognise it, and there were no further sounds to be heard, save the rustle of a light breeze stirring the treetops.

After a few minutes he stopped listening and continued on through the trees, finally reaching the riverbank, where the water was quietly meandering its way between the banks. Even as he began to unpack his rod, he noticed the flies busily flitting over the water, and the soft plop as a fish surfaced to catch one and disappear back beneath the surface once more. It seemed he'd picked the right night for his expedition.

Sitting on a fallen log near the edge of the bank, he unpacked his rod and line, expertly fixing on a worm from the small tin he carried. He caste out upstream and watched it float past him before repeating the process time and again, but he was unlucky. Although surfacing all around for the flies, they didn't seem to be interested in his worm, and he stopped casting out.

He changed it for a smaller one and sat down once again, moving further along the log so that he could rest his back against a conveniently close silver birch tree.

The shadows were fading now and night was fast approaching. The moon was already up, and although it was over towards his right and slightly hidden by the trees, he could still see the ground around him.

He cast out a few times with the wriggling worm on the end of his hook, before leaning back against the tree trunk and letting the current carry his line downstream. His arms were tiring, and he hadn't caught anything yet, despite still being able to see the fish rising. Shortly, he felt himself beginning to doze.

He felt as if he were being held in a pair of soft and comforting arms. Peace was settling all around him with a soft and rosy glow. A feeling of euphoria stealing over him, he began to drift into sleep.

The arms hugged him even tighter and he began to feel safe and warm, but suddenly he realised that the tightening around him wasn't stopping. The arms that had seemed to hold him so gently before had become a vice-like grip, and he couldn't move within their confines.

Suddenly, he felt himself being lifted from the log. He was being propelled towards the riverbank, his arms pinned tightly against his sides, and he found himself unable to break free. He kicked and fought, trying to dig his heels into the ground, but it was useless against that powerful grip. His heels couldn't find a hold in the muddy ground . . . and the river was getting nearer!

He was on the very edge now, the water right below him; when the vice-like grip suddenly released him and he awoke.

He was sitting right on the edge of the bank, his feet dangling in the water, and there was no sign of any other being. Everything around him was quiet and still, save for the hooting of a tawny owl close at hand.

Had he dreamt it all? Was it the owl that had woken him? And how had he got so near to the water? The log he'd been sitting on was a good ten feet from the overhanging bank.

Well and truly spooked now, he pulled his wet feet out of the water and quickly packed up his things. That had been too close a call, and he couldn't swim!

CHAPTER 6

Martin was already waiting for him when Riley arrived at the entrance to Havergill and parked alongside him. They exchanged a few words of greeting and shook hands before they prepared to follow the driveway towards the house.

'Afraid the rest of the way will have to be on foot,' Martin said ruefully, 'it's too overgrown for a vehicle from here on, but it will give you a good overview of things on the walk up.'

Glancing down, he nodded approvingly at the sturdy boots Riley had decided to wear.

'Glad to see you've put on sensible footwear – you may need them! I've only had a cursory look round so far, but if you want to walk the land, that might prove a bit more difficult!'

Riley grinned; from what he'd already been told, that was no more than he'd expected.

'Come on then,' he said, 'let's get started. I'm eager to see my inheritance.'

Martin smiled ruefully. If that's what he considered it, he was going to be sorely disappointed. It was more like a white elephant than an inheritance.

As they made their way towards the house, avoiding the weeds and tufts of grass that had sprung up through the pea gravel, as well as the tree saplings and the ubiquitous nettles, Riley had to contend with the unruly clump of conifers on his right. Their branches had grown far from the original trunks and were now covering most of the drive in places. They should have been cut back years ago, or perhaps it would have been better never to have planted them so close to the drive in the first place. Obviously no consideration had been given to how large they might grow.

He'd now come to accept that his knowledge of the place had only ever been a dream – the wanderings of a mind muddled and confused by the drugs they'd given him in the hospital.

However, when they rounded the perimeter of the trees, and the house stood before him, there was a certain something that struck a chord of memory in his mind – a sense of déjà vu, but there was too little of the original house left to tell him what that might have been.

Staring at it now, he realised renovation would have been far too big a project for him even to contemplate! As Martin had said, the only way was complete demolition and to rebuild from the ground up. Both aspects, and the cost of the project, would be way beyond his means! Even if he sold his own house and funded it with the proceeds, it would never be enough! Just a drop in a very large ocean!

And then there were the grounds . . . ! Spread out towards his left now, it was impossible to realise that there had once been nearly twenty acres of pristine parkland and gardens out there. It was so overgrown he couldn't see more than twenty feet or so beyond where they stood.

In the distance, he could just see the tops of the trees in the wood beyond the jungle before him. He knew from the plan that the wood marked the perimeter of his land, as he'd proudly liked to think of it. Now he wasn't so sure its ownership was something to feel quite so proud of.

'Come on,' he heard Martin's voice at his side, 'it's going to take a while to walk the grounds. Let's take a quick look at the house before we start. I warned you – it's beyond repair – only a developer might be interested in taking it on.'

He waited and watched for Riley's reaction, his own plan still in his mind, but he was already marching on purposefully towards the house, seemingly oblivious to everything around him for the time being.

Riley picked his way through the rubble which had once been a covered entrance way, and peered in through the opening where the front door had once stood; now just charred and blackened wood, crumbling away at the lightest touch. Being made of oak, it had burned very thoroughly, and nothing much was left of it.

There was little of the original dwelling left to see either. Charred roof timbers and the remains of the upstairs floor joists were piled high throughout what he could see of the interior; the whole covered with shattered roof tiles. A gaping void was open to the sky where the roof would once have been.

Everywhere was covered, inside and out, by large stone blocks which had fallen as the walls had become de-stabilised and crumbled.

About to retreat, he noticed an open patch of the floor just inside the doorway; long and narrow, but it was enough to expose the floor tiling beneath. It had once been made up of small red, black and green squares, with the odd ochre coloured tile in a relief pattern. The whole place must have once been quite grand in its heyday. So sad to see it in such a dilapidated condition now.

One thing he did notice as he looked around was a cast iron foot scraper. That too instilled a sense of déjà vu as he stared at it for a moment. It was still standing upright at the side of the demolished porch, but it was its unusual design that caught his attention. In the centre was cast the head of a lion, its teeth barred, its mane standing out; the scraper bars either side of the head. Riley felt instinctively that he'd seen it before, and even if it had only been part of his dream, how could his mind have conjured up exactly the same image if he'd never seen it before?

Martin was now at his side and brought him rudely back to the present.

'Well, what do you think?'

'I think it could do with a bit of attention!' he joked as they both laughed.

'That's an understatement if ever I heard one!' Martin said, as he stepped back so that Riley could negotiate his way back over the rubble filling the porch.

Riley smiled ruefully.

'Let's take a wander round the whole building before we do anything more. It's probably not worth coming here again, so I'd like to get an idea of what it might once have looked like before I hand it over to the developers.'

So he did have that in mind! Martin knew he had to put his own proposition to him today. There was every chance that he'd already made his decision to sell to the developer who'd shown an interest, and every chance that he intended to ring the estate agent on Monday and accept their offer.

It was now or never – but they needed to see the rest of the estate first before he put forward his own ideas. He'd already drawn out a rough plan of the estate, with sketches of where the houses might be placed to minimise their impact on the original layout, but he needed Riley to see the place for himself before he approached him with his idea. He'd already brought it with him in case the opportunity came up to broach the subject.

Having completed the full circuit of the house and returned to their starting place, Martin said, 'Where next?'

'I think I'd like to go down to the river first,' Riley said, turning towards the direction in which he could see the woods standing tall above the undergrowth.

As they approached, the path through the woods became clearer and more defined. It was obvious that it was being used by animals; and quite a large number judging by how well trodden the path was.

'Has somebody been grazing animals here?' Riley asked, indicating the prints.

'Too large for sheep,' Martin said, bending to examine them. 'I'd say they're probably deer. Many of these large properties ran herds of deer. They used them to keep the grounds cleared, and also to provide a source of meat for their own tables. When the herds became too large, they often culled them and sold them to a butcher as another source of income. Venison was very popular with the gentry at one time.'

As they followed the path and eventually reached the river, he looked for a bridge, but there was no sign of one. There were, however, small stone buttresses on either bank which had probably been used as the base for a bridge – now long gone!

Turning to follow the riverbank, there was no sign of any deer; but copious amounts of their droppings. That was another thing he needed to think about. What would happen to the deer if he sold the property to the developer? Were they wild deer? There was nothing to stop them coming in from the surrounding countryside as far as he could see. Or were they a pedigree herd his ancestor had brought in and lovingly tended during his lifetime? If they were, their bloodlines were probably well diluted now after interbreeding with the wild ones.

They continued their walk along the bank, keeping the river to their right and the woods to their left for a considerable distance. Across the other side of the river, a fence showed the boundary of his property. The land that side was much better tended and there were some sheep grazing contentedly; looking up as they passed, unused to seeing people on the opposite bank.

At the end of the woodland, the grassed area opened out and the river began to turn to the right; the fencing on the opposite bank crossing it and continuing in a straight towards the outer perimeter hedge. The sketch plan showed the land to rise slightly further on to their left; the slopes of which were covered by more woodland.

'Let's carry on a bit further to the left. We might be able to get a better view of the whole area from the side of the hill if we can find a gap through the trees,' Martin urged.

They angled away towards where they could see the trees and came across a small stream. It was heading in the direction of the river, and water was cascading over large rocks and boulders, creating small waterfalls, as it made its way to join it.

Climbing the slope into the trees, they found them quite sparse on the lower slope, but as they climbed higher, they became thicker, finally becoming quite dense.

Stopping about half way towards the densest part, Riley turned to look back at the house.

At one time, there must have been a good view of it from here, but now all he could see was what remained of the topmost stonework – the view impaired by what could only have been described as scrub, interspersed by many newly grown tree saplings. It had once been open parkland, but would now need months of work with bulldozers to clear the ground, and tons of topsoil to get it back to some semblance of its former glory.

Deciding it wasn't worth going any further into the woods, he looked round for Martin.

He was standing only a few metres away, but he wasn't looking towards the house, he was looking back in the direction of the river and the first set of woods they'd walked alongside. This time, he was gazing at something to their left, and much nearer to hand.

'What is it?' Riley asked.

'Over to the left,' Martin raised an arm and pointed. 'I see smoke, and I think it's coming from a chimney. I'm sure that's the top of a chimney pot I can see.'

Riley shaded his eyes and looked in the same direction.

It certainly did look like a chimney pot.

'Let's go and take a look,' he said, striding out towards it. 'That must be the building we've seen on the plan. It must be a cottage; but what anybody's doing in it is beyond me. That building is mine, and it's on my land.'

He felt a sense of pride welling up from within that all this land belonged to him now, and aggrieved that somebody else should be intruding on it.

As he forced his way through the last of the scrub, he suddenly found himself confronted by a sight of complete normality amongst the chaos.

There was a well beaten track in front of him, leading away to his left on one side, and in front of him leading to a stone built cottage.

It wasn't exactly as he'd imagined it to be, but it was definitely a cottage, not a barn or an outbuilding as they'd thought it might be, and it was definitely inhabited.

It was square in shape, rendered and painted in white, and curtains hung at the windows, with, as they'd noticed, smoke coming from a chimney.

A post and rail fence surrounded a garden area, with a mown lawn either side of a path leading to the front door. Raised and well filled vegetable beds filled the area to the right of the building.

They looked at each other in complete surprise.

'There's somebody living here,' Martin stated, as nonplussed as Riley himself was. 'Did you know about this?' he asked, after a few seconds pause, neither of them grasping the situation.

'Definitely not!' Riley replied angrily. 'Whoever it is, they've no right to be here – no right at all!'

Well annoyed by this unwarranted intrusion on his land, Riley started marching across towards the cottage. He'd almost reached the gate when a man appeared from round the back. He was wearing old corduroy trousers, wellington boots, and with a cloth cap perched on his head. He seemed as startled to see Riley as he was to see him.

After a few moments pause, during which time neither knew what to say, the man eventually said, 'Can I help you?' He seemed surprised to see anybody else in these parts, but his tone was conversational rather than confrontational.

Riley, however, was more taken aback by his tone, and answered somewhat aggressively.

'I think it's rather me who should be asking **you** that question. This is my land, what the hell do you think you're doing here?'

The man stood and looked at him. He was quite elderly, and seemed not to know what to say.

Martin put a placatory hand on his arm, but he was in no mood to be placated.

'You can pack your bags and get out of here. I'm the new owner and I'm selling this place – and you're trespassing! I want you out as soon as possible.'

The elderly man didn't know what to say as he just stood and looked back at them. Suddenly Riley realised he wasn't looking **at** him, but past him, as he heard a loud click from behind.

Turning, he found himself looking down the muzzle of a double barrelled shotgun – not more than a few feet away.

'And just who the hell do you think you are?' an angry voice boomed at him. 'Nobody – just nobody – talks to my dad like that!!'

The anger still strong in him, Riley replied, 'Neither of you have any right to be here. I own all this land, and nobody has asked my permission for you to live in this cottage.'

The man still held the gun pointed directly at him, its barrel unwavering.

'My dad owns this cottage – not you! He bought and paid for it fair and square after the previous owner died. You need to check your facts. Now you get off **OUR** property.'

Riley still wasn't ready to back down.

'I've spoken to the agents and they have no record of this cottage having been sold,' he argued.

Suddenly a voice cut in from behind him.

'It was many years ago that I bought it – only a few years after old Samuel died. It was in the early 1980's. If you'd like to come in, I'll show you the documents.'

Then, looking past the visitors, he said to his son, 'Put the gun down Ryan. It's all a big misunderstanding. Let's clear this up peacefully before somebody gets hurt.'

Ryan reluctantly lowered the gun. His father had been living a solitary life here since his mother died, and he felt protective towards him. Having spent so much of his life here, the old man was reluctant to leave, despite his frequent entreaties, and he was angry at the way this stranger was treating him. He was reluctant to continue any further association with him, and anxious to be rid of them both.

His father, however, was opening the gate and inviting them in. There was no way he was leaving until they'd gone, so he followed them inside, and propped his gun behind the front door. There was never a chance that he'd have used it, but the sight of it had been deterrent enough – or so he hoped.

CHAPTER 7

Martin's wife, Kate, parked her car in the staff car park, and made her way into the hotel via the rear door, where she quickly made her way to the manager's office.

Carswell Forster was already there and waiting for her.

'Hello,' he said, ardently pulling her into his arms as soon as she entered and quickly shutting the door behind her. 'It's lovely to see you again. Any problems over your little smash the other week?'

He smelt of aftershave and shower gel, and was dressed in a suit – a pleasant change from her husband's usual garb of jeans, lumberjack shirt, and work boots, all liberally coated in plaster and brick dust and smelling of the building site.

'No! No problems. I thought up the excuse of coming back from Chester early and deciding to have afternoon tea here with my friend to round the day off. He doesn't know it happened outside the rear entrance, and he's never asked exactly where it did happen, so I may have got away with it.'

He laughed.

'And if he does find out?' he said.

'He shouldn't. I filled the insurance claim in myself, and it's already gone in. I've heard nothing further, so it looks as if it's all straightforward with no questions asked.'

She didn't tell him that she'd had a letter only this morning from her insurance company.

In her statement, she'd claimed that the van had run into the back of her. Unfortunately, she didn't realise that it was fitted with a dash cam which showed the other vehicle to have been at a standstill when the collision occurred. It proved beyond doubt that she had reversed into him.

When their statements had clashed, the van drivers' firm had provided the dash cam footage to their own company to prove his side of the story. Her own company had now informed her of this and asked her to provide an explanation.

She had the feeling that they were going to refute the claim seeing as she'd lied in her statement, and the damage could run into several thousand pounds.

How was she going to explain that to Martin? With no work during most of the winter period, and no money having come in, she doubted she'd be getting her car back any time soon – if ever. She'd had to use a taxi today, but with Martin being away from home all day, the opportunity to see Carswell was too good to pass up.

'I've got some wine chilling in one of our best rooms,' he was now saying. 'There isn't a booking for it today, so you and I can make use of it. It's on the top floor so we'll have to take the chance of using the lift, but the hotel's quiet at the moment. We shouldn't see anyone you know.'

Carswell was divorced and lived in the hotel himself, not something he'd ever let her know. His own quarters weren't a patch on the public letting rooms. Not far from the kitchens, they comprised a small sitting room with tea making facilities in one corner, and a pokey little bedroom, with a small shower room and toilet next to it. Not somewhere he would ever have contemplated taking her, especially as it was often permeated with the smell of cooking from the kitchen.

However, their use of the lift didn't go entirely unnoticed.

Marianne, Martin's lover, worked at the hotel herself as a housekeeper and sometime receptionist when there was no one else available.

Today, she was just taking some linen up to the second floor when she saw them entering the lift ahead of her.

Randy old goat, she thought. He's taking another woman up to one of the empty rooms, and she tutted to herself. What they saw in him she never knew. He looked every one of his sixty odd years of age, but she had to admit, he knew how to exude charm when necessary. They might have thought differently if they'd seen him tearing a strip off some of the younger girls working in the hotel – frequently reducing them to tears for some minor misdemeanour.

Her destination was on the second floor, so she decided to avoid embarrassment and use the stairs instead of getting in the lift with them.

It was only as the woman stepped into the bright light inside the lift and turned to face out again that she recognised her with a start.

It was Martin's wife, Kate!

Although she knew Kate by sight, as she and Martin had once frequented the hotel for Sunday lunch, Kate only knew her in her role as one of the staff, and as their meetings had only ever been brief, she didn't think she'd recognise her again. Her affair with Martin had started as a consequence of meeting at the hotel, and after that, he'd started taking Kate elsewhere to be on the safe side.

Quickly running up the staff stairs, she stopped just inside the swing door onto the landing of the top floor, and watched them walking down the corridor. There was a small porthole window, and by keeping to one side, she could watch where they went, their backs to her all the time. Their best room, The Regency, was one where he usually took his victims, as she liked to think of them, and today was no exception.

She knew that up to an hour ago, that room hadn't been booked today, but Sally, their receptionist, had waylaid her not ten minutes ago. She'd informed her that she'd just taken a call from Mr. Sinclair, the hotel's owner. He and his wife would be arriving in time for lunch, and she'd booked him into that room; asking Marianne to check that everything was in order for him.

She knew it would be. She was in the habit of checking every room after the cleaners had been through every morning, from the very cheapest to the most expensive, and today was no exception.

Now she had a dilemma on her hands! Should she go and inform Carswell that Mr. Sinclair had just booked the room and would be arriving shortly, or should she let the old goat find out for himself?

She thought for a while, watching Carswell open the door and usher Kate inside, giving her bottom a proprietary little slap as she slipped inside.

A wry little grin crossed her face as she slipped away unnoticed.

It was about time Carswell got his comeuppance – it was no more than he deserved! But she'd love to have been a fly on the wall when Mr. Sinclair and his diminutive little wife arrived and let themselves into the room.

She'd always thought of them as Laurel and Hardy characters. He was a little over six foot tall, burly and cigar smoking: she just a shade over five foot, thin as a rake and always sporting some absurdly dyed hairstyle; with make-up far more suitable to a much younger woman. At over sixty years old, she seemed to be trying to cling to the remnants of her lost youth – and failing badly!

Half an hour later, having completed all her chores for the time being, she re-entered the hotel reception area, just in time to see the Sinclairs arriving through the swing doors at the front.

She smiled to herself. They were just in time to catch Carswell and Kate fully engaged in whatever sexual activity they had in mind. Neither party would realise what was going on until the Sinclairs appeared in the doorway. She'd love to have seen the expression of surprise and utter horror on Carswell's face.

Caught in the act! And no more than he deserved!

It was almost an hour later that the hotel began to buzz with excited chatter.

She was in the conservatory, a huge oak and glass edifice built on some years ago to take in the magnificent countryside views and which served as a dining room. She was just checking the table reserved for the Sinclairs in a quiet corner away from the other diners, when word reached her through the waiting staff. They'd had a lull in the lunchtime service, and they'd congregated in one corner near the kitchen entrance.

'What's going on?' she enquired quite innocently, her mind wondering if word had reached them of Carswell's dilemma, and pretending not to know anything about the situation.

A group of three young girls and one older lad were talking animatedly.

'Haven't you heard?' one of the girls said excitedly. 'Mr. Forster's been caught in one of the top floor suites with some woman. They were in bed together, and the Sinclairs arrived and caught them at it. Did you know they were coming?'

'Yes, I did, but not until just before they arrived,' she answered, trying to keep a straight face.

It must have worked out just as she'd intended.

'But I checked out all the suites myself this morning, and they were all ready for use, including the Regency, which they normally like to use.'

Her statement was accompanied by a paroxysm of laughing and giggling.

'Well, not today it wasn't!' one of the bolder girls volunteered. 'I heard they were well at it when the Sinclairs walked in!' as they all burst into more fits of laughter.

'Serves him right!' another girl piped up. 'He's always slapping our bottoms or rubbing up against us when he passes. I hope they sack him and get rid of the dirty old man.'

Just at that moment, something caught Marianne's eye. A flustered and dishevelled Kate was leaving the hotel; not by the back door this time, but by the front entrance. She seemed anxious to get away as quickly as possible as she hurried round towards the staff car park.

Marianne left the serving staff to it, trying to hide her own amusement as she went through to the kitchen to make sure everything was ready for the Sinclairs' meal. She couldn't see a small thing like Carswells' humiliation putting Mr. Sinclair off his meal in any way – he was far too fond of his food for that!

Their receptionist, Sally, was talking to a couple of guests when she made her way back into the hall. Marianne made polite conversation with them as she walked them to the door and held it open while they went through with their luggage. When they'd gone, she returned to speak to Sally.

'I've heard a story about Carswell being caught in the Regency suite with a woman. Is it true?'

Sitting behind the reception desk, Sally normally heard all the gossip before anybody else did.

'Yeh! He's just left the hotel,' Sally said, a beatific smile on her face. 'Mr Sinclair's sacked him!'

A devoutly faithful wife of fifteen years, Sally was ever dutiful. She loved her husband unconditionally and would no more have thought about having an affair than of flying to the moon. She'd heard all the stories about Carswell circulating around the staff, and he'd have got short shrift if he'd tried anything on with her; but Carswell had always seemed to have had some instinct about that and had never tried to touch or coerce her ever. It wasn't that she wasn't an attractive woman – but she'd always had that 'hands off' allusiveness about her.

Pleased with her work, Marianne went about her days work. She'd love to be able to tell Martin, but she knew theirs was only a passing fling, and she didn't want to jeopardise his and Kate's marriage.

CHAPTER 8

The older man removed his boots at the front door, and Riley and Martin followed suit. He led them through to the living room, where he stopped and turned; holding out a hand to shake theirs.

'My name is Charles Farmer,' he introduced himself, 'and you are?'

Riley, composed and more relaxed once more, introduced them both and explained that he'd inherited the property from Isaac Havers. They were here to take a good look round, omitting to mention the likelihood of an imminent sale to a developer.

'Ah yes, Isaac; Samuel's youngest son. As I remember, he was just a few years older than me. I'm sorry we had to meet like this, but I'm sure we can iron this misunderstanding out quite quickly,' Charles said.

Riley looked at him incredulously. He'd found somebody who'd actually known the family, and maybe he'd be able to learn some of their history from him. He was eager to learn more, especially how the house had come to burn down, and what had happened to them all after that.

Charles was already turning to Ryan, 'Go and put the kettle on son. I'm sure we could all do with a brew – unless, of course, you'd prefer a beer?' he continued, turning back to their visitors.

Riley and Martin looked at each other before they both nodded in unison.

'A beer would be just the ticket,' Martin replied for both of them.

'Four beers then Ryan,' he said, indicating for them to sit on the sofa, while he subsided into an armchair alongside the fireplace.

Judging by the newspapers on the small table alongside, accompanied by a tobacco pouch and an almost full ashtray, this was where he normally sat; confirmed a few moments later by him reaching into the hearth and removing a pair of rather ancient leather slippers where they'd been warming by the glowing stove.

'Now gentlemen,' he said, slipping them on and sitting back. 'I'd like to try and clear up this misunderstanding, and one which I am easily able to explain.'

Martin looked across at Riley. He was the owner here, and it was he who needed the situation clarified. He seemed to have calmed down from previously and appeared ready to listen to an explanation.

'I understood from the agents that they've been unable to sell the estate so far, so how come you own this cottage?' Riley began, looking interrogatively across at Charles.

'I'm afraid their records can't be entirely up to date then,' the man said, reaching for his pipe and relighting the tobacco already in it before continuing with his explanation.

'I was eight years old when my father became estate manager and we came to live here – in this very cottage.'

I had two sisters, both older than me, and they used to play with the Havers' girls; Emma and . . ., can't remember the other girl's name – something very similar.'

'Emily,' Riley supplied. 'She was my grandmother.'

Charles looked baffled.

'Then if Emily was your grandmother, how come you inherited this place from Isaac?'

'She died in 1976, a few months before her father, so Isaac became the only living heir. He was already living in New Zealand and he didn't want to come back to England, so he put it up for sale immediately. He'd already made a new life for himself and he wasn't anxious to return.'

Charles puffed at his pipe and nodded.

'Sad business that!' he stated. 'They never knew who set fire to it, but the old bugger died with it, and good riddance to my way of thinking.'

'Old bugger?' Riley queried. 'Do you mean Samuel?'

'Yeh, old Samuel himself,' Charles said, tamping his pipe into the ashtray and refilling it. 'That fire did everybody a favour; but it was too late for his good wife – he'd already seen her off!'

Just at that moment, Ryan reappeared with the drinks and set one down on the table in front of his father, handing the other two to their guests. He seated himself at the table under the window away from the group. He still didn't fully trust these newcomers yet.

Riley, his imagination fired from what he'd just heard, thanked him peremptorily and returned quickly to his next question.

'Do you mean he murdered her?'

'No, he didn't murder her – but he might just as well have done! He gave her a dogs' life, and the same with the rest of the family. I reckon that's why Isaac took off to New Zealand. Never said a word to the rest of the family, just up and took off one day. Don't think any of them ever heard a word from him after that.'

That didn't surprise Riley. He'd never heard tell of Isaac before; but then, he'd never known Emily either; as she'd died before he was born. He found himself wanting to learn more as Charles seemed ready to continue the story.

'Your grandmother left home when she was only 18 and shacked up with a carter from the village. She got pregnant almost immediately and Samuel was furious. He started a vendetta against the man and hounded him out of the area. Emily went with him and nobody ever heard from either of them again. Her mother had always idolised Emily and she was distraught by the breakup Samuel had caused, followed shortly after by Isaac's sudden departure. She was never the same after that.'

'So you lived here a good few years then?' Riley quizzed.

'Yes, we did – until all the trouble started over Emma.'

'Emma? So she did live past her second birthday then? I've never been able to find any record of her after her christening.'

'Oh, aye, she did. She was 17 when all the trouble started.'

'Trouble? What was that then?'

'She wasn't happy at home – spent a lot of her time here with my sisters. My mother was away from home at the same time, looking after her own mother who was ill.

Emma had just finished her education and was at a bit of a loose end, but she didn't want to stay at home with her father. Her mother was going a bit doodle-ally, I think it would have been described as dementia these days, and he was forever on at Emma for one thing or another.

She tried to keep out of his way as much as possible, and she took to spending time round the estate with my father. There was a pedigree herd of deer in those days, interbred with the wild deer nowadays, and she loved watching and feeding them.

It was all very innocent, as I often went with them when I was home from school, but the old man took it into his head that my father was messing about with her, and it all came to a head one day down by the riverbank.

They'd been out tending the deer as usual and were sitting on the grass eating sandwiches together, when old Samuel charged out of the woods and laid into her with his walking stick. My father tried to reason with him but he wouldn't listen – he was totally beyond any form of reason.

My father tried to intervene, but the old man turned on him then and pushed him away. He wasn't expecting it and it caught him off balance. He stumbled backwards and fell into the river. Luckily it was running quietly at the time, but by the time he managed to climb out, the old man was frogmarching Emma back towards the house.

Riley and Martin glanced at each other. Could anything have actually been happening between Charles's father and the 17 year old Emma? Had it all been as completely innocent as Charles obviously believed? It seemed unlikely that her father would have been so incensed with fury if they'd both been sitting innocently eating sandwiches on the riverbank. As both men were already dead, and Emma missing, with no other witnesses as to what had transpired, it was unlikely that they'd ever know the truth!

'And what happened to Emma after that? There are no records of a marriage or a death that I've been able to find?'

'I've no idea, I never saw her again. My father was sacked, and we were ordered out of the cottage straight away. We rented in the village for a while, until my father found another job on an estate in

Cheshire, and we moved right away altogether. I did hear from some of the villagers who worked on the estate that the old man kept her locked in the attic and wouldn't let anybody near, but whether that was true or not, I never knew.'

Riley's mind was now trying to make sense of the timescale. Could Samuel have kept her locked in the attic until the fire happened? Had she died in the blaze with him? Surely not! She'd have been in her forties by then! Surely he hadn't been able to keep her locked in there all that time!

No, his mind dismissed that idea as absurd! But where had she been all those years? Could she have died at her father's hands at some point in time? It didn't seem as if her mother had been in any position to stop anything that was happening.

Now Charles's voice was continuing.

'My mother and I both found jobs on the estate and I married whilst we were living there. My wife and I stayed on, until, in 1980 I met up with an old acquaintance who told me about Havergill being for sale.

I made enquiries about the property at the estate agents and told them I'd be interested in buying the cottage and a right of way to the lane leading to the main road. They really wanted to sell the estate as a whole, but they finally agreed to the cottage and about quarter of an acre of land between here and the river, although they reserved a right of way along the riverbank itself. So I've been here for about 30 years now.'

While he'd finished off the last of his story, he'd moved over to a small bureau alongside the far wall and brought out an oblong box; producing from it the Deeds of Title to the property and handing it to Riley.

'As you can see, all signed and legitimised correctly,' he finished off.

Riley gave it a cursory look before handing it back. It certainly looked a perfectly legal document, and the signature of the seller was Isaac Havers!

Finishing their beers, he apologised to Charles for his previous behaviour, and they left, realising they hadn't seen as much of the estate as they'd intended. There wasn't much left of the day to complete that now, and it meant coming back again if he really did want to see it all before it was sold and disappeared under an estate of soulless and ugly houses.

They walked back to the woods where they'd been when they first spotted the cottage and continued their exploration; or what they were able to access from its overgrown state, before deciding to call it a day.

'Fancy a beer before we make tracks for home?' he asked Martin. 'I'm sure there must be a pub in the village.'

'Yeh, fine,' Martin answered. 'I'll just call Kate and give her a rough idea when I'll be home.'

'Good idea. I'll ring Connie too. I'm getting peckish, so I reckon I'll head for home as soon as we've had just the one. It'll take me over an hour to get back, and it'll give her time to get a meal on.'

The pub was easy enough to find, right on the main road through the village; an unimposing red brick building with no outstanding features; its front door opening straight onto the narrow pavement in front.

There was a small car park at the side, nothing more than a patch of rutted earth interspersed with a few areas of gravel, but at least they didn't have to park on the main road. It wouldn't have held more than half a dozen cars, but at this time of day it was quiet and there was only one other car parked alongside theirs.

The interior was quiet too, with a threadbare square of carpet covering varnished and rather scuffed floorboards, but at least it exuded a homely and welcoming atmosphere. Their welcome was also genuine from the buxom woman behind a gleaming and well polished bar counter.

'What can I get you?' she asked with a warm smile.

'Just two beers,' Martin replied, anxious to be seated at a table and find the right opening to put his proposal to Riley.

'New to this area – or just passing through?' she queried as she pulled two frothing pints of beer.

'Just passing through,' Martin replied, before Riley cut in.

'Actually, I'm the new owner of Havergill,' he said, exuding an air of propriety, perhaps expecting envious admiration; but her reaction was far from it!

'Oh, aye,' she said, 'and what are you going to do with the place? Knock it down and cover it with houses, are you?'

That was exactly what he'd had in mind, but that didn't seem to please the woman at all. Her words had been deriding.

'That's all anybody seems to wanna' do these days,' she continued, handing the glasses across the bar and taking the money Martin proferred.

She'd given him just the opening he was looking for; a way to put his idea in front of Riley.

'Could do,' Riley continued, annoyed by her derisory words. 'There's somebody interested in doing just that; but it could also be the perfect place to build some select luxury properties. Did you think about that?'

He seemed to be trying to placate the woman, or perhaps to antagonise her, but at the same time sounding her out as to whether the locals would be opposed to any sort of building work at all on the land.

'The villagers might find that much more to their liking – but we haven't had the chance to look into all the possibilities yet,' he ended, before picking up his beer and taking it to a table under the window; foreclosing on any further conversation.

'That might not be a bad idea you know,' Martin said as he carried his own beer over and sat down opposite him.

'What? You mean a development of luxury houses? And who's going to build these luxury properties? Nobody's ever approached me with that idea. I was just winding her up and giving her something to gossip about,' Riley said, grinning.

'Me for one,' Martin said seriously. 'I could do it, with your co-operation.'

Riley's face registered surprise, but after a few seconds pause he began to seem interested.

'Go on,' he said, 'what have you got in mind?'

Martin launched straight away into the idea that had been whirling round his head for days.

As they'd been walking round, he'd been making mental notes of the layout, and how to make the best use of the available space so that no property overlooked another. He didn't want to overload him with technicalities, so kept his ideas brief and sketchy.

Riley sipped his beer contemplatively as he listened.

'And what do I get out of all this when it's finished?' he asked after a brief pause.

'Well that's something we need to discuss in detail, but I did think along the lines of a percentage of the sale price, after taking off my building costs. We both need to think about it in more detail, but you've already had the offer from the developer – that would be money in your pocket immediately – **if** he can get planning permission. The land would be worth a great deal of money with that, but if not, he may have no further interest in it.'

Riley definitely seemed interested in his proposition, but Martin didn't push his ideas any further, waiting for Riley to think it over as they sipped their beers.

'Ok,' Riley said, as he rose from his seat and took their empty glasses over to the bar. 'I'll think about your idea. I think I'd rather have luxury houses on the site than a load of little square boxes crammed together – I think I owe that to the memory of my ancestors, but will you be able to afford to build them?'

They'd reached the car park by now, and Martin realised this was his final opportunity to push forward his ideas before they both headed for home.

'I have two new builds almost completed. One of them is already sold with a 50% deposit on it; the balance of the purchase price to come on completion, which should be in a couple of weeks, and I already have two people interested in the second. We can finish that within the month. With that and the money I already have in the bank, and money coming in from other work already in hand, I'll have enough to build the first house and clear a lot of the surrounding land. We should be able to get it through planning before I'm ready to start work.'

He was becoming fired up already with the idea, but he didn't want to let his enthusiasm run away with him. He needed to give Riley time to think about it. The intricacies of where the rest of the money was coming from would be his problem to work out. If they sold the first house quickly, that should be all their problems solved, as that would then give him enough to build the next one.

Riley thought about Martin's idea all the way home, and the more he thought, the more he liked it.

His only problem being as to whether Martin would be able to afford to take on such a big job – he didn't want him walking away when the job was half completed and saying he couldn't afford to carry on, or even, God forbid, going bankrupt half way though.

He hadn't known him very long after all, although deep down, he felt he was trustworthy, and he'd already seen the houses he was building now. They looked good and solid, and the finishes seemed really good – although his was only an untrained eye. Having been in the same house since they were married, he really had nothing to compare it with.

If he sold the site to the developer it would be no further problem to him; but then again, he wasn't short of money. What he'd never had, he'd never miss. Martin's idea – if he was able to carry it through – would certainly be a more satisfying use of his property, even though it would possibly bring him in less money than if he'd sold to the developer.

CHAPTER 9

Kate was hurrying to get home, driving as fast as she dared through the narrow little lanes.

She'd had Martin's text message less than an hour ago to say he was on his way home, and she'd still been indulging in an energetic afternoon's sex with her latest conquest. She'd heard the message come through, but it was only after they'd finished their exciting and mind blowing romp that she picked it up to see who it was from.

Her mind filled with shock when she realised Martin was already on his way home.

He was earlier than she'd expected. She really shouldn't have let Bruce cajole her back to bed when she was getting ready to leave. She should have realised how late it was getting.

Carswell was long gone from her list of conquests. He'd been good for an afternoon's release from her normal routine, and she'd enjoyed the luxury hotel room, plus the bottle of champagne he always provided, but it was time to move on after that awful scene in the hotel. He hadn't managed to find another job yet and was living in a flat in a less than salubrious part of town. Once she realised that he would no longer be able to provide her with the luxury she'd become used to receiving when with him, and the many little gifts he'd bestowed upon her, she'd blocked his calls from her 'phone when he kept ringing. As far as she was concerned, that particular episode in her life was over.

Bruce was a much better proposition!

Younger than Carswell, he attended the same gym as her, and she'd noticed him several times glancing her way. The gym clothes and trainers he wore looked expensive, and so did the designer clothing she noticed when they'd left at the same time one afternoon.

It had only taken a provocative smile from under hooded lashes before he came across and introduced himself, making polite small talk as they walked out into the car park together.

It was a cold day and she was glad to be wearing gloves, covering her wedding and engagement rings from his surreptitious glance as she held the rail going down the steps.

Next time she went to the gym, she looked around for him. It was a Thursday when they'd been here together last time, and she wondered if this was his normal day to attend.

That particular Thursday there was no sign of him, as she watched for his entrance while she carried out her normal routine. After an hour, with still no sign of him, she decided that was enough for today, as she collected up her things and left.

She'd noticed him climb into a dark blue BMW when they'd last been here – but there was no sign of it as she glanced round the car park today. Perhaps Thursday wasn't his normal day after all! Perhaps that had just been coincidence.

Just as she was driving out, she saw his car signalling to turn in from the road, and she stopped in the entrance, a welcoming smile on her face.

He pulled up alongside her – both cars completely blocking the entrance as he opened his window.

'I'm glad I've caught you. Had a meeting this afternoon that went on a bit too long, and I've tried to get here before you left,' he said in a rush. 'Can we meet up for a drink sometime?'

'I'd like to,' she smiled. 'How about now?'

'Sure,' he said. 'I haven't brought my gym things – I only came along to try and catch you before you left. Would you like to follow me?'

She nodded, bestowing on him a provocative little smile that she'd perfected in the mirror.

She'd made her conquest after all!

He drove into the car park and did a u-turn before driving back alongside her and pulling out into the road, where she followed behind him. She hoped he wasn't going too far. Her own car was still in for repair, and the one she was driving was a courtesy car; much smaller and far less speedy than her own Audi.

She felt more like the poor relation in this one.

Luckily, they reached the pub within a couple of miles, and spent a pleasant couple of hours together before she decided it was time to head for home.

Martin had said he'd be working 'til the light faded. He wanted to get the two new build houses finished and some money back in the bank from the sales. The second house was as good as sold now, and he'd told her of his idea for developing Riley's property, if he was up for it.

She knew he was capable of taking on such a project, and of building them to a high standard, but was unsure of the financial side. She hoped he wouldn't be taking on more than he could chew.

That day had been the beginning of many with Bruce.

He'd told her he was divorced and was the senior partner in a firm of architects. She realised that could be a very fruitful contact for Martin, but she couldn't even contemplate letting them meet. That could have serious implications for all of them. She couldn't let him know that Martin was her husband, and one unwary word from Bruce could spark off too many complications. Far too risky!

Now, as she hurried home, she knew Martin would probably be home before her, and was trying to think up an excuse as to where she'd been. She didn't have many female friends, preferring by far the company of men, and nearly all the ones she did have were working, so she couldn't use them as an excuse.

She finally decided to say she'd gone late to the gym and hadn't got his message 'til she'd finished. She didn't have her gym kit with her, so she only hoped he wouldn't offer to take it in for her.

Luckily he was already home when she got back, sitting in front of the television with a beer and a sandwich.

'Wondered where you where when you didn't answer my message!' he said as she walked in.

'Sorry,' she answered, 'I've just been to the gym and didn't see your message until I'd finished. Thought it would save time if I just came straight home. I'll go and get some food on now.'

'No rush,' he said, turning up the sound on the television once more. 'There's a good footie match on and I've made myself a sandwich, so I'm all right for now.'

She thanked her lucky stars for that. All she had to do now was rush upstairs and get her gym kit, giving the already clean clothes another run in the washing machine to allay any suspicions he might have.

After they'd eaten, she brought a coffee through and joined him in front of the television.

They were both tired from their days' exertions – although both of a very different nature, and were happy to relax and spend time enjoying a drink and some relaxation.

'What did you do today?' he finally asked, turning towards her and muting the television. The football match had just finished, there was nothing interesting on at that time, and he was ready to chat.

'Err . . . nothing very exciting,' she stammered at the unexpected question. 'Just cleaned the house and sorted out a few things in my wardrobe. How did your day with Riley go?'

She was anxious to change the subject and move it away from her own days' activities.

Luckily, he was still fired up about the day he'd spent with Riley, and eager to talk about their visit and his ideas for the luxury houses.

'How did Riley react to your idea?' she finally asked when he paused for breath. 'Was he in favour of it?' making Martin chuckle as he described how the pub landlady had accidentally given him the opening to put the idea forward.

'I think he was up for it; in fact I'm sure he preferred my idea to that of a housing estate, but he was a little dubious about whether I could afford to complete the whole thing.'

'So am I,' she replied. 'It'll mean a big outlay before you even sell the first property.'

'I've thought along those lines myself, but I should be able to manage. Martin already owns the land, so there's no outlay to buy that before we can make a start. The money from the new builds will give me the funds to clear the site around the old manor house and demolish it. There'll probably be enough to make a start on rebuilding on the same site, and possibly enough to manage the full re-build, but I can't afford to skimp on the quality if I'm to sell it as a luxury property.

Once I have a deposit paid, the new owner can choose their own fixtures and fittings, which will be added to the bill, so I won't have to bother about them until I have the deposit in the bank.'

'Sounds a bit risky to me,' she said. 'Don't forget you'll have wages to pay as well – the workforce won't be willing to wait for their wages 'til the house is sold.'

He laughed.

'The whole thing is up in the air at the moment. If Riley is agreeable to my suggestion, there'll need to be a lot of discussion over terms. I've suggested he takes a percentage of the sale price of the property as it's his land in the first place, and I won't have to fork that out until the sale goes through.'

She wasn't convinced. Martin's small building firm had always kept them comfortably off. He'd always had a knack of finding small pieces of waste land which could be bought for a song, and one or two houses being built on it. They brought in a good profit; together with the numerous smaller jobs like the building of extensions and household repairs – but this was something else. This was something far bigger than he'd ever handled before. She felt alarmed by it.

Although she still loved Martin, she knew she couldn't lose the standard of living they'd always maintained – she just couldn't bear the thought of living in a pokey little house with the neighbour's screaming kids all around and having no money for the little luxuries of life. Things like her own car, gym membership to keep her figure in trim so that she was still able to catch the attention of other men, and holidays abroad – but only once a year. He couldn't afford any more time away from the business; particularly during the summer months when he needed to utilise every hour of daylight. Their holiday always took place in January or February and it always had to be somewhere that was warm at that time of year. She didn't mind that so much, as it was a good time to be away from the cold and miserable winter weather, but she envied their friends and acquaintances who always seemed to be jetting of somewhere on the least little whim during the summer months.

Her thoughts were interrupted as he carried on speaking.

'If necessary, I can get a short term business loan from the bank. Interest loans are cheap at the moment, and it's been a long time since I needed one. I've always managed without one for many years, but I may need one to tackle this amount and the standard of work that needs to go into it. It could make my business if it works out.'

'Oh Martin . . . no!' she cried. 'You know how my father ended up once he started taking out bank loans. They brought his business down and killed him!'

Her father, once a successful builder himself, had gone on borrowing from the bank to fund his ever larger building schemes; taking out loan after loan, until one of his projects failed miserably and he was made bankrupt. He hadn't investigate the land he'd bought thoroughly enough; only finding out later when the completed houses began to subside that he'd built over an old coal mine.

It had been the end of him too, as well as the business. Everything had been too much for him and he'd had a heart attack; dying on the way to hospital. Their large detached house that he'd built himself had been repossessed, and her mother was now living in a small terraced house with her sister. She couldn't bear the thought of that happening to her!

'It's all right,' Martin said, seeing how distressed she'd become. 'I won't borrow; even if it means only building one house and selling it before starting on another. I'll have to make that clear to Riley when we discuss it, but I don't think he'll be too bothered. I don't think it's the money he's after, so much as not having a housing estate on the home that his ancestors created.'

'Thank you,' she said, calming down once more.

She knew he always became very involved with his building schemes, spurred on not by the financial gains, although they were a big part of it, but by the reputation his business was gaining.

CHAPTER 10

Riley too had arrived home in a contemplative mood, and Connie was quick to notice his distraction.

'What's up?' she asked, as they sat down to eat the casserole she'd left simmering in the oven.

'I've a lot to tell you,' he answered, 'but let's leave it until after we've eaten. I'm ravenous.'

Meal over, dishes in the dishwasher, and a pot of coffee made, they went into the living room and sat opposite each other.

She looked at him enquiringly, anxious to know what he had to tell, and even before he'd taken his first sip from the cup, he launched into his story of what they'd found that day.

She was surprised when he told her that the building by the river had turned out to be a cottage and not an old farm building as they'd first thought – but she was even more surprised that there was someone living in it, and had been for almost 30 years.

'But where's the money from its sale? Is there nothing in the papers you got from the solicitor?' she asked when he'd finished.

'Apart from the most relevant papers, I've only had a quick look through the rest. Maybe we should have a good look through now.'

'Good idea,' she said, as he went over to take them out of the desk and deposited them on the small table in front of them both.

Splitting them into two piles, he said, 'You take those and I'll look through these.'

A lot of the papers were of little interest now, but when they'd looked through them all, they'd still found nothing relating to the sale of the cottage.

'That's me done,' Connie announced, pushing them back into a neat pile on the table. 'There's nothing about the sale in that lot.'

'Me neither,' Riley replied. 'I reckon it needs a bit of a shake up with the estate agents. They must have sold the cottage in the first place, and they must have some record of it somewhere. They can't negate responsibility for it just like that!'

'Are you sure that man had actually bought it? He could just have moved in when he heard Isaac wasn't coming back.'

'Yes, he showed us the Deeds – but come to think of it, the bill of sale was signed by Isaac himself, and I didn't see anything from the agents. Could he possibly have entered into a private sale over it, and the agents never actually knew anything about it? Could the money from the sale have gone directly to Isaac?'

Two days later, Riley dropped his last pupil of the day and made another journey to the estate agents office.

This time he wasn't going away without an answer! This time he was determined to get to the bottom of things. He wanted to find out if they had sold the property to Charles Farmer, and if so where the proceeds were; or whether, as he suspected, Isaac had done a private deal with Charles and cut the agents out of their commission.

The woman he'd spoken to on his first visit was still at the same desk as before, and after a short explanation, she remembered his visit.

'Oh yes,' she said. 'I remember. Mr. Roberts has made more inquiries with the previous agent, and he's finally found some of the old records. If you'll take a seat for a few moments, I'll see if he's free to talk to you.'

After a brief few words with the man, she showed him into the office immediately, where Mr. Roberts shook his hand and indicated for him to sit down once more.

'Mr. Gray, the previous owner, has found the papers you're looking for, but it would seem that the property, although still technically for sale with the company, has not been marketed or maintained for a good few years. It would seem that the residue of the money left in . . . . . ,' here he looked at some notes in front of him before continuing,

'Samuel Havers Trust, was earmarked for its maintenance until it was sold, but as I told you before, that money ran out many years ago.

Here he glanced down at his notes once more, a slight smile stealing over his face before regaining his composure.

'It would seem that Isaac Havers last words to Mr Gray were, and I quote, "It can rot for all I care. I want nothing more to do with it or any connection to the old bastard who owned it." Please excuse the language, but those were the exact words written to Mr. Gray – as he has attached here.'

So saying he handed the sheet of paper, a printout of a letter, over to Riley.

When he'd had a chance to read it through, he continued, 'Mr. Gray is going to drop the file in sometime soon, and I'll call you when we receive it. In the meantime, do you want us to continue marketing the property?'

This took Riley by surprise.

'But I thought there was already a developer interested!'

'There is, or should I say, has been. It's some time since we last spoke to you, and you were undecided what to do then. I don't know if they're still interested. We've heard nothing further from them.'

Riley knew now that this was crunch time! Accept the developer's offer unconditionally, or go with Martin's idea!

He knew which one he preferred, but he might be crazy to agree to Martin's offer – he definitely didn't have the money to build all the houses, and it might be a slow and complicated process, selling one house before he could start on another. It might be better to hand it over to the developer straight away and get it over and done with.

It was quite a dilemma, and he needed to talk it over and think it through with Connie first.

Before leaving, he remembered the reason for his visit in the first place – the sale of the cottage. He'd almost forgotten about it after hearing what Mr. Roberts had just told him.

'There's a cottage on the estate, and there's somebody living in it. He claims he bought it 30 years ago. Have you any record of that, and what happened to the money from its sale?'

Mr. Roberts looked at him briefly before consulting the computer again.

'No,' he finally answered, after refreshing several screens and consulting his notes. 'The plan shows a building, although what it is isn't stipulated; and there's no information about it having been sold. Can you wait while I call Mr. Gray and see if he knows anything about it?'

Riley nodded and sat back in his seat.

The conversation didn't last long, and from what he'd heard from this end of it, the previous owner had no idea about the cottage either, confirmed by the agents next words.

'I'm afraid, like me, he didn't even know there was a cottage there. He presumed it was just a shed or a barn, and there have been no dealings over the sale of a cottage. I can only presume it was a private arrangement carried out between the owner and the buyer, with the previous agents not having been consulted,' he continued, his face registering his disapproval. 'I'm afraid the only person to have benefited from that dealing would be your deceased uncle. The money in the Trust ran out many years ago, and no maintenance has been carried out since then. We sent somebody out to have a look at it when we took over the property, but it was so overgrown that he wasn't able to assess it properly – he just had a cursory look round through a pair of binoculars.'

The second of Martin's houses had been finished that afternoon; the new owners already having moved into the first one, and as it was still barely three o'clock, he decided to pay a visit to Havergill before going home. Tomorrow would be soon enough to contact the two prospective buyers who'd shown an interest in the second house.

It had been raining heavily in the morning, but the sun had come out at lunchtime, and Havergill seemed to have taken on a more inviting hue. The grass and the trees looked much greener, and the stone of the house glistened with the good wash it had just received – but it did nothing to alleviate the blackened and charred look of the interior.

Entering the building, he found a fairly sturdy roof truss, one side completely burned and charred, but the other side, touching the floor and leaning against the outside wall, was completely untouched.

Checking it would hold his weight; he climbed carefully along and upwards until he reached first floor level and could peer out of one of the window openings.

From here he could see right across the open parkland, right up to the trees on the far hillside where they'd stood previously, and his mind began to calculate and visualise where he could build five, or maybe even six houses, giving each a good area of ground around it.

Suddenly, a dark tawny shape appeared from the tree line nearest the house, completely unaware that it was being watched.

It was a magnificent red deer stag, fully thirteen hands high and with an enormous pair of antlers.

It stopped for a few moments, nose lifted in the air scenting for danger, before it lowered its head and began to crop the foliage on the ground around it.

Seconds later, its head shot up into the air and it swung round, obviously aware of some danger at hand. He knew he hadn't made any sound, and his presence couldn't have been detected, as he stood rooted to the spot, barely daring to even breathe.

As it swung its head to the other side, its nostrils scenting the air, there was a loud click, sharp and clear in the still air; followed by the loud boom of a shotgun.

The stag, already beginning to take flight, dropped to the ground, its momentum still carrying it forward as its head burrowed deep into the grass and weeds – somersaulting as it fell. It came to rest with a jolting thud – felled by a single blast to its heart.

Martin, unnerved by the sound, almost lost his footing as he heard the blast, and found himself beginning to slide down the wooden truss; sharp and jagged pieces of timber reaching high into the air below him.

Scrabbling for a hold, his fingers managed to grab the bottom of the window opening, giving him time to regain his footing on the timber as he held on for all he was worth.

Finding a foothold on the jagged stone of the outer wall and regaining his balance, he breathed deeply as he managed to haul himself back into a more stable position. Lifting himself up, he was able to look through the gaping hole once more.

There was a man strolling out of the woods leading from the river, shouldering a shotgun and making towards the animal. Martin recognised him immediately! It was Ryan, the son of Charles who lived in the cottage.

He certainly had no right to be shooting deer on Riley's land, even if they had been living right next to it for years, and he felt annoyed about this unwarranted trespass. He wanted to go down and confront the man – but staying silent and not making his presence known was the better part of valour on this occasion. He'd had that shotgun levelled at him once before! And now there was nobody around to see what might happen next!

When he peered out of the window once more, there was no sign of Ryan; the stag still lying where it had fallen. He'd probably gone to fetch some form of transport to get it home, and it shouldn't be long before he arrived back. Martin needed to steal away before that happened.

Climbing carefully back down to the ground, he was just dusting himself off before leaving when he heard a faint sound reach his ears. It seemed to be coming from within the ruined house itself, and even as his ears strained to catch the sound and pinpoint where it was coming from, it stopped as suddenly as it had begun.

He picked his way across to the doorway where the sun was streaming in before he turned to take a last look round.

He could have sworn it was the sound of a violin being played – only quietly, but the melody was hauntingly beautiful. He couldn't see where there could have been anybody in the house amongst the jumble of burnt and charred wood, mixed together with the fallen stone and roof tiles. Maybe the sound had reached him through one of the gaping window openings. Maybe somebody had been playing it round the back of the house and the sound had travelled from there; but after making a quick circuit of the house, he found no sign of anybody.

There were woods behind the house. Maybe somebody had been working in there and listening to a radio, or maybe even just walking through. Whatever it was, it had stopped now.

Shrugging his shoulders, he decided to get back to his car before Ryan reappeared. Who knows; if there was no access through the parkland for a vehicle, he may even come back through the front entrance and find his own vehicle blocking the way. The last thing he needed was a confrontation with him – especially if he was still carrying the shotgun!

He was just reversing out of the driveway when a man on a bike cycled past. He slowed as he saw Martin, and when he'd completed his turn out, he found the man had stopped at the side of the road and was obviously waiting to speak to him.

Opening his window, Martin stopped alongside him.

'You buying this place then?' the man asked conversationally.

'No, my mate owns it and I've just been looking round it for him. Why do you ask?' Martin said, wondering why the man should even be remotely interested.

'I'd keep well away if I was you,' the answer came back. 'That place is haunted! The old man what owned it burned hisself to death in that house after he'd sent his wife mad and murdered his daughter. His last son buggered off out of the country before he went the same way! I've heer'd strange things about the place from others, and I had a nasty experience meself at the river. Somebody tried to push me in, altho' I couldn't see no one, and folks are always hearing the sound of a violin, but they've never see'd anybody playing it.'

Martin was surprised and alarmed. He'd heard that violin himself, not ten minutes ago! If he hadn't heard it for himself, he'd never have given credence to the story.

Before he could recover from the shock, the man had mounted his bicycle once more and was riding away, turning into a track slightly further up the road.

His eyes followed where the man was heading, and he noticed a farmhouse set further back from the road. Inching the vehicle forward, he stopped alongside the gateway. A sign at one side gave the name as Rosehill Farm.

It was surrounded by outbuildings, and if he wasn't mistaken, if was just behind the stand of conifers backing onto the driveway belonging to Havergill. In which case, it was highly likely that they owned the woodland that ran behind the house and down to the river.

He needed to tell Riley what he'd just heard; but did he really need to tell him about hearing the sound of the violin himself? He might think he was going doodle-ally too!

CHAPTER 11

Kate had had another fulfilling afternoons' romp with Bruce in his big four poster bed.

Stretching luxuriously, she pulled the duvet back from her naked body and looked across at the clock.

'Time I was going,' she said, sliding out from beneath the feathery softness. 'Martin's likely to be home within a couple of hours, and I need to have something on for his dinner.'

She walked over to the window and pulled back the curtains.

'Not yet,' he cajoled, sitting up in bed and pulling the covers down to his waist, trying to entice her back. 'I think I could manage another round if you could.'

She turned and looked back at him. His training sessions at the gym had given him a generous six pack, and the fine line of black hair forming a Y shape across his chest and down to his navel only served to enhance the look.

She turned away quickly as he began to pull the covers even further down. She knew he was aroused again and knew she wanted more than ever to climb back into the bed with him, but she daren't be late back home again. She couldn't keep on being absent when Martin returned. He would begin to get suspicious.

'Not today,' she laughed, 'I could come back again . . . .' and then her words tailed off as she looked through the window, quickly moving to one side and concealing herself behind the curtain.

Bruce's home was an old stone house standing on a flat plateau built into the hillside not far back from the quiet country lane. Its elevated position afforded views both left and right for some distance; and she'd just seen something that alarmed her.

'What's up?' Bruce queried, getting out of bed and padding over the thick carpet to join her.

Apart from a pick-up truck stopped further along to the left, the driver leaning over and talking to a cyclist, there was nothing else to be seen.

'That . . . that pickup,' she stammered, 'it's my husband.'

He laughed.

'Are you sure? Why would he be up here? Could he have followed you?'

'I don't think so; we've been here for hours. He wouldn't have waited around that long – would he?' she said, fear in her eyes as she looked at Bruce.

'Could he have driven past and seen your car?' he replied, glancing back out of the window as the pick-up drove past and out of sight.

'I don't know,' she said, looking down towards the parking area in front of the house. Her Audi had now been repaired and she'd returned the courtesy car. 'He may have done, but it isn't very visible from the road. That big rhododendron is hiding most of it, and it's sideways on to the road, so he couldn't see the number.'

She was shaking now, her whole body feeling deathly cold as he went back to the bed and fetched his towelling bathrobe, draping it around her.

'Does he know anybody here? Could he have been visiting someone?' he queried as he pulled her close.

'That's it! He must have been visiting a client or something!' she cried, clutching at straws. She couldn't believe Martin might have been following her – and if he was, he wouldn't have waited so long – or would he? She thought she'd been so careful. She'd made sure Martin would be away for some time before making any arrangements with Bruce, and always tried to be back well before he was due home. If he'd become suspicious of her movements, she wouldn't put it past him to have followed her to this lonely little road just outside the village – but if he'd found out where she was going, why did he need to hang around? It would be easy enough to find out who owned the house. Someone in the pub or the village shop would probably have given him that information readily enough.

Pulling out of Bruce's arms, and discarding the bath robe, she grabbed up her clothes and began to pull them on.

'I'm going,' she announced as she reached the door. 'I'll call you as soon as I'm sure he hasn't found anything out.'

He heard her running down the stairs, and then the big oak door slammed as he saw her making for the car, stopping to search in her handbag for the keys before reversing across the tarmac area and driving towards the road.

Bruce had hoped at one time that she might leave her husband and come to live with him, but today had shown him that she still loved Martin, and she'd do anything not to let him find out about their affair.

Although he was glad to have parted from his wife, and to have his business to keep him occupied during the day, most of his evenings were spent in solitude.

Visits to the pub only served to unsettle him when he heard others talking about their families, and 'better get home to the wife now' being bandied about. Not only had he lost his wife – no great loss to him – but he'd also lost his two children. He heard she'd remarried after their divorce and moved away, but she'd left no forwarding address and no telephone number, and as he didn't know her new married name, he had no way of contacting her. He hadn't seen the children for three years now, and wondered if he ever would again.

At a loss for anything further to occupy the rest of his day, he made his way back to the still warm bed. A couple of hours sleep would probably leave him feeling more refreshed, and he did have some drawings he could spend the evening looking over.

CHAPTER 12

Turning into the road, Riley was surprised to see an ambulance standing in front of his house, and he panicked. Had something happened to Connie?

He quickly pulled up behind it and got out to see what was happening, where he spotted Connie standing on Betty's path near the open front door.

It was outside Betty's home that it was parked, but both driveways were adjacent to each other and its length meant that it stood across both together.

'What's happened?' he asked, walking into his own driveway and speaking across the small dividing wall when he reached Connie. 'Has Betty had an accident?'

'I don't know,' she said, concern written across her face. 'I heard the siren and I came out when I saw it stop outside. They're still inside with her.'

As they spoke, the ambulance crew came out of the house, one pushing Betty in a wheelchair, the other following behind with their bags.

'What's happened?' Connie cried, as she saw the state of Betty.

Her face was covered in cuts and bruises and her left eye was turning dark blue.

Betty turned a woeful eye on her and managed a weak smile as she followed her to the back of the ambulance, where the crew stopped at her insistence while she spoke to Connie.

'My bags still in the car and my keys are in the kitchen. Will you lock up the house and feed my cat for me. I'll be back tomorrow,' were her parting words as they bundled her inside.

'What's happened to her?' she asked of the ambulance driver as he closed the back doors and went round to climb into the driver's seat.

'Says she's fallen down the stairs,' he said, looking at her with a wry grimace, 'but I reckon there's more to it than that. You can ask her yourself when she gets back, but I think we'll be informing the police.'

He drove off before she could ask any more questions, and she went into Betty's house while Riley parked their car in the driveway.

Everything was in disarray!

The 'phone in the hallway was on the floor and the carpet runner covering the tiled flooring was in a heap against the side of the stairs.

All the drawers in the living room and the kitchen were open, and somebody had obviously been rifling through them; papers and other items lying all over the floor. Smashed crockery was everywhere.

As she surveyed the mess, Riley joined her.

'This is no fall down the stairs!' she stated. 'It looks like she's disturbed a burglar and he's beaten her up. Look at all the open drawers and the smashed crockery!'

Riley stood in the hallway; his gaze towards the kitchen.

'She's left the key in the back door, and the glass has been smashed to get to it,' he said, as she joined him and followed his gaze. 'I'd better get some wood and board it up before it begins to rain.

'No, don't do that for now. The ambulance driver said they'd be calling the police. Leave it and don't touch anything. They may be able to get some evidence from it.'

An hour later the police arrived, and Riley went to hand them the keys, informing them of their friendship with Betty. After asking him if he'd seen anything and he'd explained he'd been away from home all day, they asked the same question of Connie, but she said she'd been out shopping herself all afternoon, and had only just got back when the ambulance arrived. She hadn't noticed anything unusual when she arrived back; and there'd been no sign of Betty either.

He and Connie were just drinking their last hot drink of the night when the police called to give them the keys back; asking them not to go into the house for the time being.

They needed no second bidding, as they'd both had a busy day and were ready for a good nights' sleep.

Betty, however, didn't return home the next day, and Connie decided to go and see her in the hospital the following afternoon when she returned from work. Riley had back to back lessons that day and wouldn't be home until early evening, so she had the rest of the day to herself.

Betty was in a sorry state when she did eventually reach her bedside.

Her eye was completely closed, her cheek still blue-black from the bruising, and there was a deep jagged cut across her upper lip, held together with two stitches.

She was propped up on pillows and her arm rested across the front of her, trussed up in a sling.

She smiled with pleasure when she saw Connie.

'Thank you for coming,' she said, as Connie pulled up a chair on the side nearest her good eye. It would be easier for Betty to see her on that side without having to turn her head.

After a few minutes socialising, Connie asked the question Betty had been dreading.

'You told the ambulance people you'd fallen down the stairs, didn't you? We both know that's not true – so what did really happen?'

Tears sprang to Betty's eyes as she looked down at the sheets, unable to meet Connie's gaze.

'He broke into my house,' she finally said in a sad little voice. 'I refused to give him any more money, but he knew I always kept some in the house. He was determined to get it for those terrible drugs he's still taking. He doesn't seem to realise what they're doing to him. He's not the same boy as he was when he was a little kiddie.'

'And just who are we talking about?' Connie sat forward kindly and took her good hand in both of hers.

'I don't want to say,' Betty said, tears now streaming down her cheeks. 'He's in enough trouble already.'

'Betty,' Connie tried to remonstrate with her. 'You're not doing him any favours by keeping quiet about this. He needs to be punished for what he's done to you, and he might be able to get the help he needs to come off the drugs at the same time.'

Betty was shaking her head from side to side.

'I've been trying to tell him that myself, but he doesn't want to listen. He's got in with a group living in a squat, and they're all taking those drugs. He doesn't want to stop.'

Realising her words were falling on deaf ears, she tried a different tack.

'Betty – your house is a mess. He's broken your crockery and all the photos on your sideboard. Riley and I have cleared up as best we can, but why should you have to foot the bill for this all the time?'

Betty was now openly crying.

'I understand what you're saying, but I just can't do that to him. He's my own flesh and blood when all's said and done and I love him.'

Realising she was now getting to the bottom of it, Connie tried again.

'Is it your son?' she asked quietly, holding Betty's hand tightly and leaning towards her.

Betty was shaking her head again.

'No, Dominic would have a fit if he knew what had happened. He'd kill him. I don't want him to find out.'

'Then who is it Betty?'

Betty looked down at her hands once more, fingers now held together on the sheets, and Connie thought she was going to tell her, but she suddenly took a huge intake of breath and asked her to pass her a tissue from alongside the bed.

The moment had passed, and she became the same indomitable Betty once again.

'I won't say,' she said, her strength of mind returning. 'I'll sort it out my own way. I always have, and I always will. I'll talk to him and see if I can make him see sense before I do anything else.'

'Betty,' Connie cried in consternation. 'Look what he's done to you now. Do you think he'll listen to anything you've got to say? You're an old lady – he could seriously hurt you next time!'

But Betty wasn't listening any more. She'd made up her mind, and she obviously wasn't going to say anything further on the matter.

'What I've said is between you and I. Please don't let it go any further. I shouldn't have said as much as I have. Let me sort it in my own way.'

Sadly Connie made her way home. She had her own suspicions about who was trying to get their hands on Betty's money. He obviously wasn't going to give up so easily, judging by the lengths he'd already gone to.

She was an old woman, who knew what he might do to her next time. And even if he didn't beat her up like he had just done; too many shocks like the last one could so easily see her off at her age.

Next day, an ambulance appeared at the front of the house in mid afternoon, and Betty emerged.

Seeing her through the front window, Connie went out to greet her, taking the keys with her, and letting her in as the ambulance departed.

'How are you now?' she asked as she opened the front door and let them both in.

'I'm feeling much better,' Betty said with a bright smile.

'Riley and I have cleared everything up for you, and he's put a cat flap in the back door for you. Rumple can now come and go as he pleases, and if you want to keep him in at night, it's got a lock on it for you to do that as well.'

They'd often heard her calling the cat in at night before she went to bed, and knew she liked to have him safe inside overnight.

'Thank you so much – I must pay you for it,' Betty said, starting to look round for her handbag.

Connie held her hand up.

'No need. Let's just call it an early Christmas present shall we? Now, how about a cuppa?'

Returning a few minutes later with two mugs of tea, Betty eyed them strangely.

'I know they're not the usual ones you use, but I'm afraid all the others have been smashed. You only have these two now, and two more besides. They were saved because they were right at the back of the cupboard. I suppose they're the ones you don't use very often,' Connie explained.

Betty looked sadly at the mug and nodded her head. She'd had her favourite mug for years. It was china, with a William Morris design painted on the outside – a present from her late husband; the last present he'd ever bought her before his death.

It was on a visit to one of the stately homes they'd always liked to look around that she'd admired it when she'd spotted it in the gift shop, but she'd dismissed its purchase because it was rather costly.

Returning to the car after a quick toilet visit before driving home, Arthur had taken a little longer than her, and he'd put something in the boot before getting into the car himself.

When they arrived home, he'd told her to put her feet up and relax and he'd make them some tea. When he came back with the tea, it was with only one cup on the tray – her tea – and served in the mug she'd so admired in the shop.

At the time, he was suffering with a highly malignant and terminal prostate cancer, and knew he wouldn't see her next birthday. He'd hoped she'd keep it to remember him by – and she had! She'd used it every day for the last five years since his passing.

Trying to put aside its loss and think of the future, Betty looked around for the cat.

'Any sign of Rumple?' she asked.

The tortoiseshell cat had been given the unusual name as he'd had a slightly twisted spine when they'd acquired him as a kitten, giving him a slightly hunched over appearance, and it was her husband who'd christened him that. As he'd grown older, the deformity had become less pronounced, but the name had stuck.

'He's not in his basket, so he must be out,' Connie said, sitting down with her own drink. 'I let him out first thing this morning, and I put some food down at the same time. That's gone, so he must be around somewhere.'

Shortly afterwards, as they were sitting talking, the cat stalked in and rubbed himself against Betty's legs before jumping up on her lap and making himself comfortable, where he promptly fell asleep.

'I don't think he's even noticed I've been gone,' Betty smiled as she stroked his sleek fur, eliciting loud purrs from his throat.

'I must go and put our evening meal on,' Connie announced when she'd finished her second cup of tea. 'Riley will be back just after six. I'll put enough on for you as well and then it'll save you trying to cook.'

'Thank you Connie; that would be very welcome. I'll have a look round when I've had a short rest, and see what I've got left. There should be enough food in the freezer for the next few days until I can arrange for my son to get me some shopping. I know I have some ready meals there to keep me going for those few days.'

'I had enough milk to let you have some myself, so there's a two pint carton already in your 'fridge. If you need anything in the meantime you can ring me,' she told Betty as she left.

Betty thanked her and offered to pay for it, but Connie refused.

'You were very good to Riley when he was laid up. Let's just say I'm repaying the favour.'

Returning home, Connie was surprised to see Riley's car turn into the driveway ten minutes later.

'I thought you had a lesson at five o'clock,' she said in surprise when he let himself in by the side door.

'It's been cancelled,' he said, preparing to go upstairs and have a shower.

It had been a warm day, and he'd been cooped up inside the car all day. He felt grubby and sweaty. It was a perfect day to have a cancellation, and a perfect day to have some unexpected extra time to himself.

After they'd eaten, she took some of the cottage pie in to Betty, where she still found her as she'd left her previously – fast asleep in the armchair with Rumple still curled up on her lap.

Something must have alerted the older lady to her presence, as she opened her eyes in alarm as soon as Connie walked into the room. Knowing she must have thought it was her attacker come back again, Connie spoke immediately to put her at her ease.

'It's only me,' she said, smiling. 'I've brought you some dinner. It's cottage pie, so you should be able to eat that all right with one hand. I'll just pop it in the oven to keep warm until you're ready.'

Betty nodded but said nothing until Connie returned to the room.

'Thank you for that dear,' she said. 'I think I'll go straight up to bed when I've eaten it, I'm feeling very tired. I'll wash the plate and return it tomorrow.'

'No need,' Connie replied. 'I'll pop in when I get back from work and we can have a chat and a cuppa again, then I can check on how you're managing.'

'I don't want to be any trouble. I'm sure I can manage on my own,' was the reply, but then, anxious that Connie shouldn't feel she was interfering, she mitigated her tone and added, 'but I'm sure I'd be glad of your company if you've the time.'

'Of course I have,' Connie said in mock indignation. 'After all the time you spent looking after Riley when he had his accident, I'm sure I don't begrudge doing something to help you out now.'

Betty smiled wearily.

'I must admit, it'll be nice to have your company for a while. It can sometimes get a bit lonely living all on your own, and I don't see much of the family any more. They're all so busy with their own lives these days.'

Betty's son, Dominic, had three children between the ages of 15 and 21. His wife, Paula, was the personal assistant to the managing director of a printing company, and they all led busy lifestyles.

They hardly ever visited now, and on the occasions when she paid them a visit, she always found herself out of her comfort zone.

Everybody around her seemed to be so busy. Paula with cooking, cleaning and sorting out the problems of her often squabbling children, and they, in their turn, talking on their mobile 'phones, and with earphones plugged into their ears all the time. People always seemed to be coming and going, and doors were constantly slamming. It was impossible to hold any sort of conversation with anyone for more than a few minutes before they had to go and do something else.

Although she craved company, this was something she couldn't put up with for very long, and soon returned to her own peaceful and quiet home once more.

She also had a daughter called Sylvia, whom she hardly ever saw these days. Sylvia had always had ambition and soon acquired a post as an assistant at a city centre store in Chester after she left school. She'd worked her way up to department supervisor from there, and within three years had acquired a similar post in a city centre store in London, where she'd met Sylvan, one of the directors. He was divorced, with no children, and he was ten years older than her.

Within two years of meeting they were married and moved into Sylvan's luxury flat overlooking the river at Kingston-upon-Thames.

Betty hadn't been invited to the wedding and had never met or spoken to Sylvan, and nor had she ever been invited to visit them.

Sylvia 'phoned every so often, which she felt was more of an obligatory call than for any real need to speak to her. After a few preliminary inquiries about her mothers' health; she always prattled on about her own busy life, making Betty feel more and more like the poor relation – which she undoubtedly was now.

She always felt relief when the call ended and she could get back to her own mundane life, which she definitely preferred to that of her daughters'. She would have hated the life Sylvia seemed to be leading, even if she'd been younger. The endless round of social functions and parties that she attended was something she'd never ever have enjoyed.

A few days later, when Riley went to put the bins out for the morning collection, Betty's house was in darkness, and he realised she must already be in bed.

Quietly, so as not to wake or alarm her, he walked all round the house and checked all the doors and windows had been secured properly; something he'd taken to doing routinely every night since her release from hospital, and also checking the bins and putting out the appropriate ones for her. He knew she'd probably have forgotten all about them.

Having completed that, he returned to his own home and made his way to bed.

About two hours later, a stealthy figure crept up the side of the house and round to the back door, where he stood and listened for any sound from within. Finally, satisfied the old woman was sleeping soundly, he tried all the doors and windows around the house, and finding everything secure, he moved round to the back of the house once more. He'd gained entry once before by smashing the glass, and knew that was the most vulnerable place to gain access, as she probably still left the key in the lock. However, he found the old flimsy door with the large glass pane at the top had now been replaced by another, sturdier door, with six panes of glass at the top separated by wooden battens. That didn't seem to present much of a problem though, as the only one he now had to smash was the one nearest the lock, and, being smaller, that would make less noise than the previous large pane of glass had done.

He took off his glove and wrapped it round a large stone from the rockery behind the garage, pulling his arm back and bringing it down heavily in the corner of the pane, the place he gauged to be the most vulnerable position.

The glass cracked, but didn't break.

Listening for any sound either from inside the house or around him, he brought the stone back again and landed another hefty blow into the corner of the pane once more. This time it did shatter, and, although it sounded loud in his ears, it brought no sound of anyone looking out to see what had happened, nor did he see any lights being turned on.

He retreated to the dark passageway between the house and the garage and waited a good ten minutes, but all remained quiet, and he finally returned to the back door. He cleared the glass from the edges with the stone still wrapped in his glove, and put his hand through. The key had still been left in the lock – just as he'd hoped. These elderly people never did learn a lesson!

He hadn't found a handbag last time he'd broken in, knowing there was bound to be money in it, but this time, when he flashed his torch around the kitchen, it stood in full view on the end of the work surface leading to the hallway.

Quickly rifling through it, he found £160 in cash, and her two bank cards – one a credit, and one a debit card. He picked up the debit card and looked through the purse. Just as he'd hoped, she'd written her pin number on a slip of paper and tucked it into a side pocket inside her handbag.

He'd already learned that trick. So many people, particularly the elderly who had poor memories, often did stupid things like that and it made things so much easier for him. He could use the card to make a withdrawal from a cash machine, requesting a balance in the account at the same time. Once he knew how much was in there, he knew how much more money he could take before the account was empty and the bank notified the customer that they were overdrawn.

He'd done it numerous times before, a number of times with his own mothers' card. She never checked her statements, or kept any record of her spending, so she'd never even noticed.

The cash he'd found was good for a few fixes anyway.

Peering round the door and into the hallway, there was no sign of a light on anywhere in the house. She must still be sleeping.

Wearing trainers, his feet were noiseless on the hall floor as he crept towards the living room. She kept a desk in one corner alongside the fireplace – there might be more money in there. Some time ago when he'd visited, he'd seen her take money out of the drawer to pay the window cleaner. She may still be in the habit of keeping money in it now.

It was worth a try!

The curtains hadn't been shut, and a street light on the far side of the road created a glow into the room as he crept through the doorway. He could see the desk now. It still stood in the place he remembered.

Listening for any sound, he began to creep across the room, when suddenly a strangled yell split the air. He turned to where the sound had come from, just in time to see a heavy object whistling through the air towards him. It hit him a glancing blow on the back of his shoulder and he fell forwards into the room, hitting his head hard against the small table in front of the fire.

Stunned, he lay face down on the rug, unable to gather his senses together.

There'd been somebody in the room. They must have been there all along. They must have heard him breaking in and been lying in wait.

Stunned, he tried to stagger to his feet, but suddenly the heavy object whistled through the air again and caught him full in the middle of his back. He went down again, and this time he felt the blood trickling down his face from a deep cut on his forehead.

He felt light-headed, but even though he was anxious to make his escape, he just didn't seem able to rise to his feet.

'Once too often, Peter me lad!' he heard the angry voice from behind him. 'You've got away with it once, but this time I'm not going to stand for it. I've already called the police. It's time you got your comeuppance.'

Putting his hand to his head, he felt the blood oozing over his fingers and running down his cheek, just as he heard the squeal of tyres pulling up outside, and the room lit up with blue flashing lights.

'That'll be them now,' she said, as she went to the front door to let them in, cool and calm as you please. She was no longer afraid of him anymore. She knew this time he'd go to prison for sure; but she no longer cared. If he cared so little for her after all the love and attention she'd given him over the years, why should she care about what happened to him.

Sadly, she found she did still care, but if he'd do it to her – his own flesh and blood – he'd have no compunction about doing it to a complete stranger. This was the only way to help him now – he had to be stopped before he killed some other poor soul.

It was a warm night, and Riley was unable to sleep; tossing and turning under the cloying duvet.

Connie was already breathing deeply and he didn't want to wake her. After several sleepless minutes, he got up and went downstairs to get a drink of water; thinking to spend the rest of the night in the back bedroom. There was no duvet on that bed, as Connie just left it covered with a sheet while it wasn't in use. It would be far more suitable for a warm night like this, and being at the back of the house, he could leave the window open as well. There would be no early morning noise to wake him as people started up their cars ready to leave for work.

Taking the water back up to the bedroom, he turned the sheet down and went to open the window; leaning on the sill and gazing out at the starry night.

There was hardly any moon and the stars twinkled brightly in a velvety sky, drawing his gaze across the heavens as he stood enjoying the cool night air, the light breeze helping to cool him down.

Suddenly, he heard a loud thud, followed a few minutes later by a second, and then by the sound of breaking glass.

Leaning out as far as he could, he looked towards Betty's house. The garage hid any view of her back door – but he was sure the sound had come from there. Surely her attacker hadn't come back so soon after her discharge from hospital; and how had he known she'd be back? Betty seemed to know who he was, so maybe he was someone attached to her family; someone who would already have received that information. It seemed ludicrous that a family member would carry out such a vicious attack on her – but what other explanation could there be?

Donning dressing gown and slippers, he hurried to the front door, quickly slipping down the side path and round to the back of her house, where he found the back door ajar.

Inside, broken glass littered the floor and he could hear voices from the front room.

He looked round and spotted a heavy frying pan standing on a shelf against the far wall. Quickly picking it up, he headed stealthily towards the sound of the voices.

Suddenly, he realised the voice was Betty's, and she seemed to be well in control of the situation; her voice more angry than scared as she appeared in the hallway and went to the front door. As she opened it, three burly police officers came through as she directed them towards the living room.

Her eyes followed their progress into the room, and it was then that she spotted Riley. She'd already pressed down the light switch and the scene was now flooded with light.

'Come to join the party, have you?' she asked, smiling wanly.

Before he could answer, the police officers bundled a young man out of the room and down the path to the waiting car; the last one stopping to reassure himself that Betty was uninjured before joining them.

Just as they drove away, he heard a sound behind him and found Connie standing by the back door.

'What's happened?' she asked in dismay. 'Is Betty all right? I heard the car arrive and saw the flashing blue lights.'

'I'm fine, love,' came the cheery voice from behind him, 'and all the better for that young toe rag having been caught. I hope he gets what he deserves this time.'

Relieved that she was fine, Connie stepped over the glass and came into the kitchen.

'Would you like me to make you a cuppa?' she asked.

'Good idea,' Betty replied. 'I think we could all do with one after that little shenanigan. I'm sorry you were disturbed from your sleep.'

Sitting down together when it was ready, Betty said resignedly, 'I suppose I do owe you an explanation, and let's hope we can all sleep easier in our beds from now on.'

'I knew there was something you weren't telling us,' Connie cajoled, 'who is he?'

'That young man is my grandson, Peter, although I feel ashamed to call him that now. Heaven knows what his dad's going to say when he finds out. He'll probably disown him – although that's very hard to do when it's one of your own.

I first found out he was going wrong about two years ago when he started coming round and asking me for money. He hadn't been able to find a job, and his father was getting annoyed with his lack of trying. He just seemed content to do nothing but hang about the streets with his mates all the time, and he wasn't making any real effort.

Feeling sorry for him, I gave him the odd few pounds to tide him over, and he was good enough to meet me from the coffee morning I go to every Monday. I thought he was just being very chivalrous – wanting to see his old gran home safely.

Then word started going round from the other folk at the coffee morning that money was going missing from their handbags and coat pockets. I very soon realised that it stemmed from the time Peter started meeting me, and I had my suspicions from then on; but instead of confronting him, I stopped going to the coffee mornings altogether.

When a friend told me the pilfering had stopped, I knew then that it was definitely Peter. I couldn't confront him with anything as I had no proof – only suspicions.

He stopped coming round to see me after that, and I knew that he realised I was on to him.

Since my husband died, I often take a nap in the afternoon around two o'clock after my lunch, and a couple of times when I came down, I found my handbag open and money missing.

I always keep it on the kitchen work surface where it was tonight, but when I realised that Peter must be coming in while I was asleep, I started locking the back door and taking it upstairs with me.

You must have guessed that it was Peter who attacked me the last time. He had the audacity to break in through the back door and search through my desk looking for money while I was out shopping.

Unfortunately, I came back while he was there and found him upstairs in my bedroom rifling through my things. I told him I was calling the police and I tried to stop him leaving, but when I wouldn't get out of his way, he hit me several times before I lost my balance and fell down the stairs. I'd just collected my pension from the Post Office and I'd left my handbag in the car. He was angry 'cos I wouldn't tell him where it was. I was determined not to let him have it.

Then tonight, after my tea, I decided to watch a film on television, and when it ended, I fell asleep in the chair. I was woken by the sound of breaking glass, and I realised he'd come back again.

My husband Arthur was always a keen cricket player. He played for the local cricket team, and he kept his bat in the corner behind the settee. I've always kept it there as a memento of him.

I was determined to put up a fight this time, so I armed myself with it, and it's thanks be to my dear Arthur that it saved me.'

'What about your son? Does he have no idea what Ryan's been doing?'

Betty sadly shook her head.

'He's always been a good dad to all his children. He'll be so angry when he finds out. I'm sure he'll put Ryan out on the street when he knows, especially when he finds out it was him who attacked me and that he's been stealing from other people for some time now.'

Riley and Connie agreed, but it was done now, and his father would find out very shortly anyway; if not from his grandmother; then definitely when the police knocked on his door!

CHAPTER 13

A few days later, Riley had a 'phone call from the estate agents.

'I'm sorry to have to inform you Mr. Duncan that the developers have decided not to proceed with the purchase of your property,' Alwyn Roberts' voice informed him. 'After preliminary talks with the planners it would seem that there is little chance of their proposals being accepted. There are numerous issues against its acceptance, not the least of which being the access onto an already narrow road, and the lack of appropriate drainage facilities provided by the local council.

They have, however, intimated that a smaller development might be acceptable, but the developers have decided that is not a viable proposition from their point of view.'

Riley's hopes were dashed, and he was still thinking things through when Connie arrived home from work.

'You look thoughtful,' she said when she saw him sitting at the kitchen table, arms crossed and resting on the table in front of him; an untouched cup of coffee beside them. 'Something up?'

'Developers have pulled out of the sale,' he said, taking a sip out of his coffee and pulling a face before pouring the rest of it down the sink. 'Yuk, that's cold,' he said, pulling a face. 'So we're back to square one!'

Connie was busy unpacking the shopping she'd brought in with her, and she stopped what she was doing when she heard his words.

'You've still got the offer from Martin,' she interjected. 'You've always said you preferred his ideas anyway.'

He was quiet for a few moments, inspecting the surface of the table.

'Why don't you give him a ring and accept his idea?' she pursued. 'You've nothing to lose.'

She was right. Even if Martin couldn't complete the whole building project, at least he'd said he could complete the demolition and rebuilding of the main house straight away, as well as clear some of the grounds. The estate might remain on the market for many years to come; deteriorating all the time, and still his sole responsibility. Even if it took years to complete, there would be the prospect of it eventually being off his hands for good, and what land might be left over could be offered to local farmers. They'd bought land from the estate before. What was to stop them doing so again? Then this weighty responsibility would be off his hands for good.

Martin was delighted when he received Riley's 'phone call.

This was something he'd wanted to get his teeth into for years. A well thought out and prestigious development of luxury properties could make the name of his company, and would bring him in far more money than the mundane extensions and house repairs they'd carried out for years on a regular basis. Riley had the land, and he had the know-how – what could be better – and he wouldn't have to pay him until after he sold the houses.

Now he needed a good architect to design and see through his plans, from inception to completion. The basic ideas were already running through his head. He needed someone who could bring them to life on paper and iron out all the pitfalls.

He spent the next few hours trawling through the internet, and making 'phone calls to other people in the building game, and the same name kept coming back to him from various sources: Style and Design Architectural Services. He was told they weren't cheap; but they were the best – and that's just what Martin wanted!

With that in mind, he 'phoned the telephone number he'd found on the internet, pleased to find that they were based in a town not too far from the property, and even nearer to his own home.

The receptionist put him through to a Mr. Toomes, who turned out to be one of their principal architects, and who listened intently while Martin outlined his plans.

'I'm sure we'll be able to help you,' he replied when he'd heard his proposals. 'Perhaps you'd like to book an appointment to come and see us next week, and bring some drawings of your ideas with you. Please be aware that our costs aren't cheap, and we'll require a retainer up front if we decide to take on the work.'

He sounded rather elderly on the 'phone and Martin hoped his ideas would be more modern and up to date than he sounded. His own ideas for the properties were for sleek, open plan interiors, equipped with all the latest mod cons, whilst keeping to a more traditional look for the exteriors, with plenty of stonework and gabled frontages.

'That's not a problem,' Martin replied. 'I have some rough sketches already drawn up, so I'll re-draw them and bring them with me.'

'Good,' Mr. Toomes replied. 'Now, I'll transfer you back to the receptionist and she'll book an appointment for you.'

He worked assiduously all weekend on the designs and drawings. His years in the building trade had taught him a lot about design, and he was fairly adept at it, although he never skimped on the use of an architect's professional eye. The firm he usually used were good at their job, but for this project, he needed somebody better.

On Wednesday he arrived at the office with a portfolio full of papers and drawings to show Mr. Toomes, and was directed straight to his office. The man had obviously been awaiting his arrival.

He was much as Martin had expected from the voice on the 'phone – middle-aged, small and dapper in a light grey suit and well polished matching shoes, with short salt and pepper hair and a well clipped matching moustache.

The only furniture in the room was a desk, which, although tidy, contained trays of papers and files, together with a computer and the telephone. There was nowhere to lay out his drawings.

They shook hands as they introduced themselves, before Sidney Toomes indicated the portfolio.

'I see you've been busy then,' he said, smiling down towards the bulging case.

'No use coming unprepared, was it?' Martin said, a grin spreading across his face.

'Definitely not,' Sidney replied, walking across to another door at the opposite side of the room. 'Let's take them through here and have a look at them, shall we?'

The door opened into a similarly sized room, but here the walls were lined with work tables, angle-poise lamps overlooking each one. The one under the window was empty, and it was to this which Sidney led him.

Martin explained firstly the story of the estate and told him the available acreage, explaining that he would be building the whole project in stages, beginning with the demolition of the main building and the clearing of the grounds around it. Owing to the cost of the work needed, it would necessitate the sale of that before he could proceed with any further building work.

Sidney pored over the drawing of the building he intended to replace Havergill, saying nothing for several minutes.

'It's well thought out, and your drawings are good, but I can see a few problems which need ironing out. You do realise that a house of this size and quality will cost a deal of money to build? You say you're only a small building firm – can you raise the capital to build it? And what about the land? You'll need to purchase that first, which means buying the whole 20 acres before you even start. That could cost a packet with planning permission – and you wouldn't want to buy it without permission being granted first.'

Here Martin brought in the story of Riley's inheritance and of how they were planning an agreement for Riley to receive a percentage of the sale price as remuneration, meaning he wouldn't need to buy the land.

'Seems a fair arrangement to me,' Sidney replied, adding in a more serious tenor, 'but make sure you have the whole deal drawn up by a solicitor. It needs a legal mind to go over that one and draw up a legally binding contract – for the good of you both!'

'Already thought of,' he said, knowing he and Riley had already agreed to do just that.

'What about the plans for the other houses? And I'll need a scale map of the area in question.'

Martin brought out the map he asked for, having thought of that in advance, together with the other designs he'd drawn up, explaining that he hadn't gone into any serious placement of the other houses yet, although he had earmarked possible sites on his own plan. He was waiting 'til a later date for that. As the most prestigious part of the development, he was promising an uninterrupted view from the windows of the new Havergill itself, and he couldn't allow another house to impinge on that view.

After a quick inspection of the available land, and the other part of the projected development, Sidney pored over the main design again.

'This house has five bedrooms, each with its own en suite, and equally large open spaces downstairs. It should sell for over a million with the five acres of land that go with it, provided it's well built and you clear the land over the whole 20 acres giving it a view. It'll be equally expensive to build!'

'I've already assessed the building costs. It'll be tight, but I've just sold the last two houses I've built, and I should have enough capital to last me until it's sold.'

Toomes left the plans on the table and turned to shake Martin's hand.

'Then be assured, I'll do my best for you. I should have everything ready for you to inspect within a month, and then you can apply for your planning permission.'

So saying, he opened the door and let Martin out.

Driving home, he was ecstatic. He'd envisaged a selling price of around £800,000, and over a million was far more than he'd envisaged - but it had come with a warning from Sidney Toomes. Although houses of this calibre were much in demand in countryside areas, they often took a while to find the right buyer, and some may hesitate when they knew other houses were to be built on the land in front of them. They prized their view! It would be even more important to place the other houses where they didn't hinder that view in any way, and to be able to produce the plans to prove that.

Knowing they were there and being able to see them from their windows were two entirely different things.

He must make sure that plenty of the wooded areas were left standing, behind which could be built the other properties, each hidden from its neighbour, but leaving its own view of the surrounding countryside. With that in mind, he went out of his way to visit Havergill once more on his way home.

Climbing the roof truss once more, he took in the view from the window opening, mentally taking his time and assessing where they could be placed so as not to disrupt the view.

This time everything was quiet, save for the sound of the raucous crows and jackdaws in the woodland nearest the house. His ears strained for the sound of a violin at first, but when nothing was heard, he thought his ears must have been playing tricks on him last time, and settled down to the task in hand, soon becoming engrossed.

It was only as he felt the first heavy drops of rain falling on him that he realised how dark the sky had become, as he heard the first rumble of thunder. It was close, and he realised he'd soon be swamped by a deluge of rain.

Climbing down as quickly as he could, he made a dash for the car. The thunder was almost overhead now, and the lightening was flashing constantly across the heavens. The rain was becoming heavier and he still had some way to go.

Reaching the conifers flanking the driveway, he pushed into their branches for cover. Although the rain was heavy, they were so thickly overgrown as they crowded together for space that very little of the rain reached him, and he proceeded to push his way through them as best he could to reach the car.

Suddenly, a bright flash lit up the branches around him and the ground shook as a powerful crack of lightening found its way to earth. Pushing his way out to the edge of the overhanging branches, he saw the house had taken a direct hit, and what was left of the unburned timbers inside were now burning energetically; flames leaping many feet up into the air.

What little remained of the outer walls had been blown outwards, and huge stones littered the whole area around it. Once the dust and smoke began to settle, the flames inside showed all that was left standing were the lower few feet of the gable walls.

Well, that saves me a job, he thought as he watched, but as the storm had now passed on and the rain had turned to just a few light drops once again, he left the shelter of the trees and made his way back to the car using the driveway, skipping and hopping his way over the many puddles covering its surface.

He'd intended to ring Riley when he got back to tell him about his visit to the architects', but now he'd be able to tell him that what was left of his ancestral home had also gone too. Now it was just a pile of charred timbers and stones; no longer recognisable as a dwelling.

The masons would be able to retrieve a lot of the stonework, which he intended to use for the ground floor of the new building, but the upper floor he intended to be of rendered blockwork, painted white with decorative timber panelling relief, making it look like a Tudor style house, with chimney pots also in the Tudor style.

It was a style he'd seen in many small villages throughout the country, and to his mind, it was very pleasing to the eye. He hoped Riley would feel the same way.

CHAPTER 14

Jack Radcliffe was clearing and cutting back hedgerows when he felt the first few drops of heavy rain and looked up to see the sky clouding over.

The air had been sultry, and he felt hot and sweaty, but his view of the approaching storm clouds had been hidden by the tall conifers flanking the drive of Havergill. Those that encroached on their land he'd cut back beyond the hedgeline, but they really needed thinning out after all these years. They'd become far too crowded now, and were vying for space, their lower branches becoming denuded of greenery as they spread outwards vying for every inch of sunlight they could reach.

His tractor wasn't too far away, and he quickly made his way towards it; seeking its shelter from the heavy rain he knew was coming as he heard the rumbles of thunder approaching. It had a roof and a windscreen, but the sides and the back of the cab were open to the elements. It would be better to sit inside and wait for it to pass. There wasn't a breath of wind, so he hoped he'd miss most of the deluge and it would pass quickly.

Now the lightning was flashing around and it was becoming very dark as he reached its shelter, climbing into the cab and sitting as near the middle as possible, the rain falling heavily all around him.

Suddenly, the sky was lit up by a brilliant white light, followed by a gigantic explosion and a rending and thudding sound. He could hear the sound of crackling, as the scent of wood smoke began to drift towards him, and he knew instantly that the old house had been hit. He couldn't see it behind the thick stand of trees, but he wondered if it was lightening that had caused its demise in the first place. As the rain began to ease, from his raised position in the cab, he saw a man coming down the drive on the other side of the hedge, hastily beating a retreat to his car, which Jack now saw him climbing into.

There'd been a lot of comings and goings at the old property just recently, and he wondered if somebody had at last bought it. It had been left for far too many years now, and he wondered what they intended to do with it. From what he'd just heard, it looked as if there wasn't going to be much left of the old house now – but then there hadn't been enough left to live in previously. He'd been very young when it had burned down the first time, and he didn't remember anything about it, or what had caused it to catch fire in the first place.

After the man had gone, he drove out of the gate at the bottom of the field and into the road, going along to the driveway of Havergill and turning in; his tractor rumbling over the weed filled surface and flattening the small bushes and saplings, until he reached the house.

There really was nothing left now, just a few remnants of stonework at either end. The area in front of the house was littered with huge blocks of stone, smoking and charred timbers lining the spaces between them, and the remaining larger pieces still burning inside the shell.

As he was about to turn the tractor and head for home, his hand stopped in the act of switching on the engine. Above the sound of crackling wood, he could hear the soft strains of music being played somewhere. It sounded like a violin - totally incongruous and out of place in this arena of scattered debris! He heard only the slightest strains, before silence reigned once more and there were no signs or sounds of anyone else around.

After a few moments listening intently, the sound wasn't repeated and he decided he must have imagined it. He'd made a good start on the hedge cutting. That would be enough for today; he'd finish it off tomorrow after morning milking.

His mother, Nell, had just finished baking at Rosehill Farm as he opened the kitchen door and was turning out scones onto a wire cooling rack.

'Hands!' she cried, as he reached out to take one.

'Clean!' he replied. 'I washed them in the sink outside, and I've left my boots out there too,' as he indicated his stocking feet.

'Put the kettle on then. They're too hot to eat yet, but you and granddad can have two each when the tea's made. They should be cool enough by then.'

As she turned to remove a fruit cake from the range, he quickly picked up one of the scones. It was hot, as she'd said, and he jiggled it in his fingers as he turned to put the kettle on. He couldn't resist the smell of freshly made baking though, and dinner seemed to have been a long time ago.

Splitting it into pieces, he put it on the work surface alongside him and took out the tea things.

'I see you've helped yourself then!' the indignant voice came from behind him.

'Sorry,' he said, turning to face her with a cheeky grin on his face, 'couldn't resist. They smelled so nice!'

'Well, you're only getting one with your tea then. I was going to give you two, but as you've already helped yourself, you'll only get the one. I haven't got time to keep baking all day long!'

Her tone was half joking, but he knew her days were always busy. She had him and his brother Toby to look after, as well as his elderly grandfather, providing them with three cooked meals a day, and seeing to her own chores around the farm.

She had about a dozen chickens to see to; the extra eggs from which she sold at the farm gate, providing an honesty box for those who bought them – but not everybody was honest!

Gramps had always had his vegetable patch at the back, but as he'd grown older, and his arthritis had become worse, she'd taken that over as well. On good days, he'd go out and help her, even if it was only picking peas and beans, and preparing them later from the comfort of his armchair, but those days were becoming further and further apart. They'd now had to turn the small parlour off the kitchen into a bedroom for him, as he could no longer manage the stairs.

His wife, Amy, had died 3 years previously and he wished he'd gone with her. He'd always farmed this property since he'd taken it over from his own father, along with his son, Frank, and his two grandsons, Jack and Toby. Sadly, Frank had died 10 years ago after a tractor rolled over on top of him, leaving him and the boys to run things on their own. Aled hated being a burden on them all now; they had enough to do without looking after him as well.

Pouring water into the mugs, Jack left his mothers' tea alongside where she was working and carried his and granddads mugs through to the sitting room.

'Hello, lad,' his granddad greeted him from his armchair by the fireplace, 'did you get finished before the storm broke?'

'No, not quite,' he answered, placing the mug of tea on the small table at his granddads' side, and sitting down in the chair opposite, 'but there's not much more to do. I should finish it before lunch tomorrow.'

'Good! Good!' Aled replied. 'That's another job out of the way!'

Jack's curiosity had been fired by his thoughts when looking at the ruins of the old house, and he decided to see if his granddad could throw light on what had caused the first fire.

'Gramps, do you know anything about the fire at Havergill?' he asked.

Aled almost spluttered into his tea.

'That was a long time ago, lad,' he said when he'd regained his composure. 'What's brought that to mind?'

Jack went on to tell him of its having been struck by lightning this afternoon, and how it was now completely destroyed.

'I went to take a look after the rain had stopped, and I just wondered how it had come to burn down in the first place.'

Aled gauged his words carefully before he spoke, trying to be vague about what he told him.

'There's nothing much to tell really. We didn't have much to do with the family, and it was a great surprise to us when we saw the house burning. We heard from the locals who'd worked for Samuel that he was a real tyrant, and staff came and went on a regular basis – nobody stayed for very long, and nobody had a good word to say for him. His wife became mentally ill, allegedly he drove her to it, and he had her put in an institution.'

'Were there no children then?' Jack asked as his mother arrived with the scones and returned for her own tea.

If he'd seen the expression on her face as she looked across at Aled, he'd have known there was more to the story than he was letting on.

Aled had regained his composure by now, and was managing to think things through more clearly.

'Oh aye, there were six children, but the first two died as babbies, and another died at 15. I heard he fell in the river and drowned.'

Nell was giving him a look. He was becoming too specific for somebody who said he knew little about the family.

Aled noticed and gave her a slight nod of recognition, he'd long prepared the story in his head about what could and could not be said. Even if his body was letting him down, his mind was still sharp; he knew questions might come up at some point in his life, and he was ready to answer them as far as he could.

'Well, what about the other three?' Jack prompted.

'Emily moved away when she was only young; went to live with someone in the village and got herself pregnant out of wedlock. It was considered a great sin in those days and Samuel hounded them out of the village when he found out. We never heard of her again. The youngest, Isaac, went abroad, or so I heard tell.'

Jack was thinking all this over, and after a pause said, 'You've missed one out – that makes only five. What happened to the other one?'

Here, the look that passed between Aled and Nell was unmistakable as she paused before sitting down with her own tea.

'Emma was only 17 when Samuel caught her with the estate manager. He thought something was going on between them and he sacked him on the spot. He locked her in the attic, and kept her there, or so I heard tell. The housekeeper used to take meals up to her, but she wasn't allowed to leave.'

'And how long was she there for?' Jack's interest was aroused.

This time Nell's look was commanding. Now was not the time to tell her son everything. Not while it could still put Aled in danger.

'I've no idea, son,' he said. 'Nobody saw or heard of her again. Her fathers' body was found in the ruins after the fire was put out, but there was no sign of Emma. Nobody's seen or heard of her since.'

Jack ate his scone and sipped his tea as he pondered over what he'd heard. The look of relief and the smile Nell bestowed on her father-in-law gratified him, but he longed to be able to tell both his grandsons the truth.

He'd left a letter in a sealed envelope with his Will which would let them all know the full truth, but until after his death, it was best kept quiet. At this moment in time, there was only Nell left alive who knew the full story, and he knew she'd never tell anyone. An unwary word in the wrong place could bring about his downfall, but after his death, it no longer mattered.

A quiet moment followed as they all ate their scones and sipped their tea, after which they heard the back door thrown back on its hinges, and a cheery voice calling from the kitchen.

'I see Toby's home then!' Nell said wryly, eliciting a laugh from them all.

Toby was never one to do anything quietly, and everyone was always aware that he was around even before he appeared.

'Can I have one of these scones?' his voice came through from the kitchen.

'You can have two, but only if your hands are clean. I've left yours on a plate by the kettle. We've all got some tea,' his mother called back.

Seconds later, Toby appeared, carrying his plate of scones, a large bite already missing from one – but no tea for him. In his hand was a cold can of lager straight from the 'fridge.

'Have you seen to the cows?' Jack asked, turning to look at him.

'Yeh, they're fine,' Toby answered, flopping onto the sofa and slopping a liberal amount of lager over the top of the can, bringing a frown to his mother's face.

'How's the heifer doing?' she asked.

'She's okay. I've bedded her down in the shed with plenty of straw. Her calf's due any day now, so I'm keeping her in until she has it.'

This would be the heifer's first calf and they were all keeping a close eye on her. They all knew that Toby cared greatly for the animals, and would be up more than once during the night to check on her – that's if he even went to bed in the first place.

'Did you get caught in the storm?' Aled asked, eyeing the tee shirt and jeans Toby wore, which looked comparatively dry.

'Nah,' he answered. 'I was in the shed with the heifer putting down some more straw when it started. I just stayed there with her until it passed. Checked the others in the field after, to see if they were spooked, but they were all down the far end sheltering under the trees. They didn't seem too bothered.'

'Did you hear Havergill take a hit?' Jack piped up.

'Yeh, I did. Walked through the trees and up to the boundary fence behind the house and saw it burning. That must'a' been some hit it took.'

They all nodded in agreement. They'd all heard the explosion as the lightening hit, but at the time they didn't know where. Sobering thoughts clouded Aled's mind, but he said nothing, hoping the subject of the old house would blow over.

Toby's next words brought him straight back into the present.

'Some of the lads in the pub say the first fire was deliberate. They say somebody killed the old man and lit the fire to cover it up.'

Aled and Nell exchanged surreptitious looks before Nell changed the subject quickly.

'What rubbish!' she said, and then, changing the subject. 'Dinner's nearly ready. Get upstairs and change those clothes, Toby, they reek of cow dung – and have a shower yourself while you're at it. You don't smell too sweet either.'

'Yeh, I'll have one too,' Jack said, placing his plate on the table before following his brother. 'I've been hot and sweaty all afternoon, and I'm going out with Helen tonight.'

When they'd gone, Nell turned to Aled.

'Thanks for not telling them everything,' she said. 'Jack would probably have kept quiet about it, but you know what Toby's like; his mouth sometimes runs away with him. Time enough for them to know when you're gone. Until then it should just remain between the two of us.' He nodded. He knew she was right.

CHAPTER 15

When Martin returned home, Kate wasn't there, and he 'phoned Riley straight away and told him of the lightening strike on the old building.

He was sad to hear it was totally gone now. The house had been in the hands of his family for almost two hundred years, and heaven knows when it had actually been built. There was no documentation left to attest to that. It had probably all gone up in the first fire!

His mood was lifted somewhat when Martin told him of his visit to the architect's office, and that his plans had been acceptable, except for a little tweaking. It was lifted even more when Martin told him how much the house could be worth when it was built – it was a figure far in excess of his expectations!

Riley conveyed the news to Connie when their 'phone call was finished.

'Well, that saves on demolition costs at least,' she said, smiling slyly at him, before continuing more seriously. 'I only hope Martin manages to build it to the standard required to fetch that sort of price.'

'I don't see why not. The houses he's just completed look extremely good,' he replied, hoping he was right. From what he'd seen of them, they had looked well built, and they'd sold for a good price – one even before it was completed.

She pulled a wry face before leaving the room. She hoped he wasn't wrong. It wasn't long since he'd met Martin, and that was only through a brief association in hospital. Since then they'd only met a few times. Was that really long enough to get to know someone properly?

He should really do a bit of digging around into Martin's company before entering into any sort of legal agreement with him, and she broached the subject after their meal, finding Riley totally in agreement with her.

Whilst she sat down to watch television, he went to the computer and starting doing some research, returning to the living room just as her programme was ending.

'Everything seems okay,' he started out, flopping onto the sofa. 'I've checked Companies House and his records are in order there, and his website shows pictures of houses and extensions he's built in the past. Unfortunately, very few reviews have been posted, but those that have been seem to be glowing, with no negative ones.'

She looked at him wryly.

'You know how easily reviews can be manipulated, don't you?'

'Oh yes,' he answered, 'but I intend to ask Martin if we can go and visit some of these properties shown on line, and perhaps speak to some of the people living in them.'

She nodded sagely.

'Wise move,' was all she said before switching the television on again.

Not having found Kate at home, Martin decided to 'phone Marianne. They hadn't spoken for nearly a week, and he hadn't seen her for a fortnight.

He thought the one for business calls was on the work surface in the kitchen, but when he picked it up he found it was Kate's. They were the same make, model and colour, but hers had a piece of coloured tape across the back. She had dropped it one day on the stone flagged floor in the kitchen and it had cracked the case. He'd put the tape on to hold it together, but as he was about to put it down, he noticed the display was showing '1 missed call'.

He'd never know why, but for some reason, he checked to see who the call was from, and found it was from someone merely named as 'B'.

It was that same technique of using just the initial that he'd used for Marianne's number, and a suspicion began to creep into his mind. Could she too be carrying out an illicit association with someone? He knew his and Marianne's fling was all that it was – just a passing fling, but he was alarmed now that Kate might also be having an affair. He'd never imagined anything like that happening, and he was scared he might lose her. He couldn't imagine what life would be like without Kate by his side, and he didn't want to try. He couldn't bear the thought of losing her.

Rapidly he picked up a pen off the table and ripped a piece of paper from the notepad on the work surface; noting down the number associated with 'B' before replacing the 'phone. He didn't know what he intended to do with it, but for the time being, he'd keep it safe until he did decide. Perhaps he'd ring the number sometime from someone else's 'phone and find out who answered – maybe even pretend he'd got the wrong number and try and find out who he was speaking to.

It was then that he heard Kate's car arriving back, and quickly looked round to see if the 'phone was just as she'd left it, and that nothing else was out of place, before going back to the living room and pretending to have been watching television.

He'd keep that number safely tucked in the back of his wallet until he decided what to do about it!

Two weeks later, Martin received a call from Style and Design's receptionist.

'Mr. Toomes has some plans ready for your inspection. Would you like to make an appointment to see them?'

Of course he would! It hadn't taken as long as he'd expected, and he was overjoyed that he'd now be able to get down to business; his first actions being to apply for planning permission, and to see a solicitor about the agreement to be drawn up with Riley.

His company were working on three home extensions at the moment; one of which was almost doubling the size of the original property, and all three should be finished within a month to six weeks. He hoped that it wouldn't take long for planning permission to come through. All that were left on their books after that were some minor home improvements and numerous small repair jobs.

The money was already in place to make a start on the first house in the development, and he was anxious to get things rolling.

The appointment with Mr. Toomes was booked for the following Monday, and he told his workers he wouldn't be in that day. He knew his boys could manage things in his absence, and didn't know how long he'd be there. When he'd finished, he needed to go home and look through them properly; beginning to assess how much work was involved and how much it was all going to cost.

However, when he did arrive at the offices of Style and Design, it was to be shown into a totally different office, and to be greeted by a totally different person.

He got up from his desk when Martin entered, and came round to shake his hand; a welcoming smile on his face.

He was younger than Mr. Toomes and around Martin's own age, although an inch or so taller. He was well built, with dark wavy hair, and not so formally dressed, wearing a short-sleeved striped shirt and black, well cut and obviously expensive, jeans; together with smart, black suede shoes.

'I'm sorry Mr. Toomes isn't here to meet with you as arranged, but he was admitted to hospital over the weekend, and I've taken over from him. My name is Bruce Chambers, and I own this company. I hope you don't have any objections to my taking over. Your design is completed and I'm ready to help out with any queries you may have.'

Martin liked this man immediately. He wasn't as stiff and formal as Mr. Toomes, and he thought they'd get on well together. He seemed to be very outgoing – the sort of person you could talk frankly with and without pulling any punches.

At the back of the room was an archway, and Bruce led him through to another room behind his office, similarly laid out with tables over which hung angle poise lamps.

'These are yours over here,' he said, leading the way to the back wall and switching on the lamp. 'I'll make us a coffee while you have a good look at them, and then we can go through any questions you may have.'

Martin looked over the plans while he heard a coffee machine being put into action in the adjoining room.

They were certainly impressive and very well drawn out.

One or two changes had been made to those ideas he'd already had. He'd planned the house to be in the shape of an H, with two gables standing out from either end containing the two principal living spaces on the ground floor, and the two main bedrooms above; both looking out towards the view. The third and fourth bedrooms were situated at either end of the house; one facing the woodland leading to the river; the other facing the stand of conifers alongside the drive, which he intended to thin out once the build got under way. The front door was situated in the recessed area between the two gables, and the fifth bedroom and family bathroom were situated above that, again looking out towards the view at the front.

The main difference Mr. Toomes had made was to the kitchen area at the back and side of the house. Instead of separate kitchen, snug and study, he'd incorporated them all into one large room, with bi-fold doors opening out onto a patio and garden area to the rear. The utility room he'd kept separate, and with no intervening walls, he'd made it much larger, moving the downstairs cloakroom into the area below the stairs, while at the same time adjusting these to form three turns so as to create more space beneath them.

Martin had to admit, it had been a good improvement, and one that he'd probably incorporate into the other houses.

His next move was to work out where the other houses should be placed. He didn't want them to interrupt the view from the main house, but still retain a good view of their own. Perhaps Mr. Toomes could help him out with their placement when he returned.

At that moment, Bruce brought the coffee through.

'Well, what do you think?' he asked.

'I think it's really good,' he answered, taking the cup from Bruce, and adding sugar and milk from the small tray he'd brought through with it. 'When I'm ready, I'll probably build the other houses along similar lines, although slightly smaller and with only three or four bedrooms for the most part.'

'Are you not building the whole lot now then?' Bruce asked. He'd thought this design was to be employed for all the properties on the site.

'Can't afford to do it all at once,' he said ruefully. 'I need to sell one before I can build another.'

Bruce nodded thoughtfully. Sidney Toomes had already filled him in with the background on how Riley had acquired the land through an inheritance, and he hoped they'd make a go of this new venture.

'Take them home and study them, and make a note of anything you'd like changed,' Bruce ended. 'In the meantime, there's an invoice needs paying if you're happy with them.'

Martin **was** extremely happy with them, and decided to celebrate by paying a visit to Marianne. He still hadn't got round to ringing her yet, and as he had the rest of the day to himself, he decided on an impromptu visit. He hoped it would be a nice surprise to her.

There was a car parked alongside him, and he had to reverse out of the parking space, but as he prepared to do so, he noticed a car signalling to turn in from the road. It looked very like Kate's car! He must be imagining things! Why would she be visiting an architect's office? What business could she possibly have with them?

The car was hidden from his sight for a few moments by a passing bus, but as he regained sight of it, it was already turning in. Instead of parking in the delineated 'Customer parking' area, it turned towards the left of the building and disappeared from sight round the corner. As it passed within only a few feet of him, he saw that it definitely was Kate driving. She was concentrating on the turn, which was rather tight, and hadn't noticed him.

Stunned, he sat in the car and waited for her to reappear, expecting her to make for the front entrance to the building, but after a good few minutes with no sign of her, he decided to go and take a look for himself.

There was a wooden fence at the back and side of the building, and he found Kate's car parked sideways on, the bonnet pointing directly at the back fence. It was empty, and when he tried the door, it was locked.

He looked around. There was no gate in the fence leading to the rear of the property, but there was a door into the building next to it. If she hadn't returned to the front entrance, the only possible way she could have gone was through that door.

Did she know somebody here? It seemed unlikely. He'd never heard her mention a friend working in an architect's office. She knew he'd been researching likely architects to draw up the plans for him, so why hadn't she mentioned knowing someone here? It seemed strange that she hadn't done so.

He hung around for a few minutes to see if she came out, but then he returned to his own car and sat waiting for another fifteen minutes before her car reappeared. She reversed out and across the car park, passing the rear of his vehicle before she was able to turn towards the main road, where she had to wait for the traffic to clear before she could drive out. She hadn't noticed him!

He prepared to follow, but then he noticed that she was signalling left and not right. To the right was the way towards their home, and the way from which she'd arrived. Where was she going now? The way to the left led out of town and into open countryside – he knew that because that was also the way towards Havergill. Could she be going there? She'd never shown any interest in the place, save as another work project for his company, and he was sure she didn't know exactly where it was, so why would she be going that way? He decided to follow her!

When he caught up with her, there were two vehicles between them. Perfect! He was higher up in his 4x4 and could see her over the others, but it was unlikely she'd notice him. He was sure she'd have no idea he was following her.

They were almost there when the van in front signalled to turn into the track leading to the farm alongside Havergill, the place he'd already noted previously was called 'Rosehill Farm'. He'd need to visit them if his plans were accepted, and explain to them what was about to happen. He had no obligation to do so, in fact, they'd receive the obligatory notice from the Planning Committee asking for objections in due course, but he always thought it was best to keep on the side of neighbouring properties and try to alleviate any fears they may have about noise and pollution issues.

He had to wait while a car passed from the opposite direction so that the van could complete its turn, and he was about to speed up and catch up with her again, when he noticed the single car which now separated them was slowing down. Kate's vehicle was indicating a left turn! Havergill was on the right and a short distance further on. Just where **was** she going?

Kate was already driving up a slightly steep drive towards a house standing above the road. There was a vehicle behind him and he couldn't stop, so he continued on to the entrance of Havergill and turned in, parking across the entrance and stopping to watch.

From there he couldn't see the drive to the house because the stone wall flanking the road stood between them, but he could see the frontage of a stone house raised up on a flat plateau above the road.

Kate's car was parked alongside a large rhododendron bush covering the left of the parking area, but he couldn't see any sign of her.

He got out of the car and made his way along the grass verge flanking the road on this side. It wasn't very wide and a bit perilous with the passing traffic, but at least it was a relatively quiet road, and only one car came past.

He'd almost reached a place where he could get a better view of the front of the house when a large Council truck came from behind him and sounded its horn as it passed. It had moved well out into the road and away from him, but the shock still caused him to stumble sideways into a large bush.

Getting up and regaining his balance, he thanked his lucky stars that the bush had been there; otherwise he'd have fallen into the spiky hawthorn hedge that lined the road.

As he brushed himself off, he glanced towards the house again to make sure Kate hadn't been watching. The noise of the horn would certainly have caused her to look towards the road, and from his exposed position she would have been able to see him; but everything was just as it had been before and there was no sign of her.

Using the bush as cover, he took a proper look at the house. Apart from her car, the parking area was empty, and so was the double wooden car port on the right hand side. The house was flat fronted with a large stone built porch, in which the door stood slightly ajar. Had she had a key to let herself in, or had someone left it open after she'd gone in?

Baffled, he wondered what she was doing there when there seemed to be no other occupant present. Suddenly he noticed a dark BMW approaching from the way they'd just come, slowing down and pulling towards the centre of the road, preparing to turn in.

Taking the driveway faster than Kate had done, it executed a perfect right turn at the top and parked under the car port, before a man got out and retrieved a briefcase and jacket from the rear seat.

For a moment he couldn't see him clearly, but as he came out from under the shade of the car port and walked across to the porch, he recognised him immediately. The clothes and the hairstyle were those of the man he'd just been talking to. It was Bruce Chambers!

Stunned, he stood for many minutes as Bruce entered the house and shut the porch door after him.

His immediate thought was to go across to the house and demand an explanation from them both. To his mind it was obvious why she should have access to Bruce's home – it must be him she was having an affair with! He was probably the 'B' in her 'phone that it related to. But then a thought struck him – if she was having an affair with the architect, he was ultimately no better than her – he'd been having his own affair with Marianne for nearly a year now, and he wondered how long they too had been seeing each other.

Bruce had obviously had no idea that he was Kate's husband; otherwise he'd have shown some sort of recognition when they'd met in his office. Perhaps letting it innocently drop that night that Bruce Chambers was handling his plans for the new housing development might shock her into some sort of reaction. He didn't know what he hoped to gain from that, but he intended to tell her that night anyway. He found the idea rather amusing! It might even be enough to warn her what a dangerous game she was playing!

Oh well – if that was the way she wanted to play it, let her get on with it. If she was spending the rest of the day with Bruce, why shouldn't he carry on with his plans to visit Marianne?

What was sauce for the goose must surely be sauce for the gander!

Stopping to pick up a bottle of wine and some flowers on the way, he reached Marianne's home within the hour; but when he got there, he found another car parked under the trees where he normally parked.

She had her own space alongside the cottage, but there was only room for one car.

A stile opposite the trees led into the wooded area beyond, with a 'public footpath' sign alongside. Perhaps whoever owned the car had gone for a walk in there; perhaps giving his dog some exercise.

The lane was too narrow to park in – a car might be able to pass, but anything bigger, like a delivery van or a lorry going to the hotel would be unable to get by and he didn't want his romp with Marianne disrupted.

With some difficulty he managed to manoeuvre his car alongside the other; at the same time allowing enough room for the drivers' door to be opened and for it to be able to drive out. Any competent driver should be able to manage it easily – but then, not everyone could be classed as competent – even if they had passed a driving test.

He had to squeeze between the trunk of a large tree and his own car before he was able to retrieve the wine and the flowers from the back seat. He'd already discarded his jacket, and was now in shirtsleeves. He only hoped the back of his shirt hadn't picked up any dirt or bark stains from the tree.

He was just ducking back out of the car with his purchases when the other driver appeared from the lane. He seemed taken aback when he spotted the car parked alongside his own, and his sudden appearance also took Martin by surprise.

'Nifty bit of driving that!' the man exclaimed when he got over his surprise. 'You visiting Marianne too?'

The man wasn't what Martin would have expected from the almost brand new car he was driving.

He had a head of frizzy ginger hair that needed cutting, and he wore a black polo necked sweater and blue jeans, marked at the front by traces of white paint. He must be somewhere in his mid to late 50's in Martin's estimation.

'Hope you enjoy your ride!' he exclaimed, giving Martin a sly grin as he fumbled for his keys. 'Best lay I've had in a long time! Worth every penny! I'll be back next week for me usual.'

Martin was stunned by what he was intimating. Surely Marianne wasn't selling herself! That would make her no better than a common prostitute! He'd never have expected that of her – and she'd never asked him for money.

The man drove out with ease as Martin replaced the flowers and the wine in the rear passenger seat, undecided whether to face it out with Marianne or to drive off and never see her again.

Eventually he decided to go and see her; unsure of what he was going to say, but knowing he had to say something. He had to face her with what he'd just heard and see if it were true.

His knock went unanswered for several minutes and he tried again, eventually hearing her footsteps approaching on the stone flagged floor before the door was opened a fraction. All he could see peering out was her face, which registered shock when she realised who it was.

'Martin!' she said in a surprised voice. 'I wasn't expecting you!'

'Well, this wasn't the reception I was expecting,' he said sarcastically. 'Aren't you going to invite me in then?'

'I . . . I'm not dressed!' she blustered.

She obviously wasn't pleased to see him. Perhaps she realised he'd seen her last customer leaving and viewed his untimely appearance with trepidation.

'It's never bothered you before! You forget – I've seen you naked many times before!'

She hesitated once more.

'I . . . I was just in the shower,' she managed weakly. 'Couldn't you come back another time?'

'No! I want to talk to you now,' he said, moving into the doorway and pushing the door towards her.

She involuntarily moved back, and he closed the door after him as he stepped over the threshold.

She was wearing nothing but a bathrobe and a pair of pink fluffy slippers; her long hair wrapped in a towel.

'I suppose you'd better come in then now you're here,' she said, leading the way into the lounge, wrapping the bathrobe more tightly around her as she sat on the edge of a chair, indicating for him to do the same.

'It's nice to see you,' she said weakly.

'I don't think it is! You're very obviously not pleased to see me!' was his stern reply as he ignored her offer of a seat.

She had the good grace to look down at the floor and not to meet his gaze.

'I'm sorry,' she said. 'If you let me go and get dressed, I'll be ready to talk to you then.'

'That won't be necessary!' he answered, his tone still stern. 'I'm not stopping! I've just met your last customer – he's just informed me what a good ride you are – as if I wasn't aware of that myself – but then I gather you've had a lot of practice!'

Her face had gone pale as she looked up at him.

'How come you've never charged me then?' he asked.

'You were special!' her feeble little voice answered. 'I like you and I wanted to go on seeing you.'

He snorted derisorily.

'I mean that Martin. I don't want to stop seeing you – I think I love you.'

He looked at her angrily. There were tears springing to her eyes and rolling down her cheeks, and he suddenly knew that she meant every word.

She'd always been very self-assured and bubbly when they'd met previously, but this was a very different side to her he was seeing today. She hadn't admitted to being a prostitute in so many words, but she hadn't denied it either. He'd never known her go out to work and he'd always wondered how she made her living – now that he knew, it was more than he was willing to put up with. He couldn't bear to keep seeing her knowing she was seeing other men for money.

'Will you let me explain?' she asked before he could say anything more.

'It had better be good!' he answered, sitting in the chair she'd previously offered and waiting for an explanation.

She looked at her hands clasped together on her lap, perhaps trying to get her story straight before she began.

'George is my landlord,' she began, lifting her eyes to look at him. 'He lets me have this place rent free provided I allow him to visit me every week.'

He snorted again.

'Couldn't you go out to work like other people do?' he asked, sarcastic once again.

She looked down at her hands and shook her head.

'No, I can't,' was her quiet reply. 'I have a severely handicapped daughter. She's only three years old and she needs constant attention.'

'And where is she now? I've never seen any sign of a child on my previous visits.'

'That's because she's not here now. She's in specialist care at the moment. They don't know at this stage whether she'll live very much longer, or whether she'll progress well enough to be able to come home in the future. I have to be available for any eventuality.'

She seemed genuine and his mood of anger evaporated.

'What about the child's father? I presume you're not together any more. Doesn't he contribute in any way?'

She took a deep breath and hesitated, obviously trying to pluck up the courage before telling him anything further.

'Ray is dead,' she finally stated baldly on a long drawn out sigh of breath.

Lifting her eyes to look directly into his face and holding his gaze she continued, 'I killed him!'

He looked at her, not knowing what to say any more.

'Why . . .? How . . .?'

Composing herself now, having decided to tell him everything, she started to explain.

'I'd known Ray for a good many years before we got together. We lived in the same street, and I knew he came from what my parents regarded as a troublemaking family. His father had been in and out of prison several times for petty theft: breaking and entering, shoplifting, petty pilfering – but never anything serious, and his mother was a bit pugnacious. She had numerous slanging matches with the neighbours, mainly about her five children running riot around the neighbourhood, and she never seemed willing to keep them under any sort of control.

I'd trained as a typist and bookkeeper and I managed to get a job with the same manufacturing firm as a friend. I left home when I was 22 and we rented a flat together.

It was about two years after that that I met Ray again in a local pub, and he seemed very different from the family he'd come from. He hadn't changed much in appearance from when I last saw him and we got chatting; the outcome being that we started seeing each other on a regular basis.

He was nice and always brought me flowers and little gifts, but I soon found him a little overbearing. He seemed not to like me speaking to other men, and we often argued when I did. I put it down to the fact that it was just a bit of jealousy.

After a couple of years, he was offered a job in another town. It was a good job – something different and something he wanted to do. The pay was much better as well. He'd already managed to find a flat and he asked me to move in with him. After some thought, I decided I didn't want to lose him, so I decided to go with him. It was too far to travel to my old job, so I had to give it up and take a job in a local convenience store while I looked around for something better.

It was only after a few weeks that I began to realise what a control freak he was. He hated me going out with anyone else, or seeing the new friends I'd made. He wanted me all to himself. If I wasn't in when he got home, he started ringing round looking for me.

The situation was becoming claustrophobic, and one day, when I stood up to him, he hit me quite savagely for the first time. I was covered in cuts and bruises. When they saw me, my friends and family urged me to move out, but I still loved him and I had nowhere else to go.

My parents had my sister, her husband and their two children living with them at the time. They had moved out of their flat and were waiting for their emigration papers to come through before they moved to New Zealand, so there was no room to stay with them.

With nowhere to go, when he pleaded with me to forgive him and not to leave, I had no alternative. He'd promised it would never happen again, but after a few weeks, it started all over again. The beatings became worse and more frequent, and I was sometimes obliged to take a week or more off work because of the state I was in.

Eventually I decided enough was enough. I had to get away. My friend Sylvie came over with her car and we packed all my things into it while he was out at work, but unfortunately he came home early that day and caught us in the act. When he realised what was going on, he snatched the suitcase from her, and came up the stairs after me. He was really angry – bawling and shouting.

He hit me several times and threw me against the wall. As he did so he lost his balance and fell over a chair, and we both ran out while he was getting up.

He picked up the chair and threw it down the stairs after us, running down behind it. He caught up with us by the car and tried to drag me back inside, but Sylvie hit him with the suitcase, and he fell down the area steps leading to the flat below.

She jumped in and started the engine, but I fumbled with the door handle, and he managed to catch hold of my arm. I tried to pull away from him, but he was too strong. We ended up tussling in the middle of the road.

I managed to break free and ran towards the car, but I wasn't fast enough. He ran after me and caught hold of me again. I turned and gave him an almighty push in the chest, putting all my weight behind it. He was off balance and he stumbled backwards into the middle of the road.'

Here she stopped speaking and Martin picked up a pack of tissues from the table and handed them to her, waiting while she wiped away the tears that were streaming down her face. She was obviously finding it hard to talk about.

He waited a few moments before prompting her.

'And was it the fall that killed him?'

She shook her head and took a deep sobbing breath before continuing.

'No, that didn't, but the lorry coming round the corner did. He was sprawled in the middle of the road and the driver didn't see him in time. He ran right over him.'

He could feel a lump in his own throat as he went out to the kitchen to put the kettle on, giving her time to compose herself.

When he arrived back with two mugs of tea, she had stopped crying, and a heap of sodden tissues lay in her lap.

'What happened then?' he asked as they sipped their tea.

She seemed ready to continue now.

'All the lorry driver saw was me pushing Ray into the path of his oncoming vehicle. He thought I'd done it deliberately. He called the ambulance and the police and I was arrested. Luckily, my side of the story was corroborated by Sylvie and another couple walking up the street with their dog, as well as all the angry bruises on my face. They saw everything and I was released without charge.

There really was nothing left to say as they both sat in silence and drank the rest of the tea, before Martin thought of something else.

'What about your daughter? You said Ray was her father.'

She nodded.

'He was. Not only did he beat me up, he raped me repeatedly. I was two months pregnant when he died. He never knew about the baby, and neither did I at the time. I often wonder if the vicious beatings I endured caused her disabilities. The professionals won't comment on that one way or the other.'

After a few more minutes, Martin decided to leave. He wanted to think things over for himself. He knew instinctively now that their relationship was over, and he wondered how he was going to tell her.

'If your daughter's under professional care, what's stopping you getting a proper job for the time being?'

'I have to lie low, and I'm safest here. I told you, Ray's family are a nasty lot. They've threatened to do me some serious harm in retaliation for his death if they find out where I'm living, especially his two brothers. They've even threatened to kill me.'

A select group of clients, brought here mainly by word of mouth, earns me enough money to live on, and I've changed my name as well so that they can't find me. I hate having to do it, but I do enjoy the sexual act, so I can put up with it until I earn enough money to get away from all this. Perhaps move to another part of the country altogether where they'll never be able to find me.'

'You do realise this is the end of things between us, don't you?' he said quietly, looking down and unable to meet her eyes. 'I couldn't possibly consider seeing you again knowing what you've told me.'

She took it philosophically. It was no more than she'd expected from the angry look on his face when he'd first arrived after realising that she'd been prostituting herself.

'I understand,' she said, getting to her feet and giving him a peck on the cheek. 'I knew you were bound to find out some time. I only hoped we'd have a little more time together before you did.'

As he walked up the drive, she called after him, 'Have a nice life Martin. I love you.'

He didn't respond – just kept on walking. He knew that he might have weakened if he looked back.

CHAPTER 16

Martin had already shown the plans to Riley, and both he and Connie approved them wholeheartedly.

'They're great,' Riley exclaimed. 'It isn't anywhere near the style of the old house, but things change and we all have to move on. Whoever bought the place wouldn't have rebuilt it in the same style anyway – far too old fashioned by today's standards.'

Connie agreed and Martin prepared to present them to the planners. They came back within a couple of months stamped 'Approved'. Now he had something to get his teeth into, and his costing was pretty well finalised. All he had to do was order the materials and put together a workforce. He'd already picked out the best tradesmen for the job, most of whom he'd already sounded out, and now he was ready to approach them and agree a date to start work.

In the meantime, he put forward his proposal to visit the occupants of Rosehill Farm to Riley.

'Their house is very close to the boundary, and it would be a courtesy to approach them and tell them what we'll be doing. They won't be able to see us working, but they'll certainly be able to hear the noise.'

'Yes,' Riley said, 'I agree with you. It's only fair to keep them up updated. Bring the plans with you and then they'll be able to see what the finished house will look like. If they know what we're doing they'll be happier than being kept in the dark.'

After he'd left, Connie made them a meal, and seemed very thoughtful while they were eating.

'Something on your mind?' he said eventually.

'I've been thinking – we haven't had a holiday yet this year. How about I go with you when you visit the farm and we'll have a few days relaxation as well. It's a nice part of Wales and we haven't done any walking for a long time now. Perhaps we could find a hotel near to the site and I could have a look at the place before it disappears altogether.'

He laughed.

'You won't be impressed when you see it, I can promise you that. There's nothing to see but a pile of rubble and some very overgrown scrub where the gardens once stood.'

'Nevertheless, I'd still like to see it before it disappears altogether – see where your ancestors once lived, even if it is only a ruin now.'

'Okay,' he answered, 'but it'll have to be soon; Martin is anxious to get started.'

' I can easily arrange a few days off from the shop, but you'll have to re-arrange some of your lessons. That might be a bit more difficult.'

'I'll manage that. You leave it to me.'

He too was anxious to see the place again before it disappeared completely, and he was looking forward to meeting the owners of Rosehill Farm. Perhaps there was somebody still living there who'd known his family – perhaps someone who could tell him a few stories about them, and give him an insight into his family background. Once Martin started clearing the site and building work began, it'd probably turn into just another muddy building site, and there'd be nothing left to see anymore.

He had no more lessons that day until four o'clock and they started looking on-line for hotels in the area. They started by looking for ones near enough to Havergill, but also within easy reach of the Berwyn Mountains where they'd once done a lot of walking when they were younger. They both loved the area and were anxious to return to some of the places they'd visited in their youth.

'There are three promising ones,' Connie said, having written their addresses and 'phone numbers on a piece of paper. 'This one's in the right area, and very close to the Berwyn's, but from the photo it looks a little rundown. If I zoom in, you can see the paintwork's peeling off the veranda, and some of the woodwork on the windows could do with renewing.'

'Cross it off the list,' Riley said, without looking at the pictures. 'We haven't been on holiday for a long time and we need a comfortable place for our stay. If they haven't bothered with the outside, they're probably not doing very well, and the inside's probably the same. '

'That leaves two then,' she said, bringing them up side by side on the screen.

They scanned them both, noting the exteriors, the cost of the rooms, and the available views of the bedrooms, finally choosing one which was nearest to both Martin's home and Havergill, although slightly further away from the Berwyn's.

'How long can you spare?' she finally asked as she picked up the 'phone to make a booking.

'Better make it five days,' Riley answered. 'I'm nearly always fully booked at the weekends, so a Monday to Friday booking is best for me.'

She pulled a face. She would have preferred a full week away, but she knew he couldn't afford to lose any clients.

Having chosen to go a fortnight later, giving them both time to make arrangements to be away from their jobs, there was no problem with the booking. Being midweek they always had vacancies, and she paid them a deposit over the 'phone.

Riley also arranged with Martin to visit Rosehill Farm on Tuesday, the day after they arrived, then if there wasn't anyone available to speak to, they'd be able to arrange another day later in the week.

The hotel turned out to be as good as they'd hoped when they arrived on Monday morning, and the lunch they were served in the conservatory was excellent. So too was their room. It was very clean and contained a king size bed, with all the little accoutrements catered for – even down to bathrobes still in their original packaging, and matching shower caps.

The view from their window was also excellent. It looked out across the nearby town nestling in a valley below them, carrying on towards the distant hills; marred only here and there by the very tall conifers standing in the hotel grounds.

On Tuesday they met Martin at the entrance to Havergill and tramped up the driveway, noting that a lot of the vegetation had been flattened by a heavy vehicle.

'Looks like somebody's been up here in a tractor,' Riley observed. 'I wonder if it's one of the neighbours. Maybe they've noticed the comings and goings and decided to see what it's all about.'

'Or maybe they saw the lightening strike. It certainly made a bright enough spectacle to be seen from some way away,' Martin added. 'It might have alerted somebody's attention.'

'Well, whoever's been up here, they've certainly made it easier to get up the drive,' Riley added; all of them thankful for the easier access.

When they reached the house, Riley was stunned as he looked around.

'Wow! Well I don't know whether the lightning's made it easier or harder for you. You don't need to demolish the walls now, but some poor bugger's got to pick it all up before you can get started.'

They all laughed.

'There's machinery for that!' Martin finally exclaimed as they picked their way gingerly through the ruins to reach what was left of the once grand house.

There really wasn't much left to see and they made their way back to the cars just ten minutes later.

They left Martin's pickup where he'd parked it and all drove round to the farm in Riley's car, deciding not to take both in case the sudden invasion of cars might seem intimidating.

As they arrived, a woman was just coming out of the door carrying a basket of washing, obviously intending to peg it out on the line, and she stopped to look at them warily.

Two men climbed out; one from the driving seat and the other from the rear door. She was a little alarmed by them. She and Aled were here alone in an isolated spot, and these were two strange men climbing out. She couldn't imagine what they wanted, but when she saw the woman step out from the front passenger seat, she relaxed a little.

'Can I help you?' she asked. They weren't people she recognised from anywhere local.

'Good morning,' Riley said, still standing by the car door.

He'd noticed her alarm and decided not to approach any nearer until he'd stated his business and put her at her ease.

'My name is Riley Duncan, and this is my wife Connie.' Holding out an arm towards Martin by way of introduction, he continued, 'and this is our associate Martin Jennings. I've recently inherited Havergill from a relative in New Zealand, and we've just come to give you the news that we'll be redeveloping the old property and the rest of the site in due course. We wondered if you'd like to see the plans and discuss the matter with us before we begin work. Martin's construction company will be carrying out the work, and we wanted to give you the opportunity to put forward any concerns you might have before we begin.'

She put down the basket of washing and a look crossed her face. Was Riley mistaken? That appeared to have been a look of fear, as she turned towards the house and then looked back at them before seeming to make up her mind.

'You'd better come in then. My father-in-law owns the farm, but he's pretty elderly and not very good on his legs. My two sons work the farm.' She was going to say 'but they're out in the fields at the moment,' when something stopped her.

'They're around somewhere if you'd like me to call them,' she finally finished up.

When they made no reply, she showed them in, and as they waited in the doorway, she introduced them to Aled and explained the purpose of their visit.

Again he saw that look pass between them, before the old man welcomed them and indicated for them to be seated.

Riley repeated the explanation of what was to happen to the land and the now derelict property.

'This visit is by way of a courtesy to yourselves and to let you know what'll be going on. We hope it won't infringe on your privacy at all, but I'm afraid a certain amount of noise can't be avoided.'

The old man shrugged his shoulders but said nothing for a few moments.

'Nothing we can do about it is there? Got planning permission 'ave you?'

Here Martin stepped in.

'Yes, permission has been granted,' and he handed over the stamped paper for him to look at.

Aled had already received a notice from the planning committee about the proposed development, but hadn't sent in any objection. It was better to get rid of the old place and all its associations with the past. What was done was done, and best put behind them all.

'Would you like to see the plans for the new house?' Martin volunteered as the paper was handed back.

The old man nodded, and Martin unfolded the plan.

'May I?' he said, standing up and indicating his intention to lay it out on the table.

The old man nodded, and Nell moved forward to help him out of his chair, Riley swiftly standing to help her.

'Thank you young man,' Aled said as he eased himself into the straight-backed chair next to the table. 'These old bones don't ge' any younger, and everythin's an effort these days.'

However, his old bones didn't stop him from scrutinising the plan closely before they helped him return to his chair by the fire.

Having got the preliminaries out of the way, Riley was anxious to hear whether he had ever known his family and whether he could tell him anything about them.

'Did you know the Havers family at all?' he asked.

The old man nodded.

'Yeh, knew them all. Lived here all me life and me tad – father to you lad – before me.'

'Can you tell me anything about them? I didn't even know I had any family in Wales until I heard from the solicitor that I'd been left the property by a great uncle in New Zealand. His name was Isaac Havers, and I'd never even heard of him before.'

'Oh aye. I knew Isaac well. We were near enough the same age and we used to play in the woods together and fish in the river when we were younger.'

'What about the rest of the family? Emily was my grandmother,' he prompted, taking out the sheet of paper showing the Family Tree and handing it across.

Aled picked up his glasses from the table and scanned down the sheet, but when his eyes alighted on Samuel's name, they became hooded as he prodded a wrinkled finger towards it.

'Now he were a nasty old bugger if ever I met one. I swear he hated everyone he met, including his family.

Never knew the first three kids. Two of them were dead before I were born, and poor Bernard drowned in the river when I were only three - wouldn't mind betting the old bugger had a hand in all their deaths.'

'Aled!' Nell's voice piped up. 'That's no way to speak of him. He is a member of Riley's family after all.'

'My great grandfather, to be precise,' Riley prompted as he glanced towards her.

She'd moved to stand alongside Aled and was now looking over his shoulder at the paper.

'Don't care what relation he was to you – he drove poor Mary insane, and then put her in an asylum. She never come out of there alive again, and I'm sure it was him that made sure of that.'

At the mention of his great grandmother, Nell began to get agitated. 'Aled! Please!'

Riley looked up at her. Was there some mystery here, or was it just that she didn't like him speaking ill of the dead.

The old man reached up and put a hand on hers, now resting on his shoulder. He patted it several times and then returned to the paper in front of him.

'Emily was a nice little thing. A bit older than us, but she never had no friends neither. Often used to come fishing with me and Isaac down by the river, and we went swimming when the water was calm, but the old man didn't like her being with boys and he forbade her to go with us in the end. Her and the other girl, Emma, only had each others' company after that, until he locked Emma in the attic.'

Here Nell's hand tightened noticeably on his shoulder and Aled stopped speaking, obviously trying to work out how much more he should say.

'Put the kettle on Nell, and we'll all have a drink – and some of your cake if there's any left.'

She seemed reluctant to leave his side, but her hand had apparently stopped him saying too much else. Connie volunteered to help her make the tea, and they both left the room together, although Nell made sure the door was left open. She needed to intervene if Aled started to say too much.

'How long was Emma in the attic for?' Riley asked, anxious to find out more about her awful existence.

Aled had obviously heeded Nell's warning hand.

'Couldn't say,' he answered.

Riley noted the word 'couldn't' instead of 'can't'. Did he actually know how long she'd been there for? But Aled was already changing the subject.

'Now your grandmother, Emily – she was more feisty than the others! Wouldn't be put down by Samuel! She had nobody when Emma was shut away, but she managed to get away from the house and go down to the village or come here when he wasn't around.

There's a gate into our fields behind the conifers along the drive and she could find her way here without being seen. My two sisters lived here then and she came over to play with them. Mind you, she had a fair few hidings when she got home, but she always said it was worth it to get out of his clutches for a while. She was really lonely shut away in that big house with no friends.'

Nell and Connie brought in the tea when he'd finished speaking and the next few minutes were taken up with handing them round, together with some slices of fruit cake, but Riley was still anxious to find out more.

As soon as it was convenient, he pressed the old man again.

'How did Emily get away then, and was Emma still locked away when she left?'

'Emily met a farmhand who came to work here one summer. She was just seventeen, and it was obvious straight away that they were taken with each other. It was a hot summer that year, and they spent a lot of time in the fields together when he'd finished his days work. We often saw them walking round hand in hand – unfortunately, so did Samuel.

He'd been out one evening, and when he drove back up the drive, he saw them walking the field alongside. He shouted at her to get back home, and she had no choice but to obey. Forbade her to see the lad again, and kept her confined to the house for a couple of weeks before she made her escape. This time she packed up all her belongings and went back to the village with him.

His mother had heard the story from her son, William, and she let her stay there, but one day Samuel found out where she was and went to the village to bring her back. He didn't know which house William lived in, and by the time he found it, word had reached them and William and Emily had fled. I never heard anything of her after that.'

The long story seemed to have tired Aled and he was leaning back in his chair.

'I think that's enough for today,' Nell said, going to his side.

'Just one more question for now, and then we'll leave you in peace,' Riley implored.

Aled nodded.

'What about Isaac? I know he went to New Zealand, but when did he get away?'

'It was when he was 21 that he left. His father wanted him to go into the family banking business, but Isaac hated the idea of being cooped up in some stuffy city office. He'd taken over the job of looking after the deer when Denzil Farmer, the estate manager, was sacked, and all he wanted to do was work with animals. He just up and left one day when his father was out at work. We never knew where he went.'

'And was Emma still locked in the attic then?'

He'd promised one last question, but he couldn't resist asking that as well. He was anxious to know just how many years she'd been locked away, but he never received a reply.

'That's enough,' Nell snapped. 'You said one last question. Aled's very tired and I'd like you to go now.'

She'd already walked over to the door and was holding it open for them to leave.

Riley apologised on his way out, but her mood softened as she saw them out.

'I know you're anxious to find out about your family, but perhaps make it another day now when he's had time to rest,' and with that she shut the door behind them.

CHAPTER 17

Riley and Connie arrived home late on Friday afternoon.

The weather had stayed kind to them all week and they'd enjoyed a few sightseeing trips around the area; also enjoying a couple of long walks in the Berwyn's.

There was one particular place they'd visited when newly married, where they'd found an old ruined farmhouse. It was in a beautiful spot in a wide flat valley with high hills all around, and when they were younger they'd had a vision of buying it and making a home for themselves out of it.

It stood on a flat area of land, with a small river meandering past just a few metres away from the front door. It was certainly a very idyllic spot – but ultimately, a very impractical place to live, which was probably why it was abandoned in the first place.

It was at least a mile from any sort of road, and that only over a dirt track. It was miles from the nearest town of any sort, and they'd laughed when they'd arrived home after their visit. There was no sign of any electricity supply, and the valley would probably have filled with snow during the winter months. Access in or out would have been impossible – probably for weeks at a time. And where would they have found jobs? The nearest town of any size was probably about ten miles away; the first mile or so from the house over boggy ground that looked as if it might be liable to flooding even in the shortest period of rainfall – as might the house itself have been, seeing as it was so near the river.

They'd marked the place on an old Ordnance Survey map that they'd kept for many years, and with its help, they'd managed to find the valley once more; but the area was so changed that they'd never have found it without the help of the map.

The farmhouse was no longer there, and in its place stood a plantation of conifers – row upon row reaching up to the sky and filling the whole area. There was nothing left to see of the beautiful flat grassy valley, grazed and kept that way by the sheep which had surrounded the old farm building. The river, still meandering through the trees, was the only recognisable feature still left.

They paid a cursory visit to Havergill before they left, but nothing had happened yet and there was nobody present on the site.

When they reached home, Betty was cutting back and deadheading roses in her front garden as they pulled into the driveway. She greeted them with a smile and exchanged a few words of welcome with Connie while Martin took in the suitcases.

'Had a good holiday?' she asked.

'Yes, very good,' Connie replied, 'but it's been a long drive and I need the toilet. Come and have a coffee tomorrow around eleven and we'll have a chat. Riley is booked solid with lessons all day so he probably won't be home 'til early evening and I'll be on my own all day. I'll be glad of a bit of company once I've got all the washing in the machine, and the bit of shopping I need to do can wait 'til the afternoon.'

'Yes, I'll do that,' Betty replied. 'I have a bit of news of my own to tell you as well,' and she returned to her pruning as Connie made her way quickly inside.

She was there exactly as the clock struck eleven the next morning, and Connie put the kettle on before she answered the door, welcoming the offering of another homemade cake from her.

'Just a little something to welcome you home, and some milk in case you need it,' she said, handing them both over.

'Thanks so much – that's very thoughtful of you. I brought a small carton of milk in with me yesterday, but there's only enough left for our coffee this morning,' Connie replied. She'd intended to have her tea black at lunchtime until she could get to the shops.

When coffee and cake was set out in front of them, and they were both comfortably sitting down, Betty enquired about their holiday and

Connie told her of the places they'd visited and how good the hotel had been, before she decided she'd said enough. It was a boring subject to other people, even though it had been so stimulating to them, and she inquired about the news Betty had to tell her.

'Well, I'm afraid my own news isn't as pleasant as yours,' she said, pausing for a moment before going on.

'My grandson was in court while you were away, and he's been given a five year jail sentence.'

Here she took out a tissue and blew her nose. She was obviously upset by the news, but in Connie's eyes it was no more than he deserved.

'I'm sorry, Betty,' she said, 'but after what he did to you, I have to agree with the sentence. It might make him realise that the life he's been leading isn't right, and he might get onto a drug rehabilitation programme while he's inside.'

'That isn't all,' Betty said, tears running openly down her face now. 'My son is angry with me for calling the police. He says I was mean and selfish to call them, and I should have called him instead. He thinks we should have kept it as a family matter and dealt with it ourselves.'

'How could you?' Connie exploded. 'It wasn't just you he's been stealing from – it's other people as well! Who knows what might have happened if he'd been allowed to carry on – he might have ended up killing someone.'

Betty nodded.

'That was my thinking as well when I decided to call the police.'

'Forget it Betty. He'll come round when he's had time to think about it I'm sure.'

'No, he won't. He's told me he wants nothing more to do with me, and not to try contacting him or his family again. He put the 'phone down before I could say anything, but when I tried to 'phone him back, he'd blocked my number.'

Connie couldn't think of anything to say. This was more serious than it had sounded at first, but then Betty seemed to brighten as she wiped away the tears and imparted another bit of news.

'Anyway, I've nothing to keep me here anymore, so I've decided to move away. My house is going up for sale on Monday.'

Connie showed her surprise.

'But where will you go? You've been here since before we arrived.'

'I don't know whether I've told you, but before we married, I lived in Lincolnshire where I was born, and I have a cousin living in Rutland. She and her husband bought a house overlooking Rutland Water when he retired. I've been there for a holiday a couple of times since Arthur died, and it really is a lovely little spot.

Her husband died two years ago and she's been thinking about selling up and moving back into a town. It's a lovely place to live, and she doesn't really want to leave, but it's a little lonely when you're on your own, and she's asked me to sell up and go and live with her. I've always said no because of my family still being here, but if they don't want to know me anymore, I've decided to take her up on her offer.'

It was a complete surprise and Connie would be sad to see her go. She'd been a good neighbour for so many years, and good neighbours were often hard to come by, but she knew it was probably the best thing for Betty. She too was probably a little lonely after her husband had died, although she'd never spoken about it.

'I'll be sad to lose you,' she said. 'I'll miss our little chats, but I've some news of my own as well. Please keep it to yourself for the time being – I haven't told Riley yet.'

Betty looked at her with interest.

'Of course I won't. What is it?'

'I've decided to go back to nursing. I've already had an interview at the cottage hospital and there was a letter waiting for me when we got back. I've been offered the post and I start at the beginning of next month.'

'Wow! It's all going to be a bit of a change for both of us from now on, but I'm really looking forward to the move!' Betty said, smiling once more. 'And I wish you well in your new job.'

Riley wasn't quite as pleased as Betty when she told him that evening. He'd become used to having her at home for lunch and their evening meal together. It was going to mean a complete change of routine for him as well if she had to work shifts, but he said nothing. She wasn't tied to him, and she had every right to enjoy something she loved doing, even if it did mean radically changing their daily routine. He'd just have to get used to it.

He was even more surprised to hear that Betty was moving.

'I suppose there's nothing much here for her anymore. She may as well join her cousin and they can keep each other company. It'll be a refreshing change of scenery for her as well.

I still wish it'd been possible for us to live at Havergill; but that'll have to stay as a pipe dream.'

She looked at him wryly. She hadn't realised he was still hankering after that old place, but living there was as totally impossible as their dream of living in the cottage in the Berwyns had been.

CHAPTER 18

Within a few weeks the site at Havergill had been cleared and the masons had started work on identifying and preparing the stones that could be saved. These would be used in the building of the ground floor, and the pile in one corner was already beginning to pile up with those that were ready for the rebuilding work to begin.

Soon afterwards the foundations had been laid and a firm of contractors were already clearing the ground which was to form part of the garden.

Over the next few weeks, Riley went down on several occasions to see how things were progressing, and was longing to call at Rosehill Farm for more information from Aled, but Nell's attitude on his last visit held him back. He didn't want to pester the old man, but he hoped he wouldn't pass on before he managed to learn anything more.

Martin was only present on one occasion when he visited. His time seemed to be taken up with making all the arrangements with contractors and ordering supplies these days, and he only managed a quick ten minute chat with him before he was off again.

Connie had now started work at the hospital, but because she'd been away from nursing for so long, they were keeping her on day shifts for the time being, so it wasn't too much of an upheaval to their daily routine as yet. He found he quite enjoyed the time to himself when he sometimes had one or two hours free during the day, and began to look forward to it. She always managed to conjure up an evening meal when she got back, or if she rang to say she'd be late or was very tired, he'd go out for a takeaway.

Martin, however, was more stressed with the amount of work he'd taken on. He seemed to be constantly rushing around and chivvying people along.

Sometimes deliveries didn't arrive on time, or were late, and he had to keep contractors waiting; eating into his budget as he had to go on paying them for their time.

He hadn't seen Kate's car parked at Bruce's house since that day weeks ago, and began to wonder if she'd been there for some other purpose; other than that which he'd suspected. Perhaps he'd been making too much of it.

It had been on the tip of his tongue to ask her a few times, but he'd never ventured any further. If she'd blustered and reddened as she did if caught out in a lie, he'd have known the truth and that she was trying to hide something. He didn't, ultimately, want to find out that she was having an affair!

Kate, in the meantime, was becoming very bored with the hours he spent away from home and was constantly looking for ways to fill her time. She'd already discovered that Havergill, almost opposite Bruce's home, was where he was working, and couldn't chance him seeing her. She had no idea that he'd already followed her there from Bruce's workplace, but, knowing that he was using the services of Style and Design, although back in the hands of Mr. Toomes once more after his recovery, she couldn't go there either. Meeting up with Bruce was becoming more difficult.

Finally, at Bruce's insistence, they devised a plan to meet up. When he was ready to leave work, he'd 'phone her and she'd drive into some woodland near to his home. There she'd leave the car and he'd pick her up and drive her back with him. As the windows at the rear of his car were tinted, there was no chance of her being seen if she sat in the rear seat, and so they continued to meet when he managed to get off work early.

Martin and the boys hardly ever arrived home before seven o'clock these days, so she managed a fair amount of time with Bruce, but he still hankered after having her all to himself. She knew he loved her – he never tired of telling her, and he was still trying to convince her to leave Martin and come to live with him.

For her part, it would be a big step to take. Ultimately, she still loved Martin, and although he was always very busy these days, she still wanted to spend what little time they had together with him. She wasn't ready to break up the family home yet, if ever.

She couldn't contemplate the thought of losing her boys. They worked for and with Martin, and were very close to him. They wouldn't take kindly to her leaving him for another man, and might even cut off all communication with her.

Bruce was a very kind and considerate man, who would have fallen over backwards to do anything for her – but ultimately, she felt he was just another distraction. If there'd been any hint of Martin finding out about their relationship, she'd have dropped Bruce without a moments' hesitation.

She'd always be able to find another man to fill her days with – she always had before! She never considered that time was marching on. She wasn't getting any younger – and young, fit males wouldn't be so easy to pull once the wrinkles started appearing.

She was just living for the moment!

Once the building work started, things moved on quickly. The weather stayed fair and the stonework on the lower floor was already completed when Riley made a visit, bringing Connie with him on one of her rare days off which managed to coincide with a time when he had very few lessons booked.

Martin was there when they arrived, and while they were looking over the building together, and Riley was inspecting the plans and being shown where everything was to go, Connie took a walk into what were soon to be the grounds.

The contractors had cleared most of the undergrowth and the small trees, and at least it resembled the beginnings of a garden now. It would remain like that until further work was carried out to turn it into a lawn; but that wouldn't be until the house was completed. They'd decided to lay turf, which, although more expensive, would make it look more attractive to prospective buyers.

Martin was elated when he received a 'phone call while they were making their inspection. It was from the estate agent, and it seemed that they had somebody already interested in viewing.

He explained the position, saying that it was only up to first floor level as yet, but they were welcome to come and view it. The plans were available for them to see if they'd care to give a time to make sure he'd be there.

The prospective viewer was already there with the estate agent, and they decided to come straight away. It would take around twenty minutes to get there if Martin was willing to wait.

Of course he was! Nothing would have stopped him – and they didn't seem to be put off by the price tag of just over a million pounds that was placed on it. Of course, it was only an asking price, but they hoped to get somewhere near it; somewhere above the £900,000 mark at least.

Riley decided to hang around and meet him – after all, he was still the owner of the property, and he was anxious to meet the person who might buy the first house.

They made good time and it was exactly twenty minutes later that they arrived.

Riley wasn't sure what sort of person the prospective buyer might turn out to be: perhaps a prosperous businessman; even an American tycoon looking for a base in Britain, or even a pop star, but he was surprised when the man alighted from the car. He was surprisingly ordinary looking; in his late thirties to early forties and dressed in a dark blue polo necked sweater, tan chinos and navy trainers. His upper body was well muscled, and it looked as if he kept himself fit.

'This is Mr Martello,' the estate agent said by way of introduction as he stepped out of his car. 'I presume you are the people we've come to meet?'

Riley stepped in quickly, holding out his hand towards the man.

'I'm pleased to meet you Mr. Martello,' realising he sounded a bit gushing and moderating his tone as he held out his hand to shake the other man's. 'I'm Riley Duncan. I'm the owner of the property; and this is Martin Jennings. He's the builder and overseer of the project.'

Martin stepped forward and held out his own hand.

'Nice to meet you both,' the man said, shaking their hands in return, 'and I presume this is the property I've come to look at,' turning towards the house.

His accent was English. Riley thought that with a name like Martello, he may have been of foreign extraction somewhere in the past, but there was no hint of any sort of accent.

He'd already left the group before they realised it and was striding towards the house, using the duckboards they'd provided for when it was muddy.

He stood some way in front of the house and surveyed it for some time, before he walked round the back and inspected that too, returning to the waiting group when he'd finished his inspection.

'Can I see the plans then?' were his first words.

'Certainly,' Martin answered, indicating the metal shipping container which served as a site office. 'I've laid them out on the table for you to see.'

Once inside, Riley and the estate agent stood back while Martin went over the plans with him, explaining the layout in detail and preparing to answer his queries.

He made few comments on what he was seeing, nodding his head and saying nothing. He took out his 'phone and photographed them before he turned away. He seemed very non-committal.

'Thank you for that,' he said, holding out his hand to shake theirs once again. 'I'll need to think about it before I make any decision.'

Once outside, he asked about the acreage and surveyed the amount of ground allocated. Martin had staked out the perimeter boundary with red and white poles, which disappeared into the woodland at one side.

'Is the woodland part of it?' Martello asked.

'Yes,' Martin answered. 'There's a narrow area of grass on the other side, but the land allocated goes right down to a river. That's the boundary of the property. It's just farmland owned by a neighbour on the opposite bank.'

At this point, Martin indicated the pathway near the house which led towards the river, which had already been cleared and new gravel put down.

'That's the footpath down to the river,' he said. 'Would you like to go and take a look?'

Martello shook his head.

'Not now,' he said. 'I'd like to think about things first. Thank you for your time.'

With that, he walked back to the estate agents' car leaving him to follow.

'What do you think?' Riley asked when they'd gone.

'Could go either way,' Martin answered, 'but don't get your hopes up yet. He doesn't look the type to have that sort of money, and he wasn't very forthcoming with his questions. We'll just have to wait and see.'

The building workers were just packing up for the night, as Riley started looking round for Connie. He finally found her alongside the driveway when she answered his shout. She'd been talking to a man on the other side of the hedge who was sitting in his tractor, the door flung open.

'This is Aled Jackson's grandson, Jack,' she said. 'I've been asking about his grandfather.'

Riley acknowledged him and asked how the old man was.

'He's been in hospital, but he's back home now,' was the reply, 'He's far from well. We don't think he'll be with us much longer. Between you and me, I think they've sent him home to die with his own family.'

Riley was dismayed by this.

'I'd like to talk to him if I can. I'd like to hear if he can tell me anything more about my family. Do you think he'd be up to it?'

Jack merely shrugged.

'Mum vets all his visitors these days, although he's always glad of some company. It tires him out though, so I'll ask her for you.'

Riley fished out a card from his pocket and reached across with it.

'That's my number if she'd give me a ring. I really would like to have a few more minutes with him if I can.'

Jack nodded and put it in his pocket, starting up the tractor and driving off across the field.

'Really, Riley,' Connie said when he'd gone. 'The old man's dying. Do you really need to bother him?'

'Who else is there left?' he answered as they climbed into the car and headed for home. 'If I don't find out about my family now, I'll never know anymore. There's nobody left to ask once he's gone, and by the sound of it, that won't be much longer.'

Martin cleared up the desk and tidied away his papers. The others had all gone now and he was the only one left.

Taking a quick look round the site to make sure no equipment had been left out; he locked up the container and made for his own car.

They'd all left early tonight. It was starting to rain, and from the look of the sky, it was only going to get heavier. For the moment, there was no shelter inside the new building and it was impossible to work in the rain.

Driving out into the road, it began to get heavier and his wipers came on. It was then that he saw Bruce's car coming towards him, signalling to turn into his driveway as he approached. Martin slowed down to allow him to complete the turn. He didn't seem to have recognised Riley, and drove in without a glance.

Heading back towards the town, there was a car ahead of him which began to slow down, allowing another car to pull out of an entrance up ahead. The sign on the side of the road read:

The Lake
←
Parking area

As he slowed and pulled up behind it, the driver turned to acknowledge her thanks. Her window was open so that she had a better view of oncoming traffic through the rain, and he got a good view of her face. It was Kate!

What was she doing in some woodland on a lonely stretch of road so far away from home? The only answer blatantly staring him in the face was that it was something to do with Bruce!

CHAPTER 19

It was just over a fortnight later that Riley received a call from Martin.

'Something wrong?' he asked, fearing some serious complication.

'No, nothing wrong,' Martin answered. 'It's just that we've found something just inside the woodland next to the house. We were clearing some of the ground to put in the foundations for the garage when we found it just in amongst the trees. It's an old metal box, a fairly large one, and it looks as it if might have been thrown there when the lightning hit the house. I thought you'd like to be the one to open it.'

'Oh yes, of course I would,' he answered, the idea firing his imagination. 'I'll be there around lunchtime tomorrow.'

He had three lessons in the morning, the last finishing at twelve. If he cancelled the two o'clock one, he'd just be able to get there and back before his next lesson at four.

His eleven o'clock lesson was with a middle aged woman who'd already failed one driving test, but today she wasn't feeling too good. Having been driving rather erratically during the whole lesson, she eventually called it a day and asked to go home. She didn't know what was wrong, but she didn't feel up to carrying on.

Free a quarter of an hour early, he filled the car with fuel and made his way into Wales. He'd already 'phoned Martin and he was waiting when Riley arrived.

They went straight into the office where the box was lying across a chair.

'It was padlocked when we found it, but it was only one of those small ones and it easily came off with a good whack. Nobody's opened the box yet – I've left that for you. You should have the privilege of being the first one to open it.'

Eager to see what was inside, Riley tried to open it, but it was badly battered and stuck fast. Fetching a wide chisel, Martin pushed it into several places around the lid and after a few thumps with the heel of his hand it suddenly sprang open, making a metallic squeal as it did so.

They both looked down into it.

The box seemed to have been made into two compartments; a small flat one on the bottom, and a larger one on the top, separated by a drawer-like fitment covered in green felt, much discoloured and singed by the heat of the fire it had once endured.

Lying in the top one was a violin smashed into many pieces, the only thing intact being its strings, now almost completely separated from the once highly polished outer surface of the instrument. That had been stripped of most of its varnish, and the raw wood beneath was blackened by the heat it had also endured.

Martin felt his pulse race! He'd heard a violin before when he'd been in the house. Could it have been this one? Could someone have been playing it before the lightning struck? If so, it would never be played again!

The inner fitted drawer had once been lifted out by the use of what looked like ribbon loops at either end. These had melted and shrivelled to almost nothing, but Riley, after a couple of attempts, managed to get hold of the ends with a pair of long nosed pliers and lifted it out.

The thin plywood of the drawer was smashed, but still held together by the well glued felt. He lifted it out and placed it on the floor.

Beneath were some sheets of paper. Most of them were badly singed and unreadable, but those that were protected by those above and below them were yellowed with age. The writing, some in ink, and some in pencil, would need a magnifying glass to be able to read them properly, if at all.

Where the tops of the papers were visible, it was clear to see they'd been ripped from some sort of pad – maybe a writing pad or a journal of some sort.

'I'll take this home with me and see if Connie's got any ideas on how we can stop the paper falling to bits before we try and read them. They look like some sort of diary,' he told Martin before replacing the drawer on top and shutting the lid once more.

After loading it carefully onto the back seat of his car and securing it with a seat belt, he decided to take a look round the house.

It was coming along well; the upper floor had now been added and the roof timbers were in place ready for the roofers to begin laying the slates.

'I'm hoping they'll be able to make a start next week. Once that's on, we can start on the interior without any holdups from the weather. Things should start to move quickly after that,' Martin said, indicating a pile of slates that were standing in a corner of the site. 'Those were delivered yesterday. So far everything's going smoothly, barring a few small hitches.'

'Any news from that Martello guy who came to view it?' Riley asked.

Martin shook his head. He was as disappointed as Riley.

'Nothing so far, and the agents haven't heard anything either. They've made a follow up call to him, but his 'phone just goes to voice mail and he hasn't rung them back.'

'And no further contacts from anyone else?' he asked, wondering if they were perhaps asking too high a price to attract interest. After all, there couldn't be many people out there looking for a million pound house!

'My son said there was a woman nosing around a few weeks ago; but she drove up in an old Ford, and they didn't take her seriously. She was only here about ten minutes and drove away without speaking to anyone. They thought she was just one of the locals being nosy.'

Riley frowned. It was remiss of them not to have made an effort to speak to her. Who knew what lay below the surface? He'd once had a very ordinary looking woman take her driving test in his car. She'd passed easily enough as he'd assessed she would, but when she went over to tell him she'd passed, a car honked its horn impatiently from across the road.

'I'd better go,' she'd said. 'My husband doesn't like to be kept waiting,' and she'd crossed the road to where a gleaming Mercedes was waiting at the kerb; a uniformed chauffeur behind the wheel!

He'd laughed about it afterwards with Connie, but it had taught him never to judge anyone at face value.

After spending a few more minutes with Martin and asking some questions relating to the build, it was time to make for home. He should just make it for his four o'clock lesson if he went straight to the pupils address.

That evening, he finished his last lesson at seven and Connie had a meal waiting when he got in.

'I'm glad you're late,' she said as he walked through the door. 'I worked an hour later myself, so I'm afraid it's only pork pie and salad. I haven't had time to do anything else.'

'That'll do me,' he answered, and went upstairs for a wash while she put it on the table and made a pot of tea.

After they'd eaten, he went and retrieved the box from his car, and while he unpacked it on the living room floor, he explained its discovery.

Connie picked up the papers carefully with finger and thumb, placing them on the palm of her hand and spreading them out between her thumb and index finger.

'I don't think I can do anything with the pencil markings, but maybe the ink might come up better if I go over it with a cool iron, and it will certainly flatten the paper out.'

She carried one of the larger pieces of paper with less writing on it into the kitchen and got out the ironing board and a tea towel, setting the iron to a cool setting. Flattening the paper, she placed the tea towel over it and ironed it gently.

It worked! But there were only two lines of writing visible:-

are so dreary, and all I . . . .
. . . . . . I've already read over again

That was all that there was of the page! The top was torn away, as was the bottom; and the sides were too charred to make anything more decipherable out of it.

'You know, I think somebody ripped all this up deliberately. Whoever it was probably didn't want anybody to see this or to read it,' Connie commented. 'I wonder who they were trying to hide it from.'

After having heard the previous story from Aled, Riley had his own ideas on that!

The next day Connie was on early shift and was home by mid afternoon. When Riley arrived back just after six, he was amazed to see what she'd done. She'd carefully ironed each piece of paper and stuck it onto a sheet of flat card which she'd received with a dress ordered on-line.

'I'm afraid most of them are illegible, but these few have some writing on them, although I'm afraid they don't give any insight as to the writer. Do you think they could have been written by Emma when she was locked in the attic?'

He read through them without comment, reading some of them a second time. Most of them were ambiguous and said very little. They gave no clue as to the writer. His thoughts were turning more and more to that writer having been Emma. They certainly might have been written while she was incarcerated in the attic? Had she done it to fill her lonely days, or to make a record of her imprisonment in case she didn't get out again?

Or could they perhaps have been written by Mary? Had she realised she was becoming more and more confused as the dementia took hold? Had she written some sort of journal to help her keep a hold on reality? Both scenarios were highly possible.

Both of them could have had a fear of Samuel finding them and might have been trying to hide them if discovery were becoming imminent.

It was as he was thinking this over that Connie brought out her biggest coup.

She'd found a larger piece of paper; one that had more writing on it, and had remained more intact than the others. The writing on this was more distinct, and she'd stuck it to a piece of stiff card from the back of a writing pad.

'I think we can safely say you'll be interested in this one!' she crowed – proud of the coup she'd managed to pull off. 'This one is far more interesting!'

He took it from her. The ink was more prominent on this one, and there seemed to be more writing; but what was most interesting still was that there was part of a date at the top!

It read:-

ber 1948

... been over a year now. I want to ...
... leave this prison he's been keeping me ...
... I want to run free in the fields and ...
... in my hair. All I have is my violin ...
... books I've found. I've read them all.

Why does he hate me? What have I .... deserve this?

This was only the top part of the page, that to the right hand side and the bottom had been torn away, and although they searched through the other scraps of paper, they couldn't find a matching piece to bring together the rest of the story.

'I don't think we've got all the papers here,' Connie observed after they'd given up all chance of finding the rest. 'I think they might have been put somewhere else, or destroyed altogether.'

'Why do you say that?' Riley asked.

'Didn't you notice how tightly packed the papers were into the bottom of the box? Even if they hadn't been torn up, they'd still have been a very tight fit into the bottom layer. This shows she was kept in the attic for over a year, so there were probably many more sheets that we haven't come across, unless, of course, she ran out of paper. Her pen seems to have run out of ink at some point, and she completed the rest in pencil. Maybe she hid the rest somewhere else – that's if there were any more.'

He frowned.

The house was gone, and with it all hope of ever finding them if there had been more.

A couple of weeks later he was on his second lesson of the day when he received a text message from Martin: 'Good news. Ring me when you can.'

When he'd finished the lesson, he rang him back, and Martin answered almost immediately.

'It's good news. I've had a call from the estate agents. That Martello fella' who came to see the house – he wants to have a second viewing. It looks promising.'

'When's he coming?' Riley asked, hoping it might coincide with a time when he could manage to be there.

'He wants to come tomorrow afternoon at three.'

That was a blow to Martin. He was solidly booked with lessons from twelve o'clock onwards, and his last lesson didn't finish until six. It was too short notice to cancel them now – much as he'd have liked to. His clients were his bread and butter, and he couldn't afford to alienate any of them.

'Sorry, I'm fully booked from twelve onwards tomorrow – you'll have to handle it yourself.'

'No problem. I'm used to it, and I'll be able to answer any questions he asks anyway. I'll ring you in the evening,' Martin said cheerily.

Much as he liked Riley, he had no idea about the intricacies of the build, and it would probably be easier handling the buyer on his own without any interruptions from him. He did have a habit of trying to provide everybody he met with a potted history of how he'd come to acquire the property, and proudly stating that it had once been owned by his family. It seemed to him like a form of showing off, and not something other people would be interested in when they'd come to view a prospective house purchase.

It would be quite a coup if he could close the sale himself that day!

Sean Martello arrived ten minutes later than expected in a gleaming black Jaguar, pulling up well away from the mud and grime of the building site. Before he ventured over to the site office, he changed his shoes for a pair of sturdy green wellingtons before using the duck boards to reach it. He was again wearing a polo necked sweater, but this time he'd changed his chinos for a pair of dark blue jeans.

His greeting of Martin was peremptory. He seemed anxious to complete their business as quickly as possible, and strode away towards the house before Martin had even closed the door to the office.

The house was well on its way to completion, and all the interior partition walls were already in place. The plumbing was nearing completion and the electricians were inside now installing the wiring.

He followed Shaun round the house, carrying the rolled up plans under his arm in case he needed to look at them, but the man had very little to say until they were outside.

He pointed to the foundations laid for the garages.

'How many garages will there be?' he asked.

'We've allowed for three, but we can easily find room for more if you need them. Of course, there will be an extra cost for that.'

Shaun merely turned away and walked back to the site office, saying 'Three will do,' as he went.

At the door he stretched out a hand and shook Martin's.

'Thank you for showing me round,' was all he said, before he turned on his heel and walked back to the car.

Martin couldn't think what to make of him. A strange and rather cold fish if ever he'd met one. He had no idea of whether he'd liked what he'd seen; or whether he'd lost all interest after his second viewing.

He rang Riley after they'd eaten that evening.

'Is he still interested?' Riley asked animatedly. He really thought that having been interested in a second viewing, the man might be ready to make an offer.

'I really have no idea,' was the only answer Martin could give. 'He's a cold fish if ever I met one. Didn't offer any opinions or ask any questions. I guess we're back to the waiting game again.'

Dejected, Riley replaced the receiver after a few more minutes and relayed the news to Connie.

'Everything may not be lost yet,' she said, trying to console him, 'he may well still make an offer. All we can do is wait and see. You never know, somebody else may come along soon if he's not interested.'

CHAPTER 20

The smartly dressed woman left the hotel entrance and walked down the steps towards the pavement. The night porter, dressed in his dark green uniform, held the door for her, as he appreciatively admired her sleek appearance and shapely figure. He knew exactly what she was, and what her business had been in the hotel that night, as she gave him a half-smile in acknowledgment of the courtesy.

She was wearing a bright red wool coat, tightly belted at the waist. On her head was a matching red beret, from beneath which her dark hair curled out and covered the lower part of her face. On her feet she wore patent leather shoes in a matching shade of red; much too high a heel from those she usually wore – but she'd been out to make an impression that evening.

She daintily put a gloved hand out towards the railing as she descended the three steps to the pavement; wary of falling.

Reaching the pavement, she prepared to cross its width to reach the car waiting at the kerbside, the uniformed chauffeur already holding the door for her.

Suddenly the sound of a motorbike reached their ears and they both turned to look in its direction. It was just after 3a.m. and no other traffic was around. Its sudden appearance took them both by surprise!

Just metres away, it mounted the pavement and roared towards her, the sound of its engine echoing back from the silent and unlit buildings in the quiet city street.

Heading straight for her, she saw it was two up, and as it cut across in front of her, she involuntarily stepped back, thinking it intended to hit her.

The pillion passenger reached out and grabbed the large clutch bag she held under her arm, the bike momentarily slowing down almost to a stop as he did so. She tried to hold on to it, but she was too much off balance in the over-high heels she wore, and he easily ripped it away from her.

As he saw the bike coming towards her, the chauffeur was already taking action.

He removed a pistol from his jacket and thrust out his arm, taking careful aim. As the rider changed down gear and prepared to roar off into the night, a single shot rang out. The bike skittered across the pavement for a few wild moments and then dropped onto its side, still continuing to slide in an arc; eventually coming to a halt as its front wheel buried itself between the hotel railings.

The driver lay where he fell; part of the bike on top of him, but the pillion passenger, almost uninjured, picked himself up and began to limp off, still clutching the bag.

As he reached its junction with a side street, another shot rang out in the still night air, and he dropped to the floor like a stone.

Calmly, the chauffeur walked over and picked up the bag, before returning to the car. The woman was already sitting in the rear seat and he handed it to her before going round to the drivers' side and climbing in. He started the engine, and drove smoothly away into the night, slowly and inconspicuously so as not to draw attention to their departure.

The night porter had heard the sound of the motorbike, which didn't faze him. They often got late night revellers from the city centre clubs and pubs driving past in the early hours, but the two shots had caught his attention. He'd been busy talking to one of the night staff at the rear of the lobby and was just walking back to his post in the lobby when it all happened.

He opened the door and walked out to the top of the steps.

Most of the buildings around the hotel were office blocks; unoccupied at night, and there seemed to be nobody about on the street when he looked out. Thinking it must have been a car backfiring, he turned and prepared to go back inside, but as he did so, he glanced along the pavement and noticed the motorbike lying on its side. Its engine had now died and its rear wheel had stopped turning, but it was the dark shape beneath it that made him take notice.

The top half of the figure was partially hidden behind a pillar box. It looked like the rider might have been hurt!

He quickly descended the steps and made his way over, but it was only when he reached him that he realised the man was beyond help. His eyes were wide and staring and a pool of blood covered the flags around and beneath him.

He took out his mobile and called for an ambulance and the police, before he noticed another man lying further on. Most of his body was hidden by the corner of the building, but when he reached him, he saw the bullet hole in the back of his head. Unlike the rider, he hadn't been wearing a crash helmet, and he'd been an easy target for a fatal head shot. Blood and brain matter had oozed from the hole.

His legs turned weak and the police and ambulance crew found him sitting on the steps, head in his hands and looking unseeingly down at the pool of vomit in front of him. He'd never seen anything so callous in all his life – and he hoped never to again!

The ambulance crew were sympathetic towards him after they'd ascertained that both men were dead, but the police weren't quite as generous with their sympathy. They needed to try and find these people before they could commit any similar crime in the future. Robbery was one thing – but murder was something else altogether!

Similar bag and 'phone snatches had been carried out previously all around the area, and always by two men on a motorbike, but they suspected there'd been a third man involved. One who retrieved their booty from them and took off down the quiet side streets unnoticed, while the two robbers continued innocently on their way home. If they were stopped, they had nothing on them and were just two people making their way home from a night out.

The woman involved posed as a high class call girl, and while her punters were sleeping off their exertions, she relieved them of their wallet and any other valuables they might be carrying; making good her escape before they even knew she'd gone.

The man she'd robbed tonight had just made a withdrawal from the bank that afternoon. It was for a shady deal he'd been about to do, necessitating a payment in cash, and he'd unwarily left it in his briefcase. Not only had she left with the £300 he'd paid for her services, but she'd also taken with her the envelope containing his £10,000 withdrawal.

She'd told him her name was Trish, but apart from that, he knew nothing else about her. He'd found her card in the hotel washroom, and being on his own for the rest of the night, he'd called her straight away.

The hotel porter knew which room the woman had been in, but when questioned, the occupant found he no longer had the card. She'd taken that with her as well when she left.

Forensics took samples from the room, but being a hotel room, with many people coming and going, they could have come from anybody. The database found no matches from anyone already known to the police.

CCTV failed miserably as well when they accessed it. It showed her leaving the hotel, but she'd kept her head down, and her face was masked by the beret, pulled low over the upper half, together with her hair, which swung forward and covered the lower half. The car itself was just out of sight of the camera, and the so-called chauffeur couldn't be seen. He'd obviously checked where the cameras were beforehand, and planned it so that he was just out of their line of vision.

The police inspector in charge thought this was going to be a hard case to crack. The couple seemed to be forensically aware, and the driver seemed to know the area well. The car hadn't been captured by any CCTV on the roads in the city centre, and they soon realised he must have been using side roads to make good their escape.

The car was dark coloured, but they could tell nothing else apart from that. Their only witness, the hotel porter, had failed to notice what make it was. He'd been anxious to get back to the hot pie that was waiting for him in the kitchen, and he'd been far more interested in the woman than her mode of transport.

CHAPTER 21

The black Mercedes had left the city via a series of back roads, eventually resorting to quiet country lanes where he was unlikely to have been picked up on CCTV, and was now rounding the final bend before having to cross the main road.

This was the final obstacle to reaching their destination. The road was quiet and unlit on this stretch, and it was devoid of any CCTV cameras – he was already well familiar with the area – but there was always the chance of a car or a lorry being on the road, even in the small hours, and he couldn't afford to take any chances.

Nosing the car forward toward the junction, he rolled down both front windows and listened for the sound of an engine approaching. All was quiet and he quickly put the car in gear and crossed over. The lane immediately opposite was narrow, and the old station house on the corner, once part of the railway network which meandered across the countryside, and long since closed in 1963, was all in darkness.

Negotiating the slight hill beyond, the lane lined with unkempt hawthorn hedging on either side, he came to a fork. The one on the right led to a small hamlet of just sixteen houses dotted across the top of the hill, and the one on the left led to a disused quarry, now filled with water and used as a wildlife habitat.

He took the turn to the left and up an unmade track, at the end of which stood several disused buildings, once belonging to the now defunct quarry company.

One of these had been used for offices and was sturdier than the rest. It was built of brick and had double doors to one side, leading into a garage used by the staff. In the days when they had used it, it had been open fronted, but the man had installed sturdy wooden ones to hide the Mercedes from prying eyes.

The woman, now in the same clothes but wearing wellington boots in place of her red high heels, took the keys to the padlock from her companion and went to open them before he drove in and right to the far corner of the building, closing them after him and bolting it on the inside. Another door at the side led into the office block, where they quickly changed from their disguises and hung them in one of the metal lockers, before donning normal everyday clothes and going to a Ford Fiesta parked on the opposite side of the garage.

They drove out in this and padlocked the sturdy door behind them, before driving down the track once more and taking the opposite fork to the top of the hill.

The small hamlet lay before them on the right, but they took a single track road on the left, skirting the bottom of a hill, and winding its way for a couple of hundred yards through gorse and stunted hawthorn bushes before it reached an area of open ground. Here they turned sharply to the left and through a five barred gate, pulling up in front of a farmhouse, hidden from view on one side by a small hillock of ground and on two others by woodland. The front looked out onto a large, rather unkempt lawn, containing no flowers or shrubs, but with an open view over the valley beyond.

They hadn't seen a soul since they'd left the hotel – and what was more – nobody had seen them. They'd come and gone like wraiths in the night, and nobody knew who they were or where they came from.

Now was the time to count their booty and check what the nights' haul had brought them.

She knew that the envelope contained cash – and a great deal of it – but she had no idea how much it actually was!

Both were now dressed in jeans and warm sweaters, as the heating had gone off some hours ago, and she went to make coffee while he counted the cash.

She heard his low whistle as she brought the steaming mugs through.

'There's ten thousand here!' he said in awe. 'With the three hundred he's already paid you, we've made the best haul yet!'

She put the coffee down and looked at him with trepidation.

'D'you think we've got away with it? It's a great deal of money. He won't be willing to let that go so easily.'

The man shrugged his shoulders.

'Looks like he's going to have to! I made sure the car was out of range of the cameras, and nobody'd know you now from what little they could see of you. You look totally different now. There's nothing to worry about. We're home and dry. Let's get this coffee down us and go to bed; I'm whacked.'

When she'd clipped back her long blonde hair and put the black wig in place, she had to agree that she did look totally different, especially with the beret at an angle and shading her eyes. It would probably have needed a good hard look from anyone who'd known her well before they could be sure it was her, especially with the full-on red lipstick, a shade she never ever wore. She always wore pale pinks or mauve – never ever red!

After he'd gone up to bed, she sat for some time on her own.

What they'd been doing was a risky business. The rewards were certainly high. She could stand being pored over by men she didn't really fancy to earn £300 for an hour's work, but she was worried about what had happened tonight.

What they'd done before was just theft, something that hadn't come to the notice of either the police or the public so far.

The men who hired her services were usually businessmen, or reps travelling the country. Unwilling to bring the theft into the open and have their wives or families find out what they were doing whilst away from home, they'd never made any allegations against her, and everything had just been swept under the carpet and put down to experience – but tonight had been something else! Now he'd shot two people! She had no idea if they were still alive, but if they died, he'd surely go to prison for life – and so would she. It wouldn't be any use her protesting she didn't know he had a gun, she was his accomplice, and as such, she'd be equally guilty.

He'd assured her that it was just an air pistol, and wouldn't have done any serious damage at that range, but she wasn't so sure. She thought air guns didn't make such a loud noise as the one he'd used.

This was getting far too hot to handle, but she wasn't in any sort of position to change the situation.

When she'd thrown in her lot with him, she'd given away all her security, including the nice little place she rented. There was somebody else living there now, and no prospect of her moving back in.

He'd told her the money they earned was going towards buying somewhere larger, but what he hadn't told her was why he needed somewhere larger. His intention was that they could take in several girls to entertain more well-to-do clients, who'd bring in much more revenue, but it had to be somewhere unobtrusive and off the beaten track.

Once they achieved that, she'd be able to oversee the girls and not have to perform tricks herself. She wasn't getting any younger and her days of being fancied by men were fast draining away.

The man had inherited this farm from his parents, and he'd lived here since they'd died. He'd sold off the two hundred acres that went with it, and had kept only the garden and the woodland surrounding the house. The sale of that should finance the rest of the purchase, perhaps with the aid of a small mortgage.

There seemed to have been some sort of controversy about his parents' deaths – something to do with a shotgun. From what little he knew, it seemed that she'd shot his father and then turned the gun on herself, but nobody seemed to know what had caused the dispute that had erupted in such violence.

CHAPTER 22

'Mr. Jennings?' the woman's voice on his mobile queried.
'Yes.'
It was a formal voice as she introduced herself as an associate of Alwyn Roberts, the estate agent.
'We've had another inquiry about the property you have for sale.'
'Havergill, you mean?'
'No, not Havergill. This is one of the other houses you're planning to build. Mr. Roberts is already in negotiation about the sale of Havergill.'
That was news to him. He'd heard nothing further since the last visit Sean Martello had made.
'I'm not sure what's happening with that sale. Mr. Roberts will be in touch as soon as he has something to tell you. The one I'm ringing you about is another shown on the plan, marked only as Plot 2.'
He knew exactly where she was talking about. Plans had now been finalised as to the siting of the other properties, and he'd given the agent a copy of the plan as it would be built.
Plot 2 fronted onto the road and was further away from Havergill. It was situated along a short driveway which opened straight off the road and would access plots 2 and 3, both of which would be hidden from Havergill and from each other by trees.
There were still to be four bedrooms, but built to a much smaller scale, with the bedrooms being built into the roof space. They would all have large dormer windows and skylights to let in plenty of light. This would mitigate their height and the impact on the landscape, as well as the building costs, but only two would have en suite bathrooms, unless more were requested at an additional cost.

Consequently, their price tag would be lower, but he did hope to realise around £600,000 for each one.

Those would be the next two houses to be built, but unfortunately, he didn't have the money to build another house until Havergill was sold. He could manage to clear the ground and perhaps squeeze out enough to lay the foundations, but there his plans, and the money, ended, until its sale went through.

But he couldn't afford to lose the sale of a second property!

'Can I speak to Mr. Roberts?' he asked, anxious to find out what was happening over Havergill.

'I'm sorry, he's not here at present, but I'll get him to call you when he gets back,' was her friendly reply. 'In the meantime, would it be all right if I bring Mr. Hunter round tomorrow. He's seen the plan, and he wants to take a look at the site for himself.'

Martin felt his chest tightening. There was nothing much to show the man, except some overgrown ground and a very unkempt hedge fronting the road.

Once the call was over, he enlisted the aid of some of the men on site and went straight to Plot 2, taking with them some marker poles and some green and yellow tape to mark out the plot. At least he could show him where the house would be, and the land it would occupy. Both plots 2 and 3 were being sold with 2 acres of land attached to them, but even if he marked out their perimeters, it would be impossible to see them through the jungle that stood between them and where the house was to stand. He'd just have to point out where they'd be situated when it was all completed.

The biggest dilemma now was where the money was going to come from if the man wanted it built straight away.

After they'd finished running up and down with the dumper truck, putting in the poles and joining them together with tape, a lot of the undergrowth had been flattened, and it was possible to see the area which the plot would occupy.

When they'd finished and the workmen had gone back to their jobs, he had a brainwave. If Mr. Hunter did want the house built, he'd explain that they had Havergill to finish before work started on the next phase of construction. If he wanted it built straight away, he'd have to hire in extra workforce, at extra cost, and he'd need a good sized deposit up front to cover the cost. He had in mind something like 50% of the purchase price, but even a quarter of that would go a long way towards it. He could always ask for more later if he needed it.

The man was obviously interested in the house, so he may just go for it.

The woman from the estate agents, Paula Smith, as she introduced herself, was medium height and dapper, wearing a straight black skirt and a fitted matching jacket, her long mousy coloured hair pulled back into a chignon. She arrived around ten o'clock, Mr. Hunter following behind in a white Range Rover Sport.

Seeing the state of the entrance, they both got out of their cars at the roadside and began donning wellingtons as Martin saw them and began to walk towards them.

'Good morning,' he greeted them both.

'Good morning,' the woman answered, raising a hand to meet his. 'This is Mr. Hunter. He's come to see Plot 2.'

Martin let go of her hand and reached out to shake that of the man.

'I'm afraid there's not much to see,' he said, 'we haven't started work on it yet, but we've marked out the site for you. You'll be able to see where it'll be built, and we've tried to flatten out the ground so you can get a rough idea of the area it'll cover.

The man was around fifty to sixty years old, olive skinned and with very dark hair. He looked to be of Mediterranean extraction, but his accent was all British.

'I've already been told,' he said in rather clipped tones. 'Now I'd like to see the site. I'm a busy man and I don't have much time. I'm going straight from here to Cardiff, so could we get on with it.'

Martin exchanged looks with the agent, who seemed as if she was trying to contain a smile. She'd obviously been privy to some of this treatment before and was finding it amusing.

Turning back to the man he said, 'If you wait here, I'll go and get my pickup and take you down there. It's far easier to access it from the road at the moment, and that's where the driveway up to the house will be when it's completed.'

The man gave him an impatient look, before nodding and making a point of consulting his watch, showing his displeasure at being kept waiting.

He wasn't going to be an easy character to deal with, and Martin would have to be very careful with his handling of him.

Once they arrived, Paula took out the plan and laid it across the bonnet of his pickup. Luckily, he'd put a hosepipe across it that morning when he'd first arrived, and it didn't have its usual coating of mud and dust.

Mr. Hunter pored over it for a few moments, occasionally asking questions, with Martin answering and pointing out the various boundaries. He used an expansive arm to indicate where the 2 acres of land would be, but obviously they couldn't see where it would end until the rest of the ground was cleared.

'Havergill has 5 acres of land in front of it, and your land will abut that on the right hand side. On the left, it will abut that of your neighbour, whose house will be built across the entrance road from yours. At the far side will be the woods next to the river. Some of that belongs to Havergill, but the rest will be up for sale to anyone who wants it. It stretches along the riverbank until it reaches a small cottage at the far side of the land which is privately owned.

'Will it join up to my property?' Mr. Hunter asked.

'If you want it to, yes,' he answered. 'It's just beyond your far boundary, but you'll have to buy the rest of the land joining the two together as well.'

'Is there good fishing in the river?' was the next question.

'I believe so,' Martin answered, surprised, 'but I'm not a fisherman myself so I can't vouch for it.'

The man certainly didn't look the type to be a fisherman. He seemed much too impatient. He couldn't see him being the type to sit on a riverbank all day long waiting for a fish to bite.

With that, he rolled up the plan and handed it back to Martin.

'Ok, you've got yourself a deal. I'll buy it if my wife approves,' he said. 'How long will it take to build?'

Martin hadn't expected him to make such a snap decision, and it took him completely by surprise.

'Let's discuss it back at the office,' he said, trying to give himself time to think.

'No time for that! I've got to be on my way. Talk it over with this young woman and I'll get my wife to come over and see where it's at. She'll be the one making the decision, and if she's says yes, I'll call in to discuss the details when I get back.'

Martin and Paula exchanged glances as the man hurried back to the car.

'Chop! Chop!' he called over his shoulder. 'Time is money, and I need to be on my way!'

Hurrying after him, they dropped him at his car and gazed after the receding vehicle as it drove away.

'D'you think he's genuine?' Martin asked.

'Who knows? All we can do is wait for him or his wife to get in touch again, but don't go making a start on anything. We need a deposit and a signed contract from him before committing to any work being carried out.'

When she'd got in her car and driven away, Martin heaved a sigh of relief. The agents wanted money on the table before they'd commit to the sale, and he needed money before he could start to build. It was working both ways at the moment, but first they needed to get Havergill sold, then he'd have all the money he needed.

Martin was surprised when Paula rang him again just two days later.

'Do you remember Mr. Hunter who came to see Plot 2?' she asked.

Who could forget him? He wasn't the type of man you met every day! Or wanted to!

'Yes, of course I do,' he answered, putting innuendo on his words and making her laugh quietly.

Pulling herself together she continued, 'His wife's been in touch and she'd like to come and see things for herself. Would tomorrow be convenient?'

'Of course, I'll be here all day.'

Would he not? With the prospect of a sale, he'd move heaven and earth to be there, but he'd intended to spend all the next day there anyway. Havergill was nearing completion and he wanted to be there to make sure the finishing touches went in smoothly and efficiently, and more importantly, to his satisfaction.

It was just before her arrival that Riley also arrived. He hadn't managed to get there for a couple of weeks, but by careful manipulation of his bookings, he'd managed to wangle almost a whole free day.

'Any news from Martello about Havergill?' was his first question.

'No, nothing. I think we can assume he's not really interested after all this time.'

He said nothing about the negotiation the agent was in for its sale. Time to tell him if, and when, something materialised out of it.

Riley nodded. He knew Martin would have rung him straight away if he'd heard anything.

'Still, there's the prospect of the Hunters buying Plot 2, although I haven't got the cash to build it unless I get a hefty deposit from them.'

This was what Riley had been afraid of ever since he'd gone in with Martin on this venture. He was overstretching his resources, and Riley was in no position to help out. There'd be rich pickings at the end, but that would only be if they could overcome the small problem – or should it be very large problem – of money.

Without any capital behind him, and all his money having been spent on the main house, he wasn't able to build the smaller houses, which would probably have sold more easily. Perhaps it would have been better if he'd concentrated on them first.

The legal agreement they'd had drawn up between them stipulated that Riley only got his cut of the profits when each house was built and sold. It would be a substantial sum when he received it, but until then, he'd receive nothing. At the present moment, it looked as if that wasn't going to happen, and Martin may have to walk away from the rest of the project, leaving him with the liability of an extremely large and expensive house to sell.

He'd have to find the money himself to clear and landscape the land, as the house wouldn't sell looking out onto a vista of nothing but scrub. The estate agents' brochure promised 5 acres of land, and although the scrub had been cleared, it would soon grow back if not kept attended to. It would need grass planted and nurtured until it was well established enough to take care of itself, after which time it would need constant mowing to keep it in trim, not to mention the cost of the fencing that needed to be erected around it. Five acres would be unmanageable for him alone, especially with him living so far away, and that would necessitate bringing in a gardening contractor. All he could see was more expense for him in the future and possible deterioration of the house itself if a sale didn't materialise soon.

Martin took him round Havergill, which was virtually completed now save for the fixtures and fittings – kitchen and bathroom fitments, floor coverings etc. An allowance was made for these in the purchase price and the buyer would be able to choose from a provided selection, which Martin had managed to source from a supplier who would give him a good discount, promising to use him for the rest of the properties as well. If none of these was acceptable, they could source their own, but it would probably cost extra.

Once these were in place, the house would be ready for occupation and the buyer could move in – provided the full purchase price had been paid.

It was just as they were leaving the house that Mrs. Hunter arrived, in the company of Paula once again.

She was more sensibly dressed than her husband, wearing jeans, parka and wellingtons, and her demeanour was totally different to that of her husband as well.

She was a tall woman, just slightly older than Martin, and very friendly, greeting both he and Riley as old friends.

'I hope my husband wasn't too rude,' she said, as they showed her into the office where Martin had already laid the plans out on the table – once he'd cleaned off the cup rings and the spilt tea stains.

'He can be a bit gruff at times, but it's only because he's a busy man. He's just bought another restaurant in Cardiff, and he's spending a lot of time going backwards and forwards while it's being refurbished.'

Martin and Riley exchanged glances. It looked like the couple had cash to flash, and that explained his abrupt departure last time he'd been here.

She asked them to call her Naomi, and while she was examining the plans, the estate agent had a call on her mobile. Excusing herself, she took it outside to answer. When she came back inside, she smiled expansively at Riley who'd turned to look at her while Martin was busy with Naomi, and gave him a thumbs up. He didn't know what that was about, but he was prepared to wait until later to find out.

While Martin took Naomi to view the site, Riley stayed behind in the office with Laura, anxious to know what the 'phone call was about.

'Good news,' she said when they'd gone. 'That was Mr. Roberts, Sean Martello has been into the office and made an offer on Havergill. They'll be over later on to see you both.'

Now that was good news if ever he'd heard it! The last he'd heard was that Mr. Roberts was still receiving no answer to his telephone calls. The man seemed to have suddenly materialised in person after all this time.

Naomi Hunter spent some time looking around the site with Martin before they returned to the office, during which time Riley spent some time talking to Paula. She seemed as if she needed someone to talk to.

She told him she was newly divorced, her husband having taken off with another woman. She never knew they were having an affair until one day she came home and found all his belongings were gone. A brief note explained the situation and asked her for a divorce.

She wanted to stay on in the house they'd bought together, but the mortgage was too high for her to afford on her own, and she'd had to sell, receiving little remuneration from her share. They'd only bought it 5 years ago, and little of the mortgage had been paid off. She was now living in a rented flat near the estate agents' office. It was handy for work, as it was near enough to walk to, but it was also rather small and she couldn't afford anything bigger at the moment.

He felt rather sorry for her. It wasn't the sort of thing anyone wanted happening to them, but he was also brimming with excitement and relief to tell Martin the news about Havergill. He felt he hadn't given her the full attention he should have done. She so obviously needed someone to talk to.

Just at that moment, Martin arrived back.

Naomi was pleased with the plot she'd been shown – in fact, if anything, it was far better than she'd expected.

'It'll have a lovely view at the back when it's all cleared, and at the front it'll look across the road to the woods. I didn't see or hear another car go past, so I expect the road's very quiet as well. There's enough land to exercise the dogs, and if they need a change, we can have a ramble through the woods. I really like the area, and I'm a country girl at heart.

At the moment we live in a city centre flat in Liverpool, and although it's handy for shopping, I feel more isolated than I ever did when I was growing up on my family's market garden.

I really must have this house! I'll ring my husband tonight and let him know.'

Paula looked ruefully at Riley as they left. She'd found him an easy person to talk to, and would have liked to continue their conversation, but that wasn't to be. Tonight she'd go home to her lonely existence and pour out her feelings to her Persian cat, who never listened anyway. All he seemed interested in was where the next meal was coming from – and when!

Martin was delighted when Riley told him that Sean Martello was going to buy the house and was coming to discuss it today. He rushed straight over, leaving Riley in the office in case they arrived before he got back. He made sure everything was left spick and span for his visit, ascertaining that the electrician and his mate who were still finishing the wiring would be away by lunchtime with everything completed.

He gave the floors a final brush when they'd left, making sure everything was left clean – or as clean as a newly finished house could be. It smelt of drying plaster and wet paint but it wasn't unpleasant. It gave the feeling of everything being fresh and new.

Riley hadn't intended to stay on into the afternoon, as Connie finished work at lunchtime that day, but he couldn't pass up on an opportunity to speak to Sean Martello for himself and make sure he really was going to buy the house. He needed assurance in person from the man himself before he could go home and tell her the news.

He rang her when he judged she'd have arrived home, and told her he wouldn't be home for some time yet and explained the reason. She was as delighted as he was with the news.

'Don't worry about me,' she said. 'I've plenty to be getting on with. Just stay as long as you need to.'

As he disconnected the call, he saw Sean's sturdy figure striding up the drive in the company of Alwyn Roberts, the estate agent, and called Martin out to join him.

They all shook hands and made their way to the house, Riley and Alwyn waiting in the hallway while Martin showed him round. He took a considerable amount of time, and when he arrived back with them, he was carrying the brochures of fixtures and fittings that Martin had given him.

They all walked back to Martin's office, Sean talking adamantly to Martin, and stopping once to point out an area on the right of the house. This was an area with the house on one side, the conifers flanking the driveway and swinging round to the side of the house at the other, and the rather rambling woodland at the back belonging to the neighbouring farm.

Martin had left this area untouched, considering it to be a good place to build stables if the new owner had horses. It was well sheltered on three sides, and was near to the back of the house for easy access from the large utility room.

They all stopped to look as they listened to his words.

'I want a large brick garage built there with an extra wide door at the front,' he said as they all listened.

'I can do that,' Martin said. 'There's plenty of room for it, but there are already three garages on the opposite side of the house and it'll cost extra. I'll clear some of the trees back if you still want it.'

He couldn't understand why the man should want another garage when there were already three provided.

'No!' Sean said imperatively, then mitigating his tone, 'Leave the trees as they are, and give me a figure for the extra garage. I want it in this corner.'

No further explanation was given, and Martin didn't question him any further.

'Okay,' he said, trying to pacify him. 'I'll work something out tonight and give you a ring tomorrow.'

No further explanation was given, and after another look at the plans in the office, Sean Martello left; but when Martin rang him the next day to give a figure for the extra garage, the 'phone once more went to voicemail.

Strange man, he thought. He never seems to answer his 'phone, but he does seem to get the messages that are left. With that in mind, he gave his quote and waited for a return call.

There was nothing else he could do!

CHAPTER 23

Larry and Franny Barnes, from the good old U.S. of A: California to be precise, were 'doing' Wales this year on their annual month long vacation.

They both thought of Britain as where their roots were planted, but truth to tell, it was nearly two hundred years since their ancestors had left Britain's shores bound for New York. How the family had ended up living in California, the opposite side of the country, had never been explained, but it had a far better climate than New York, and they enjoyed living there.

For the last five years, ever since Larry had decided to step back from the business his father had started in the 1930's and let their two sons take over, they'd spent their month long yearly vacation 'doing' England, but this year they'd decided to have a change and 'do' Wales instead. He'd heard it was a much quainter country than England and they spoke a strange lilting foreign language, although he was assured that they all spoke English when they wanted to.

Larry's father had started by opening his first business producing reels of film for the movie industry. When Larry and his brother had taken over from him, the company had moved on into producing video cassettes, and finally into the production of DVD's and CD's, but his brother had died some years ago, and Larry had brought his own sons into the business. They were all keen to move on with new ideas, and Larry was soon finding himself out of his depth.

Once on-line games started being introduced, Larry was getting on and found himself unable to cope with the intricate technology any more. It was all becoming much too complicated for him. He finally gave in to the inevitable and decided to take a back seat, handing the business over to his sons who were the ones with all the ideas, although still keeping a controlling interest himself, and retreating to his sprawling villa on a hillside overlooking the sea, where he could relax and sit by the pool enjoying the sun.

Larry had wanted to ship over his large Cadillac to drive them around, but he'd been warned that Welsh roads were much narrower and far less hospitable than those in England, often with only room for one car at a time. These roads had what were called 'passing places', which were often rutted and muddy, and there were many of these on the small mountain roads that they wanted to visit; they'd be far better to hire a smaller car while they were there.

Today they'd decided to visit Betws-y-Coed. They'd heard about the quaint little town nestled in the Conwy Valley, and of the famous waterfalls, and were anxious to see them for themselves. They were staying in Conwy itself for a few days, and had decided to travel down the A470, branching off onto the A5 to reach it.

Having spent a good part of the day there, they decided to return by a circuitous route taking in some of the mountain scenery, but as they passed through a small village, Franny espied a chip shop right alongside the road.

'Ooh, look!' she almost screeched, 'a fish and chip shop. Do stop and get some. They're supposed to be an English delicacy.'

They hadn't yet had any lunch, so Larry pulled into the kerb and stopped.

He'd never get used to this idea of just stopping at the side of the road to visit a single shop situated on its own – not something usually found in their own country, but he did as she asked; hungry himself. He came back with a good sized portion of both fish and chips – but where to eat them was the problem.

'Let's see if we can find somewhere off the road where we can sit in peace. I don't fancy eating them here with people walking past on the sidewalk and staring at us,' he said, starting the engine.

Unfortunately, it was some way before they both spotted a sign pointing towards a lake, and they were both worried about the food getting cold by the time they reached it.

'I'll pull in here,' he said. 'There's sure to be somewhere to park.'

Just as he'd foreseen, there was a small rough parking area a few metres off the road, with another sign pointing down a footpath towards the lake.

Theirs was the only vehicle there and they sat and ate their food ravenously, finding them delicious.

'Oooh! That was well worth the journey back to England,' Franny crowed, licking the remains off her fingers. 'We must have that again before we leave. It sure is a delicacy!'

Looking around for somewhere to leave the papers, she spotted a litter bin alongside the footpath to the lake, and left the car to rid herself of them, where she got a glimpse of the lake itself.

'There's lots of birds on the lake,' she told Larry when she returned. 'Why don't we go take a looksee at them? We've got plenty of time before they'll be serving dinner at the hotel.'

After that big helping of food, Larry would far rather have returned to the hotel and had a snooze on the bed before dinner, but she wouldn't stop pestering him if he didn't, so he finally got out of the car and followed her, muttering under his breath as he did so.

They didn't walk very far round the lake, neither of them being keen walkers. These days the most walking they usually did was to the pool and back, but occasionally, if they were feeling energetic, they'd take a leisurely stroll round the gardens surrounding the villa, admiring the work their two gardeners did in keeping it neat and tidy.

Both of them were at least thirty pounds overweight these days, but they shrugged that off, putting it down to just a consequence of their growing older, and neither of them doing anything about it. It hadn't occurred to either of them that it may shorten their lives, but would they really have cared if they had. They were both contented with the lifestyle they lived and had no intention of changing it.

Finding a rough hewn wooden bench alongside the lake, they sat down, and while Franny looked at the birds and tried to work out what they were, Larry snoozed and finally began snoring loudly.

Franny was annoyed by it and tutting to herself, she dug him in the ribs.

'Eh . . . wha'? Whassa' matter?' he spluttered, coming back to the land of the living. 'Somethin' up?'

'You're snoring again,' she said indignantly.

They had separate bedrooms at home because of his snoring, but while they were staying in the hotel, they'd had to share a bedroom. She hadn't liked to ask for a separate room of her own, in case the staff thought her strange, but neither had she got much sleep while they'd been on vacation because of it.

He'd been deeply asleep, and was annoyed she'd woken him.

'I'm going back to the car,' he said. 'I can sleep in peace there without having my ribs caved in.'

Annoyed that he was spoiling the day, she got up to follow, and by the time they reached the car park, a full scale row had erupted.

Both incensed by their own anger, neither of them noticed the car that was parked a short way from their own as they carried on rowing. Finally in a fit of temper, he climbed in and started the car.

'I'm going back to the hotel for a sleep. Come with me or get out and walk,' he shouted.

She screeched something unintelligible at him and aimed a sharp thump to his shoulder. He glared at her and engaged reverse gear before shooting backwards out of the parking space – anger increasing his aggression.

Suddenly they heard a loud thump from the rear. He knew he'd hit something and stamped hard on the brake as he looked in the rear view mirror. He could see nothing there!

Franny was looking round in consternation.

'You've hit something,' she said, glowering at him. 'That's your pig headed temper for you. Go and see what you've hit.'

Even before she'd finished speaking, he was out of the car and making for where he thought the sound had come from, but when he looked, there was nothing there. He looked all round the area behind, still not seeing anything.

'Nothing there,' he said as he got back into the car. 'I'll bet it was one of those damn birds you're so keen to look at. It's probably long gone now and with a gawdamighty headache I hope. There's no damage to the car either.'

He completed his turn, and made for the entrance, just as another car came into view. It did nothing for his temper when he had to wait for it to clear the way before he could drive out.

'Stupid roads these British have! Why don't they make them wide enough for two cars at a time!?' he growled under his breath, before heading recklessly out into the road beyond and turning wildly to make his way back to the hotel.

He'd almost forgotten that he should be driving on the left hand side of the road before he spotted a lorry coming towards him head on, and sounding its horn loudly. It shattered the stillness of the afternoon and brought him back to his senses as he swerved back to the left to avoid a collision.

Doing nothing to alleviate his bad temper, he muttered angrily under his breath, more determined than ever to return to the hotel and have a couple of very large bourbons before taking himself back to their room for a well earned snooze.

Franny could go hang – he was finished with sightseeing for that day at least – and any more of her company was the last thing he needed.

Bruce was surprised to see Kate's car already in the car park, but no sign of her. Usually if she was there before him, she'd walk down to the road and wait just behind the hedge where she couldn't be seen, stepping out to meet him when he turned in – but not today.

He parked alongside, glancing across and noticing that she wasn't in the driving seat. He got out and walked round the car, but when he tried the door, it was locked. He walked to the back of it and looked around before calling her name, but there was no answer.

The area was so small, barely room for half a dozen cars, that it would be impossible to miss her if she was anywhere in that space. Maybe, if she'd arrived early, she'd decided to take a walk down to the lake and wait for him there. It seemed a strange thing for her to have done, and she'd never done it before, but then, there was nowhere else she could have gone.

Walking over to the footpath, he continued down the short slope, but as the trees gave way to open countryside on all sides, and the lake came into view straight in front of him, he was able to see all around, and there was no sign of anyone else.

He stood for a few moments and called her name several times; turning in all directions as he did so, but there was still no answer.

Retracing his steps, he returned to the car park and looked around again. She still wasn't there and he was puzzled as to where she could be. He shouted one more time

It was then that he heard his name being called, only faintly, and it was followed by a low groan. He listened, trying to work out where it had come from. There it was again! If the afternoon air hadn't been so still and quiet he'd never have heard it. It seemed to be coming from somewhere beyond the right hand rear wing of her car.

Walking round the back, he saw it was parked only a short way from a steep bank leading down towards the trees, and as he went towards the edge of it, he heard another groan, louder this time.

Reaching the edge, he peered over, and saw her immediately.

She was almost at the bottom of the slope, her progress having been halted by the trunk of a tree, against which she was lying. He scrambled down towards her.

Earth had been piled up to form a plateau on which to park the cars, and the slope hadn't had time to grow much in the way of vegetation as yet. It was dusty and stony, and large stones rolled towards where she lay as he made his way down. He tried to keep well over to her right so that none of them fell on her.

'Are you all right?' he asked as he reached her side. 'Can you get up?'

'No,' she answered weakly. 'I . . . It's my hip. The car hit me . . . knocked me flying.'

'I'll get an ambulance,' he said, reaching into his pocket for his mobile, before sitting alongside her and comforting her as best he could while they waited. She tried to move a couple of times, but each time it caused her too much pain and she cried out in agony.

'It's my hip,' she gasped. 'It hurts so much . . .!'

'It may be broken,' he told her. 'Lie still until the paramedics arrive. They'll know what to do.'

Twenty minutes later, he heard the siren and scrambled up the bank to meet them. They quickly assessed the situation and gave her painkillers before strapping her to a stretcher and whisking her away to hospital.

They were kind and sympathetic, treating her gently and with a great deal of empathy, but also swift and efficient in getting her up the slope and into the ambulance.

'Are you her husband?' one of them asked as he closed the rear door.

'No. I'm just . . . a . . . a friend,' was all he could say.

'Then I suggest you call someone to inform them of her whereabouts – her husband perhaps – or a close relative?' the man said, guessing at the situation, and also having noticed the wedding ring Kate was wearing.

Once they'd driven off, Bruce was torn.

Kate had now informed him of who her husband was, but he wasn't aware that Martin already knew they were having an affair. When Martin had visited their firm on the few occasions when it was necessary, he'd kept strictly out of sight, and let Sidney handle all the dealings with him. He'd only met him the once, and perhaps Martin wouldn't remember him. It was only a slim chance, but best be on the safe side.

He knew he was going to have to come clean and ring Martin.

He was worried sick about Kate, and knew Martin needed to know. He'd have to put a brave face on it and do the right thing; then the recriminations and explanations would have to begin.

He knew this would probably be the end of their affair, but he still hoped that he might be able to persuade her to leave Martin and come and live with him when it was all over.

It was only a faint hope, but he knew he needed to try. Life would be almost unbearable without her.

CHAPTER 24

Martin had received a strange request from the estate agent.

Sean Martello had confirmed that he was going to buy Havergill at the full asking price, and had already deposited 50% of the purchase price with his solicitor, but required a few alterations to be carried out first: these all to be at no extra cost to himself. He had also agreed to pay for the extra garage to be built and submitted the dimensions he required. The kitchen and bathroom fitments had also been agreed from the alternatives already given to him; but the alterations he needed seemed to be very strange.

The upstairs landing stretched right from one end of the house to the other. On the side nearest the garages, he required a door to be let into the end wall, and a fire escape built on the outer wall to reach the ground. The garages also needed to be left open fronted and with no doors fitted.

It was strange, but not unreasonable. The cost of the garage doors which wouldn't now be needed would go some way towards the extra cost of the changes; and as he hadn't really expected to get the full asking price for the property; that would well cover the rest.

It seemed Sean had already signed his side of the contract, which the solicitor would hold until he was happy that everything was finished to his satisfaction.

Why he needed the fire escape was beyond Martin. That usually only applied to commercial properties, and unusual for it to be fitted to a private dwelling; but his wasn't to reason why. He'd make the changes as quickly as possible and get some money back in the bank, when he could concentrate on getting Plots 2 and 3 built.

Naomi Hunter had already rung the agency to confirm that they were going ahead with the purchase of Plot 2, and saying that her husband would be in touch as soon as he got back from Cardiff in a few days.

She'd also informed them that her sister was interested in buying Plot 3. Martin had given her a printout of the plans, and without saying anything to anybody, she'd taken her to see the plot allocated to them, indicating where the other house was to be built to the same design. Both houses would share the same access road, and both would face towards the road, but would be built almost 100 metres apart, and would share a boundary fence of the two acres of land behind them.

Martin hadn't yet heard from her sister, but he needed to crack on with preparing the ground for the Hunter's house to be built. Once they received confirmation from her husband and a hefty deposit was received, he'd start work immediately.

Now that they'd made a start, things seemed to be moving better than expected, and he rang Riley with the news.

He'd just arrived back from his last lesson of the day and was overjoyed when he heard the news. After all this time, Havergill had at last been sold – or as good as – and the next two plots were well on their way too. Now that things were beginning to move, they were beginning to snowball, and he once again had his doubts as to whether Martin would be able to cope; but he realised that money in the bank meant Martin would be able to hire in more labour, and that way he should be able to cope admirably well. He'd done a cracking job so far, so why should he doubt him now.

It was just over an hour later that Martin received a call from Bruce Chambers, and wondered what the man could want with him.

'Hello, Martin,' he said, somewhat hesitantly. 'It's Bruce Chambers here from Style and Design Architects.'

He'd already seen who it was from his caller display screen. He still had his number stored from the last time they'd met, but what could he want with him? He'd had no contact with him since their last meeting.

'It's about your wife, Kate,' he continued, sounding somewhat intrepid, wondering what Martin would say when he realised they must have been together.

'Yes?' Martin said quietly, a cold feeling creeping up his spine.

What was he about to be told? Had Kate decided to leave him and go to live with Bruce? He'd sometimes wondered if it would come to that. Had she bottled out of telling him and left it to Bruce? Maybe he should have faced them both with it when he realised what was going on. He might have been able to nip it in the bud if he had and it wouldn't have come to this.

Now Bruce's voice continued, still sounding intrepid.

'She's had an accident. She was hit by a car and they've taken her to the hospital at Bodelwyddan. I think you'd better get over there straight away.'

'How . . . ? What . . .?' Martin asked, completely taken by surprise. This wasn't what he'd been expecting to hear, but now was not the time to start asking questions, he needed to get to her and find out if she was all right. Without waiting for an answer, he disconnected the call and rushed out through the door.

There was nobody else on site at the moment and Havergill was all locked up, so he quickly padlocked the office and made for his pickup, dropping his keys several times as he fumbled them out of his pocket.

He didn't care any more that she'd probably been with Bruce, all that was in his mind at the moment was to get to her side.

He arrived in twenty minutes and made his way straight to A & E, where they were still assessing her injuries.

The department was busy, and Kate was lying there all alone, the curtains open at the bottom of the bed. She was awake and smiled weakly as he reached her side. Thank God she wasn't at deaths door was all he could think of.

She raised her hand slightly to take his, but he noticed the movement caused her pain as she winced, and her face and arms were covered in cuts and grazes, a large dressing above her left eye.

'Are you all right?' he asked.

Stupid question really, she wouldn't be here if she was, but it was all he could think of to say at the moment. There was a huge lump in his throat and his voice was already breaking.

A man in shirt and trousers came over when he saw Martin at her side, and from the stethoscope he carried round his neck, Martin deduced he was the doctor.

'Are you the husband?' he asked.

Martin nodded, unable to find the words.

'I'm the A & E consultant on duty today. Don't worry too much – we're not. She's been hit by a car, and we think she may have broken her hip. She's going for a scan soon, so we'll have to ask you to leave then, but stay until they come for her. We'll have more news by morning if you'd like to ring then. The switchboard will tell you which ward she's on.'

With that he was gone to attend to another patient.

Martin looked down at Kate once again. Her eyes were closed, but as he leaned over, she opened them and a smile flickered over her face.

'I love you,' he whispered, taking hold of her hand. 'Please don't ever leave me.'

He knew now how much she meant to him, and didn't know how he'd manage without her.

'I won't,' she answered. 'I love you too.'

In that moment he realised that she meant it, and also that her affair with Bruce was probably over for good now, as he held her hand until they came to fetch her.

Knowing that he had to tell the boys, he went straight home where they were already wondering where she was, and broke the news.

They were concerned and asked many questions, but there was nothing more he could tell them. Luckily, they didn't ask where it had happened, as that would have meant more probing questions, and if she meant what she'd said about her liaison with Bruce being over, there was no need for them ever to know anything about it. It would remain a secret just between the two of them.

Next morning, he rang the hospital before leaving for work. He was told that she had broken her hip, but that she didn't need an operation. They'd fitted her with a pelvic binder and she was resting comfortably now. He was given the ward number and told he could visit later on that day.

The alterations and the building of the new garage at Havergill were almost completed now, and he rang the agent to say it would be ready for occupation in two weeks.

The news they imparted in return was that Mr. Hunter had been in the previous day and confirmed that he was going ahead with the purchase of Plot 2, and he was seeing his solicitor today.

Things were going better and better, but at the moment, it was overshadowed by what had happened to Kate. She was all he could think about while he was arranging for the clearance of Plot 2 to begin.

As soon as he could get away, he picked up a hot pie from a roadside stall on the A55 and gulped it down before continuing his journey to the hospital, where he found her reclining in the bed.

She smiled and held out her hand as he reached her, and it felt like they were newlyweds all over again. Even better was the news that it was only a minor fracture and would heal by itself. Luckily it had caused no internal bleeding.

Just before it was time for him to leave she became more serious.

'How did you find out what had happened to me?' she asked.

Looking straight into her eyes and watching for her reaction he said, 'Bruce rang me.'

Her face clouded over, and she was obviously struggling for words.

'I know what's been going on,' he continued, 'I've known for some time.'

'How did you find out?'

'I'd been to Style and Design and I was parked at the front. You didn't see me and I watched you park at the side and go in through the side door. I knew then that something was going on. I waited, and when you came out, I followed you to Bruce's house and watched you go in. It was obvious then that you had a key. I didn't know whose house it was at the time – until I saw Bruce arrive and follow you in.'

He said nothing more for the moment as she looked down at the starkly white sheet turned back and tucked in around her, and he saw a tear drip down onto it.

'I'm sorry Martin,' she said in a teary little voice. 'Can you forgive me? It's over and I won't be seeing him again – I promise. I don't want to lose you.'

'And I don't want to lose you either,' he said, taking both of her hands in his rough calloused ones. 'I want to be with you forever, and I don't want to share you with anyone else.'

Her eyes lifted to his face.

'You won't have to. I won't be seeing him ever again – and that's a promise.'

As he left the hospital, a less worried man than when he'd arrived, he found himself thinking about his own affair with Marianne. He was glad that he'd ended it when he did. If he hadn't, he might have felt compelled to confess it to Kate, and although he was ready to forgive her, would she have been so willing to forgive his affair with a woman who was nothing more than a common prostitute?

CHAPTER 25

Sean Martello opened the five barred gate and drove up to the front of the house, stopping to shut it behind him before going inside.

The house was warm, and the fire in the living room stove was crackling with logs, but there was no sign of the other occupant.

'Jess, where are you?' he called from the hallway.

'Be down in a minute,' her voice called back, echoing from the fully tiled bathroom.

He went through to the kitchen and poured himself a very large Scotch, taking it through to the living room as she came down the stairs and followed him in.

She was dressed in a white bath robe and fluffy pink slippers, a towel wound round her long blonde hair.

'I've got some news for you,' he said as sat in an armchair and sipped the whisky. 'We're moving soon.'

'Moving? Where to?'

She stopped towelling her hair dry and looked over at him.

'I've bought a house out in the country over towards the Wrexham area. It'll be perfect to set up our own little operation. It's got five bedrooms, all up on the first floor, with five acres of land. It's surrounded by trees; perfect for privacy.

I've even had another garage built to hide the limo out of sight. It'll be ready in a fortnight.'

'What operation are you talking about?' This was the first she'd heard about his idea, and their move was a total surprise to her.

'We can set up five girls in the upstairs bedrooms, where they can entertain clients. There's an outside staircase leads straight to the upper floor from the garage area, so they'll be completely separate from below, and I intend to turn one of the downstairs rooms into a bedroom for ourselves where we can live on the ground floor, completely separate from the activities upstairs.

The dining room would be perfect for that. The full-sized downstairs bathroom is right next to it, and we could knock a doorway through between the two.'

'And what will we do? Will we still be going out to punters away from the house? Surely we won't be entertaining them in our own home?' she asked.

'We can close down that side of the operation if you want to. I'll still carry on the chauffeur business, and you can become a lady of leisure. All I ask is for you to be around and keep an eye on what's going on. Keep any noise down to a minimum. We don't want any rowdy behaviour alerting the locals. This is to be a high class venue, and the rent we receive from their activities will bring in all the money we need to live on.'

And where will you find the girls from?' she asked, thinking it might be a tall order to find five such girls.

'My brother will source them. He's already got two of them interested.'

She'd never met his brother – never knew where he lived, or what he did for a living, but he always seemed to be very good at finding and fixing appointments with rich clients for her. That had always been one of his many talents.

Come to think of it, she'd never known a great deal about the man she was living with either.

They'd been together almost a year now, and she had no idea whether he loved her, or whether this was just a convenient arrangement between them.

She knew he owned and ran a limousine hire company, but where he ran it from had never been disclosed – not that she'd ever asked or been interested in where it was. If it paid the bills, that was all she cared about.

He'd come into her life at the birthday party of a mutual friend, held in a hotel near her home. He'd just been another of the guests but they'd hit it off immediately, spotting each other sitting alone as wallflowers.

When he saw her smile in his direction, he'd come over and sat beside her, where they'd talked animatedly for the rest of the evening.

They'd both come alone, but they went home together at the end of the evening and stayed together at her home for the rest of the following day.

From then on, they'd seen each other regularly until he'd asked her to move in with him, and she'd felt it incumbent on her to explain how she brought in the money to live on. She was surprised when he said he already knew – her friend's boyfriend had felt it necessary to tell him when he saw them together, but he didn't really care. Her activities could become another source of income for them both.

From then on she'd stepped into his world of high class dates only, where he made all the arrangements, and she merely serviced the men he provided. Her dates were usually at hotels where he ferried her backwards and forwards, and acted as a minder. He always stayed near at hand in case there was any trouble. He'd provided her with a panic button which activated on his 'phone, but she'd never had to use it yet.

The idea of looking around and robbing the punters if they fell asleep was a new idea to her – one that she wasn't entirely happy with, but so far there'd never been an allegation of theft made. She soon realised he'd been correct in thinking they wouldn't want to make any sort of fuss and advertise to their families that they'd been with a prostitute.

When they'd taken the £10,000 from the last one, no allegation had been made about that either. The police had quizzed him and all the hotel staff about the shooting, but he'd kept quiet about the loss of the money. He knew his wife would be furious about him being with a prostitute, and even more so about the theft of the money.

There'd been only a few staff present at that time of the morning, and only the night porter had seen anything of her. He remembered her clothing, but of her features he remembered little. If he saw her as she was now, he'd never have recognised her, which was the whole idea of the disguise.

She also knew Sean had been in the army during his earlier years and had seen active service, but he seemed reluctant to talk about it.

She thought he must have bad memories, and so left the subject alone. She never knew he'd been highly trained as a sniper, and until he'd shot the motorcyclists, she never even knew he had a gun, nor that he was such a crack shot.

Having towelled her hair dry, she quickly put a brush through it and went to the kitchen to check the dinner she'd left cooking in the oven.

'How do you fancy one last job tomorrow night?' he asked. 'A swan song you could call it.'

She thought for a moment before replying. The last few nights had been cold and frosty, and it was forecast to continue all week. It would be nice to curl up in front of a warm fire in the evening, watch television and not have to go out again.

'How much is it paying?' she finally asked.

'£300 an hour,' he replied, 'and he wants two hours. Could be rich pickings too – he's something high up in government circles so I'm told.'

She thought again.

'Okay, I'll do it, but let's make this the last one will you? If we're moving in a fortnight, there'll be a lot of packing up to do.'

He laughed.

'All we need to do is pack the personal items in boxes. The removal firm will do the rest. That's what I'm paying them for.'

She kept the appointment the following night, finding this time that it was at an exclusive country club, and they were instructed to park round the back before she was met by the manager. He asked her to wait in his office, from where she was shown up to the suite by a security man sent down to accompany her.

They used the service lift to reach the top floor where he led her down the corridor to the room and handed her over to his companion who was waiting outside the door, leaving via the staircase this time.

The second man instructed her to divest herself of the warm fur coat she was wearing, after which he checked the lining and the pockets before draping it across a chair next to the door.

'Hold up your arms,' he commanded.

Realising what he intended to do, she protested violently, but he didn't listen and went ahead anyway, pushing her arms roughly aside. He ran his hands all over her body, and finally groped between her legs before pulling out the front of her dress and peering down.

She was wearing a tight black and silver sheath dress, with short cap sleeves. It was obvious that she couldn't have concealed anything beneath it.

'Enjoy that, did you?' she asked angrily when he'd finished. She wished now that she'd declined this visit.

'What do **you** think?' he said, grinning lasciviously before knocking and opening the door to the suite, pushing her roughly inside.

The man who turned to greet her was tall and elderly, but still very upright and with a military stance. His hair was grey, and he had a bristly well-clipped moustache.

He was standing by the drinks trolley when she entered, and turned to smile at her.

'Well you're a sight for sore eyes,' he said. 'You're a very pretty young woman.'

His tone was kindly, rather like a grandfather speaking to his young granddaughter.

'Would you like a drink?' he asked.

She would have liked a very large gin and tonic, but she declined the offer. She needed to keep a clear head if she was to pull off another theft, but somehow she didn't feel like robbing this man. He seemed far too nice, and his security was pretty tight. She might even be frisked on the way out. She wouldn't put it past the guard to do it again, even if he hadn't been instructed to.

'No thanks,' she answered, 'but I'll have a tonic water please.'

He poured himself a large whisky and brought them over to the end of the divan bed, where he patted the space alongside him and invited her to sit with him, where he seemed anxious to talk for a while first. She sensed there was an air of embarrassment about him.

He told her it was his first visit to this part of the country. He lived most of the week in his London flat, and spent weekends at his country house in Berkshire. He'd never been to Wales before and was on his way to Scotland where he was joining his wife for a house party in a Scottish castle.

It wasn't a lifestyle she'd have fancied herself, and she found talking about it rather boring too. It was some time before she finally got him down to business.

'What is it you want today?' she asked. 'I understand you want me for two hours at a total cost of £600.'

He nodded, seeming somewhat abashed at her bringing the purpose of her visit to the forefront.

'My security man has an envelope with cash in it as requested. He'll already have handed it to your employer. I've never done this before,' he continued more quietly, tending to gabble a little, 'but a friend gave me your number and recommended you.'

'I'm as good as he told you,' she said seriously, 'so what would you like today?'

'Erm . . .!' He didn't seem to know what to say.

Trying to alleviate his embarrassment, she finally took the lead and said, 'How about you go and take a shower and I'll wait for you here. I take it you'll want me to undress in front of you?'

His face was almost puce as he hurried through to the adjoining bathroom. She couldn't remember the last time she'd had a client look so embarrassed before.

While he was showering, she took the opportunity to text Sean and make sure he'd received the cash. His answer was short, the message reading simply "Yes" and nothing else.

When the man returned, he was wearing a bathrobe, and he'd put on a clean pair of white Y fronts underneath; functional, but very old fashioned.

She helped him take them off and gently pushed him down onto the bed, but he insisted on keeping the bathrobe wrapped around him.

Next, she dimmed the lights, and began undressing slowly and lasciviously in the light from a single bedside lamp, running her hands along the contours of her body as she did so, making heavy breathing and mewling sounds as if she was enjoying the experience.

She heard him suck in his breath a few times, hoping he was getting well turned on and ready to get things over quickly, but when she was naked and lay alongside him, she found that he was still very flabby. Try as she might, and using all the tricks she'd learned, she still couldn't bring him to an erection, and he finally took hold of her hands to stop her.

'I'm sorry,' he finally said. 'I'm trying, but beautiful as your body is, it's just not happening. Maybe we could try again later.'

She didn't mind. This was going to be an easy, if very boring way, to earn £600.

After a couple more whisky's, she talked him into having another try, but by this time he was far too relaxed, enjoying her company and talking to her rather than getting horny. Finally, she gave up in her efforts, and pulling on her clothes again, she poured herself that gin and tonic she'd missed and sat in a chair by the window, continuing to listen to his talk and letting her mind wander. He was getting drunker and drunker as he poured yet another whisky, and it wouldn't be long before he slipped into a drunken stupor, but her two hours were almost up and she had no time left to have a good look round.

Perhaps he'd be able to manage it tomorrow when she returned, and then she could check around. She hoped it wasn't going to be as boring as tonight had been. Thank God this was to be her last punter!

The next evening, when Sean arrived home from work, he brought with him a message.

The man she'd met last night didn't require her services again, as he'd decided to continue his trip into Scotland instead of staying on for another night. He had, however, left a small present for her, and if somebody could call at the country club, it would be waiting in the manager's office.

She was intrigued by what it could be. She'd already received £600 for doing absolutely nothing, so why did he think he needed to give her a present? A new phase in their life was about to begin, so perhaps this would be a fitting end to her old life.

Although she'd hoped it might bring the situation to a head between them, Sean had made no mention of marriage as yet. Now she wondered if he ever would! Was he just taking her along to keep a hold on the new venture he was planning – a sort of manager cum caretaker? Or was he taking her along as his partner? No sort of remuneration had ever been mentioned. When she'd been earning money from her punters, it had been a 60/40 split, with her taking the lion's share, but that was all about to stop.

Before she committed to the move, they'd have to talk about the money side of it. She wasn't being mercenary about it, but with the farmhouse being his, there'd never been any question of who paid the bills and provided the food, and she'd kept her own earnings to herself. Now she wouldn't be earning anything – where would her own money be coming from?

Next evening Sean arrived back with a padded envelope.

'Whatever it is, it's all yours,' he said. 'Keep it yourself.'

'Thanks,' she said, taking the envelope from him.

'Sean,' her voice stopped him as he was about to leave the room. 'When we move, what'll my role be in your operation?'

'How do you mean?' he said, a frown crossing his face.

'Well, I'll be virtually a lodger myself. If I give up taking on punters, I'll have no money to pay for my own keep.'

He laughed.

'Have I ever asked you to pay for your keep?'

'No, but I've always earned enough money for clothes and my own needs, and I've often bought things for the house as well as some food at times. Now I'll have nothing to buy anything with.'

He laughed again.

'How do you fancy becoming Mrs. Martello? Then you won't have to earn your own keep, but it'd be in name only – there'll be no wedding – I'm still married to my former wife.

This was the first she'd heard about a wife. She'd no idea he'd been married before.

Her face must have held a look of inquisition as he decided to continue with the story.

'I was married when I was 25, but it was short-lived. We were only together for 2 years before we split up. Somehow neither of us seemed to feel the need to get divorced, and it's a costly business, so we just carried on as we were. I haven't heard from her in 10 years, and I've no idea where she is now.'

She was surprised at hearing this. Now that he'd bought this house, she'd expected them to be married, but obviously that wasn't about to happen. Her own position in life was about to continue without stability, and she'd so hoped they'd be married sometime soon.

When he went upstairs to shower, she took the envelope up to the bedroom. Inside was a small note of explanation. He'd enjoyed her company very much and was sorry he hadn't been able to participate to the full. He hoped she'd understand the cancellation of their second meeting, as he felt it would be a waste of her time, and asked her to accept the small gift enclosed by way of his apology. It had once belonged to his grandmother, and as his wife had never liked it, he hoped she'd accept it as something to remember him by.

She tipped the long envelope out onto the bed, and out fell something small wrapped in tissue paper. Carefully opening it up, she finally held a ring in the palm of her hand. In the centre of the setting was a beautiful sapphire, its facets sparkling and shining in the light from above the bed, and it was surrounded by a ring of smaller diamonds. At first glance, the metal seemed to be silver, but when she showed it to Sean, he held it up to the light and examined it from all angles.

'You know, I don't think it is silver,' he finally announced. 'I think its white gold. We need to get it valued for insurance purposes. It could be worth a lot of money.'

The jeweller whistled when he saw it.

'At a rough guess,' he said when pressed, 'probably in excess of £80,000, but I need to examine it properly before I can put an accurate price on it.'

When his estimate did come back, he'd put it on proper headed paper – with a value of £85,000, saying it was a very old ring, probably dating back to the late 1800's, and the setting was rather old fashioned, but it may sell well in the antiques market.

Wow! It was the easiest money she'd ever earned, and all for merely talking to the man for two hours, but she had no intention of selling it unless in dire need of the money. She intended to keep it as a reminder of him and how lucky she'd been.

She would have liked to thank him, but he obviously had no idea of the rings true value, and neither did she know his name or where he lived. Besides which, it might compromise his relationship with his wife if she found out what he'd been doing while they were apart.

She did, however, find out his identity a few months later.

It turned out he was a minor member of royalty, and his daughter was splashed across the pages of the tabloids when she married a member of the aristocracy. She was pictured with the groom and both sets of parents on the front page.

CHAPTER 26

Bruce was very worried about Kate.

He couldn't accompany her to hospital in the ambulance as he wasn't a relative, and he didn't dare try to visit her, as he knew Martin would go straight there, but he badly wanted to know how she was. How to find out was going to be tricky, and at the moment, he couldn't think of a way round it.

He 'phoned the hospital, but as he wasn't a relative, they wouldn't give out any information. When he 'phoned again, he said he was her brother, and this time they did give him the information as to which ward she was in, but still wouldn't give out any information as to her condition.

He couldn't visit in case he bumped into Martin, or one of their two boys, but he did, in the end, try to 'phone her. He wasn't sure whether she'd have her 'phone with her, or if she'd be allowed to use it in the hospital, but he knew he had to try.

It rang several times before it was answered, but it wasn't her who answered, it was a man's voice.

'Kate's 'phone,' the voice said.

He disconnected immediately, he was sure it had been Martin.

Now he was in even more of a pickle! Did she have his name on caller display? If she did, Martin would know it was him calling.

Martin, on the other hand, realised it must have been Bruce. Caller display had merely shown the initial 'B' on the screen. Who else with that initial would have been calling her and have disconnected when he answered? He needed to put a stop to this here and now – he had no intention of losing her.

With that in mind, he called the number back but, as he'd guessed, it wasn't answered. After a few rings, it went to voicemail, and he left a terse message of his own.

'I know who you are, and I know you've been seeing my wife. This ends here and now. She won't be seeing you again, and I'm erasing your number from her 'phone. Don't try to contact her again or you'll have me to answer to.'

He hoped he'd put an end to it once and for all, but the next step would be to have it out with her. She was too bad for him to bring it up now, but when she was home again, that would be the time to bring things to a head.

She was much brighter and more cheerful when he saw her that afternoon.

'Did you bring my 'phone?' was one of the first questions she asked.

'Sorry, I forgot it,' he said, pretending regret.

She looked disappointed.

'Was it anything urgent? I can make a few 'phone calls for you if you like.'

'No,' she replied rather quickly and hesitated before continuing. 'It's rather boring sitting here all day, I thought I might ring round my friends and have a chat.'

He knew Bruce was going to be one of those so-called 'friends', and decided not to let her have the 'phone for the time being. She probably wouldn't know his number without it. He didn't think the man would have the balls to come to the hospital, so for the time being he could keep them separate until she was well enough to come home.

Next day, Sean Martello and his new wife were due to move in, and Martin had laid on a bottle of Champagne to toast their arrival, but unfortunately Mr. Hunter had also 'phoned to say he needed to see him that same morning.

'What time will you be here?' Martin asked.

'Eleven sharp,' the man's rasping voice answered, 'and I can't leave it any later than that, I need to be on my way to Cardiff again.'

That was a bit of a blow to him. Sean had said they'd be arriving between eleven and twelve. Luckily, Riley had already arranged to be there to welcome them, so there would at least be somebody to greet him, even if Mr. Hunter did make him a bit late.

With money from the sale already in the bank, he and the crew were now working flat out on Plot 2, but when they closed operations for the day, he decided to go back and take a last look round Havergill and make sure everything was clean and tidy for their arrival.

He checked upstairs and downstairs, making sure everything was in order and locked the house up before leaving.

It was then that he heard the strains of the violin again! Soft melodic notes that seemed to linger on the breeze and then finally die away into nothing; leaving just the raucous cawing of the rooks and jackdaws going to roost.

He listened for a while, but it wasn't repeated, and glancing at his watch he realised he just had time to get home for a quick shower and change before he went to visit Kate. He'd pretend that he'd forgotten her 'phone again in the rush to get the house ready for its new occupants.

Tonight when he arrived she was sitting in a chair alongside the bed.

'I've been having physiotherapy today,' she told him, 'and they're going to try and get me back on my feet soon; then I should be able to go home.'

There was no denying that was good news.

It was bad enough being a patient in the hospital, but it was just as bad for those at home having to fit numerous visits into their busy work schedule. Once she was home, he could arrange for his boys to take over some of the work and allow him more time off to look after her. He could always leave her alone for a few hours if there was anything he needed to attend to himself.

'Did you bring my 'phone?' she asked again.

'Oh sorry luv! My bad, I forgot it again. I left it sitting by the front door and I must have walked right past it.'

He had the good grace to look sorry, but he was secretly pleased that he'd thought up the excuse once more.

'Never mind,' she looked resigned to his lack of memory. 'You're here now, so I've at least somebody to talk to for the next hour.'

'What about all these people around you?' he asked, glancing round. Every bed in the ward was occupied. 'Surely there must be somebody here you can talk to.'

She looked at him as if he was a moron.

'Have you not noticed? They're all elderly – decrepit old wrinklies! All they want to talk about is their aches and pains and the medicines the doctor's prescribed for them. I'd go bonkers if I had to listen to them all day! I at least have my I-pad and there's open Wi-fi in the hospital.'

He'd forgotten she had that. She'd be able to look at Style and Design's website and manage to get through to Bruce that way if she had the use of a 'phone. Luckily, she wasn't able to walk yet, so she couldn't get to a public payphone, but would there be someone here who might lend her one? He realised she'd be able to get through to Bruce if she was determined enough, and there was nothing he could do about it!

Next morning Mr. Hunter arrived on site at the same time as Martin; and in a rush as usual.

The main structure of the house was already taking shape and he wanted to have a look at how it was getting on for himself. He wanted perfection, with no corners cut, and he was going to make sure he got it! Donning wellington boots and overalls, he accompanied Martin round the outside shell of the building, peering in through every orifice he could find. Martin wouldn't allow him inside because of health and safety regulations; much as the man wanted to.

'I'm sorry sir,' he said firmly. 'I can't risk you having an accident. It's just not safe for you to go inside.'

The man was disgruntled, but he'd had the same reaction from the builders refurbishing his restaurant in Cardiff, and knew they were right in what they said. At least Martin had had the manners to call him 'sir' and not 'mate' as the builders in Cardiff always did.

He was there for twenty minutes before he decided it was time to leave, and Martin was able to get back to Havergill, arriving at the front entrance just at the same time as the furniture van.

He followed them in, leaving them to go up to the house while he went into the office and put the plans away, before divesting himself of his overalls and boots ready to greet the new owners.

When he walked over to the house, Sean was just removing suitcases from the back of the car and about to carry them inside.

'Welcome to your new home,' he said with pride. 'I hope everything's to your satisfaction.'

The front door was standing open. Riley must already have opened it and let them in.

'Seems fine,' Sean replied. 'Jess is inside and busy inspecting everything. This is the first time she's seen it. I want you to meet her when I can find her.'

'It'll be a pleasure,' Martin replied.

He picked up two of the suitcases and carried them into the hall with Sean, and just as he put them down to ask where they were going, he heard a woman's laugh from upstairs.

Riley must be up there with her and they were laughing at some joke or other – but it was the sound of her laugh that stopped him dead in his tracks.

He'd know that laugh anywhere!

Just at that moment, she and Riley appeared from along the corridor and prepared to descend the stairs. Too late to do anything about it now! She'd spotted him too!

Both stood rooted to the spot staring at each other in horror.

Luckily, Sean had already gone back out to the car to bring in more luggage and he didn't see their reaction to each other – but Riley did! He looked from one to the other – a perplexed look on his face, but before he said anything, Martin put his finger to his lips just as Sean returned with the rest of the luggage.

The woman in front of him, whom Sean was calling Jess, was actually the woman he'd known as Marianne! The woman he'd been having an affair with for so long, and who he now knew to be a prostitute.

Could Sean be aware of that? Possibly not – but the situation needed careful handling. Neither of them would have wanted Sean to know about their association, and Riley had probably guessed about it already. He hoped he would have the common sense to keep quiet until he could explain it all to him.

He did!

Descending the stairs, he picked up the boxes Sean had already brought in and followed him along the corridor, calling loudly to find out where he was, and giving Jess and Martin the opportunity to speak.

She came down quickly and they both stepped outside, walking to the far side of the house and out of sight.

'What are you doing here?' she hissed.

'Me?? I should be asking you the same question. I built this house, and until your husband bought it, Riley owned it. All this estate was left to him by a relative.'

Her attitude changed.

'I'm sorry,' she said. 'I remember you saying you were a builder, but I had no idea it was you building this house. Are you going to say anything to Sean?'

'Of course not,' he answered. 'What do you take me for? And by the way, what is your real name? And what do I call you now?'

'My real name **is** Jessica,' she said. 'I changed my name to Marianne so that my boyfriend's family couldn't track me down after he was killed by the lorry. I've been living with Sean for over a year now. I'm very happy with him, so please don't spoil things for me.'

'I've no intention of doing so,' he answered indignantly. 'I've my own marriage to think of as well.'

Before they could say anything more, they heard Sean's voice calling her.

'Wait here for a while,' she whispered, 'I'll keep him busy inside the house before you make an appearance.'

He did as she asked, before going back to Sean's car and lifting out the rest of their belongings to leave them in the hall, just as if he'd been there all along.

The furniture van was almost completely unloaded by now, and Sean and Jess were busy directing the positioning of their belongings within the house. It looked as if he hadn't been missed – save by

Riley, who gave him an odd look when he arrived back shortly after Jess.

'I'll explain later,' he said quietly, as they stood side by side in the hallway.

He caught sight of Sean at that moment hurrying from one room to another.

'The site office will be gone on Monday. There's heavy haulage coming to move it around ten o'clock, and I'll have workmen on site making the ground good after that,' he called.

'That's fine,' Sean acknowledged as he disappeared again.

Once back in the office, Martin put the kettle on as Riley sat down and waited for an explanation.

'Well, what's the story with you and Jess?'

Martin turned back to him with their coffees and set them down before sitting down himself.

'We had an affair some time ago,' he said, 'but her name wasn't Jess in those days; she called herself Marianne.'

'Why?'

He should have realised that Riley would be curious, but he wasn't prepared to say she'd been a prostitute.

'She'd left her husband. It was an abusive relationship and she didn't want him to find her,' was the simple excuse that quickly came to mind.

Riley nodded. He'd had a similar temptation some years ago and knew how easy it could be to fall into the trap.

He'd given a young woman lessons; a woman much younger than himself, and she'd obviously fancied him right from the start. She kept giving him gentle hints in things she said and the looks she gave him. She was a good driver and passed her test easily at the first attempt; but when she invited him out for a drink to celebrate, he knew it was going to be either go along with it, or nip it in the bud immediately before things progressed any further. He'd chosen the latter, and often wondered what the outcome would have been if he'd succumbed, but he was already married to Connie, and decided to stick to the straight and narrow. It was so much less complicated, and he did like an easy life.

When she realised Martin had gone, Jess was relieved, but sad that he wasn't around any more. She'd realised when she saw him standing at the bottom of the stairs that she still loved him, and had wanted more than anything to run into his arms and hug him close, but that could never be now. She belonged to Sean, and having seen what he was capable of by shooting the two motorcyclists in cold blood, she couldn't risk him finding out about her and Martin.

Her thoughts were interrupted by Sean asking her which room she wanted to use as a bedroom. He pointed out how easily the dining room could be combined with the bathroom to form an en suite and she agreed with his choice.

It looked out towards the front of the house, and would have a nice view once the gardens were completed, but it also had a smaller window to the side as well. That way looked out onto the conifers which swept round and into the driveway, but also gave a view of anybody trying to get to the garage where he intended to keep the limo.

He wanted Martin, and anybody else who might still be around, out of the way before he brought it in. When they'd been out on one of her 'dates', he always used false number plates, which were changed for the real ones when he was using it in the legitimate side of the limo hire. That way, if somebody managed to take down the number and the police tracked it down, they'd find that it belonged to another similar Mercedes and not to the one he owned. He'd spotted the other car one evening parked outside a hotel where he'd been picking people up from a function, and had the plates cloned.

Jess had chosen the path of a lady of leisure when he'd given her the choice, realising that she didn't want to 'date' the punters through his business any more.

The money they'd receive from the use of the rooms should be sufficient to live on, but the money she sometimes managed to bring home from her liaisons would be sorely missed – the last £10,000 she'd managed to pick up having been the best by far. As far as they knew, its loss had never been reported to the police.

If he could, he wanted to try and persuade her to carry on the odd visits in the future. The limousine hire was a lucrative business, but the cars were expensive to run and even more expensive to buy when one had to be replaced, and he'd noticed that trade had been falling off quite significantly just lately. Having paid out his hard earned cash to buy this place, it needed to earn its keep – and so did she!

Martin and Riley saw the furniture van drive past the office as it left, leaving in its wake a cloud of dust from the unfinished surface. He'd have to see to laying the tarmac as soon as the container had been moved to its new position between Plots 2 and 3 on Monday.

It seemed Naomi's sister and her husband were very interested in Plot 3 and had already been to see it twice now. He expected them to make a down payment any day now, and even if they didn't buy it in the end, he now had the money to develop both Plots at the same time.

It was just as the dust was settling that they heard another car arriving, as it parked right outside.

They both peered through the open doorway to see who it was, but although the man who emerged looked familiar, neither of them could place him.

'Mind if I come in,' he said as he reached the door, and it was then that Martin recognised him. The last time they'd come face to face, he'd been looking down the barrel of a shotgun!

'Ryan Farmer,' he announced, 'my father, Charles, has the cottage on the far side of your land down by the river.'

Martin nodded, wondering what the man could possibly want with them. They hadn't been anywhere near his father's cottage since their previous encounter, so there was no way he could have come with a complaint.

Seeing Martin's hostility, he continued with what he'd come to say.

'My father hasn't been well for some time now, and he's had several health scares over the past couple of years – mainly to do with his heart.

He'll be 80 next month, and I've been trying to persuade him to come and live with us for some time now, but he's always said he wouldn't leave the cottage where he and my mother had so many happy years together.

Last month he was rushed into hospital and we all thought he was a gonna', but he pulled through in the end. The staff there finally persuaded him he shouldn't be living on his own, so he's agreed to come and live with us now.'

Martin looked at him quizzically.

'So what can we do for you?' he said, not seeing the point of all this explanation.

'I'm just letting you know the cottage will be going up for sale. I wondered if you might be interested in buying it from him and making it into part of your development. It already has its own entrance and exit, but it's only over rough ground, and you'll probably want to improve it.'

Martin gave a small snort.

'These are luxury houses we're building here,' he said. 'It doesn't fit in with those in any way, and I don't think we'd find anybody interested in it.'

'Hang on a minute,' Riley said, putting his hand out to Martin. 'I know somebody who might be interested, but it'll probably need a lot of work to bring it up to modern day standards. It'll all depend on the price you want for it.'

Martin glanced at him in surprise but said nothing.

Riley had long held the dream of living here on the land his ancestors had once owned, but he'd never be able to afford one of the houses Martin was building, and they were far too large for just him and Connie anyway. The cottage was much smaller and had a lovely view from the back across the river and onto the farmland beyond. In time it would have a similar view at the front once Martin had finished the landscaping.

All he had to do was persuade Connie!

'Mmmm . . . let me think about it,' he said.

The price might go up if he seemed too eager.

'It's up to you, gentlemen,' Ryan said as he turned to leave. 'I'll be seeing the estate agents after the weekend.'

As he drove away, Martin turned to Riley.

'I presume it's you who's interested in buying it,' he laughed.

Riley nodded.

'I'm very interested – but I don't know if I can persuade Connie. I might just buy flowers and a nice Chinese takeaway on the way home before I put the idea to her.'

They both laughed as Martin shut up the office and they prepared to leave for home, but when Riley did arrive it was to find a very glum looking Connie.

'What's up?' he asked as he put the Chinese takeaway onto the table.

'I've just heard some bad news. It seems Betty from next door died yesterday. The cousin from Lincolnshire she's been living with just rang to tell me.'

Riley too was upset by the news. While he was recuperating from his accident, she'd been very good to him, and they'd become buddies during their chats over morning coffee. Although it had been some time now since they'd seen her, he was sad to hear of her passing.

This was not the time to bring up the subject of buying the cottage!

CHAPTER 27

Bruce still hadn't managed to see Kate, or to find out how she was, and he was getting more and more anxious.

Throwing caution to the wind, he decided to go and try to visit her.

Seeing Martin's pickup parked outside their offices one day, he realised it was almost visiting time, and Martin was still in the office with Sidney Toomes.

When he listened at the door, they seemed deep in discussion, and he decided to go straight to the hospital. Even if he only managed a few minutes with her, he'd make do with that, but he was desperate to see her and find out when she was coming out. He'd be able to visit her at home with little fear of discovery while Martin and her boys were out working.

He already knew which ward she was in, but when he arrived, there was no sign of her.

'Mrs. Jennings?' he queried of the nurse at the desk. 'Where is she?'

She knew immediately.

'Oh, she was discharged yesterday. She's probably at home now.'

He left the ward in a hurry, but it was too late to go and see her now. Martin would probably have gone straight home when he'd finished his business.

Too late in the afternoon to go back to work and get on with anything, but he was pleased she was at home now. In the morning he'd wait to see Martin's pickup arriving for work, and then he'd go straight there.

As expected, Martin arrived just after nine the next morning, and Bruce saw the pickup drive past the window. He'd already told them he wouldn't be in work that morning, hoping to spend most of it with Kate.

Quickly gathering his things together, he left the house and went straight to her home. He knew there was work waiting for him at the office, but that could go hang for the time being, he wasn't going to miss this opportunity.

The lane where she lived was a dead end and he parked right at the far end, where it took a right turn into a farm entrance, and where a high hedge hid his car from sight of the house.

Hurrying back, he noticed there were no cars parked at the side of the building, or in the open parking space at the front. He was in luck! She must be there alone.

He peered through the bay window at the front and saw her sitting on the sofa, a blanket tucked round her. She was watching television, and she looked up as his head cast a shadow on the glass.

She looked startled, and he smiled and gave her a small friendly wave of greeting.

'Come in,' she called, 'door's on the latch.'

He wasn't sure whether she was pleased to see him or whether she just wanted him out of sight of prying eyes.

'What are you doing here?' she asked rather curtly when he entered the room. 'Martin could be back any time.'

'He'd just arrived for work when I left. He'll probably be there for some time now,' he said, feeling pleased with himself, but her next comment pulled him up short.

'No, he won't,' she said. 'He was dropping the boys off and going to pick up some groceries, and then he's coming straight back here. What do you want?'

She sounded churlish and he was puzzled by her attitude. He'd felt sure she'd be pleased to see him after so long apart.

'I've been worried about you. They wouldn't give me any information at the hospital, and I had no way of finding anything out. How are you now?'

'I'm okay.'

Her tone was offhand, and she kept glancing towards the window.

'What's the matter Kate? Aren't you pleased to see me?'

'No, I'm not.' Her tone was aggressive now. 'It's over Bruce! We're finished! I've had a lot of time to think things over while I've been in the hospital, and I don't want anything to come between me and Martin. He's been very attentive, and it's made me realise just how much I love him. I don't want to see you again. Now please go before he gets back.'

'But Kate . . . I love you! You can't finish it just like this! I don't know what I'll do without you!'

'Bruce,' she said, giving him a determined look, 'it's over! Please do as I've asked and go now. I'm sure Martin knows about us, and I don't want to compromise the situation any further.'

His shoulders drooped. He knew she meant it.

Sadly he turned and left, but as he walked down the lane back towards his car, he heard the sound of a vehicle coming from behind. Theirs was the last house in the lane, and it could only be Martin arriving home.

Quickly he strode the last few yards back to his car and peered up the lane from behind the cover of the hedge.

It was Martin returning, as he watched him take out a bag of groceries and carry them into the house, locking the car behind him. He'd probably be unpacking them in the kitchen, which was right at the back of the house. He'd noticed the open door and seen where it was when he'd first entered the house.

Once he judged Martin would be busy unpacking everything, he jumped in and started the engine, driving out quickly and quietly past the house – but he'd missed that little thing in life called chance – that little thing that could turn out to be either destiny or disaster. This time it could have been called either.

Martin had taken the bag of groceries through to the kitchen as he'd thought, but when he'd put them on the table, he remembered the bottle of Kate's favourite German Riesling that he'd bought for her as a treat. He'd put it in the elastic pocket at the back of the driver's seat in case it might get broken on the journey home.

He returned to the car to get it just as Bruce's car drove past, and he quickly walked out to the road. He'd recognised the car immediately, and watched as he saw it gather speed up the lane. He was angry that the man had had the temerity to come to their home.

Going back inside, he marched straight into the living room, his anger still raging, and confronted Kate.

'What was Bruce Chambers doing here?' he stormed.

She realised he'd seen the car and she couldn't lie.

'He just came to see how I was,' she said brightly, trying to mitigate the reason for the visit.

'Don't lie to me!' his voice was thunderous now. 'I know you've been seeing him. Are you going to start bringing him to our home now as well?'

'No . . . no!' her voice was adamant. Far from feeling timid now, she only felt anger herself at Bruce's audacity in coming to her home, and she knew it was no use pretending any more.

'I've finished it! I've told him I don't want to see him again!'

Martin had calmed down a little now, mindful of how ill she'd been and what she'd gone through. He sat down in the armchair opposite her and tried to talk calmly and rationally.

'I've known for a long time you were seeing him, but I hoped it would all peter out in time.'

Too late to lie anymore! She had to come clean!

'I have finished it, and I didn't ask him to come here today. I was as surprised as you to see him!'

'You were supposed to be meeting him when you had your accident, weren't you?'

She nodded.

'How did you know?'

'I spoke to the paramedics who took you in. They were still there when I got to A & E, and they gave me the name of the person who made the 999 call, but I already knew you were using that as a meeting place. I saw you driving out one day just after I left work. It didn't take a genius to put two and two together.'

She looked suitably abashed, before lifting her eyes towards him and looking straight into his face.

'I'm telling you the truth Martin. I've finished it. I wasn't expecting him to turn up here, and I told him to leave straight away.

It's you I want to be with and not him. He was just a diversion, and I never loved him. Please believe me!'

He did! He was hardly the one to criticise after his own little diversion with Marianne – now known as Jess. He knew how it could be to need a little bit on the side after so many years of being married to the same person. He had no intention of letting that happen to him again either, after he realised the heartbreak it could bring to both of them.

'Let's just put the whole thing behind us and start again,' he said. 'I've brought a little something back for you.'

She looked surprised and waited with anticipation while he fetched the bottle of wine and a glass.

'Just one glass?' she quizzed when he came back.

'I prefer a beer,' he said, putting down his own glass with a can alongside. 'You can keep all the wine to yourself.'

Cuddling up alongside her, he poured the liquid into both glasses and put his arm round her shoulders while they both drank.

It seemed a cosy little scene, with both their dalliances put behind them – but Martin wasn't finished with Bruce yet! He'd think of a way to get back at him!

It was just over two weeks later that that chance arrived!

He was just driving along the road from one part of the site to another in a dumper truck, when he saw Bruce's car coming towards him in the distance.

He'd just bought another brand new BMW, and he'd only had it a couple of weeks, so it still looked brand spanking new.

Quickly checking both front and rear views, Martin saw no other vehicles on the road, and decided now was as good a time as any.

Taking a calculated risk, he deliberately continued on past the entrance to the site, and headed towards Bruce's brand new vehicle, veering onto the wrong side of the road as the gap closed between them.

Bruce's face was a picture of sheer terror as the vehicles came closer and closer together, sounding his horn over and over again, but

Martin was completely set on what he intended to do. An eye for an eye!

There was a deep ditch to the left of the road, and Bruce's only options were to swerve into the ditch, or be hit by the heavy dumper truck.

The last thing Martin saw was the look of terror on Bruce's face as he let go of the steering wheel and put his hands over his face as the two vehicles came together, and the truck side swiped the BMW with a loud squealing of rending metal. He knew he'd done damage to his own vehicle, but then, it was already covered in deep dents and scratches from working on the various building sites, and he kept on going as he saw the car veer nose down into the ditch.

Victory was his – retribution had been extracted – and there'd been no witnesses!

Shortly afterwards, Bruce scrambled out of the ditch, covered in cuts and bruises – but that was more than could be said for his new car!

He knew instinctively that it was a write-off! And he also knew who the other driver had been!

He'd never known how much Martin must have hated him for his affair with his wife – but he knew now just what he was capable of! Knew he'd never be able to go near Kate again!

CHAPTER 28

Alan Kirkbride was riding his motorbike home from the tyre depot where he worked in the nearby town. Friday was a late night for them as they were open until 7p.m. on that one evening of the week. All the commuters had already gone home, and the road ahead of him was quiet. He'd passed very few cars since leaving the outskirts of the town and he was enjoying the ride home to the farm where he lived with his parents. His tea would be ready and waiting in the oven and he was looking forward to it. He was ravenously hungry!

It had been a warm, sunny day; the sun just beginning to set beyond the far mountain range. It was low down on the horizon ahead of him and it was dazzling him a little as he slowed down to wipe a hand across his visor.

He was approaching a small crossroads where he turned left to reach his home, but just as he was preparing to change gear to negotiate the turn, a vehicle appeared from the right hand side. It crossed the road in front of him, and went into the lane he was about to enter.

He stared in surprise. It was a black Merecedes limo; a complete surprise to see one so far from town, and especially in the narrow country lanes surrounding his home.

He turned up the lane after it and followed. He knew that car! He'd seen it before, and in very different surroundings! He'd also made a note of the number plate when he'd last seen it, committing it to memory.

Going past his own home, he followed it for a couple of miles until the road widened and they entered a village. Here it slowed down, and he had to moderate his speed and hang back; but when it left the village, it continued on down the lane once more, eventually signalling to turn into a driveway.

He gave it a few minutes before he followed cautiously on foot. There were conifers to his right which hid him from view, and the unmade driveway helped to deaden his footsteps.

He stopped when they ended and he found himself facing a large house just ahead and to the right. He heard the sound of a garage door being opened and concealed himself amongst the overhanging branches.

To the right of the house was a large garage, and he saw the man drive in and park the limo inside, before coming back out and closing the doors behind him. He padlocked them, and as he turned to walk towards the house, the setting sun shone full on his face.

Alan knew that man! He'd never forget that face as long as he lived! The street lights had been bright outside the hotel, and the man was facing him when he took aim and shot his brother in cold blood.

Now he knew where he lived – punishment would be extracted!

Alan had been the third man in the scam to grab handbags and mobile 'phones from unwary pedestrians.

His brother and his cousin had roared up out of the blue on their motorbike and snatched whatever items they were carrying from the unwary punters. They were so taken aback by the noise, and so surprised when the snatch came, that they were left reeling from the shock, and just stood staring after them, not knowing what to do.

The two assailants would then hand whatever they'd snatched over to him as they passed, where he waited out of sight of any surveillance cameras, and could make good his escape through the quiet side streets. If the others were stopped, there was nothing on them, and no proof that they'd been the ones involved – they were just two innocent lads coming home from a night on the town!

It was an audacious robbery, but it had always worked well so far – until the day they'd met up with this man! Now both of them were dead – and this was the man responsible!

He watched the front of the house for a while, but there was no further sign of him, although a woman did come outside for a few moments and put a bag full of rubbish into the bin.

As darkness began to fall, he decided there was going to be no further sighting that night, and he began to hatch a plan.

There couldn't be too many firms in the area supplying limos for hire, so it shouldn't be too hard to find out where he worked.

A couple of weeks later, Sean took a call just as he was about to leave work. Everybody else had already left and the distraught man on the other end of the 'phone was begging for assistance.

It seemed his two daughters and four of their friends had been invited to a hen party in a large hotel in Ruthin. They were excited and looking forward to it, and had all bought new outfits for the occasion. Unfortunately, the company they'd contacted for a minibus to take them there and back had just rung to say that it had developed a fault with the engine, and wouldn't be able to fulfil the booking.

The man was desperate not to let them down, and Sean's was the only other hire company in the area that was still open.

Sean hadn't expected such a late call, but after thinking about it for a few moments, he knew their own minibus was sitting idle in the garage, and he wasn't doing anything himself that evening either.

He agreed a price with the man, and although bookings were usually paid for in advance, in these circumstances, he'd be willing to accept cash when he arrived to pick them up.

It was a fair arrangement for him too. With cash being paid, he wouldn't have to run it through the company's books and it could go straight into his own bank account.

With that in mind, he unlocked the garage where the hire vehicles were kept. Most of them were already out, and the minibus came out easily enough with only one car having to be moved.

Putting his own car back into the slot it had vacated, he drove the minibus back home. He wasn't due to pick the girls up until 9 o'clock, and then return to fetch them at 2a.m. If he went to bed straight after dropping them off, he could snatch a few hours sleep before picking them up again.

Jess was surprised when he arrived in the minibus and told her he'd be going out again that night. He usually only did the limo runs these days, spending the rest of his time in the office, but after he explained, she understood his reasoning and being able to pocket the money himself.

They still hadn't found anyone to occupy any of the upstairs bedrooms. The possibilities he'd first had for their occupation hadn't materialised, and this place was high on overheads. They'd shut down all the radiators in the house and closed off the upper floor for the time being. They'd also done the same with the downstairs rooms, using only the dining room they'd turned into a bedroom, the bathroom and the large kitchen as their living quarters.

The kitchen was big enough to accommodate some of the lounge furniture and the television at one end, with a small table alongside the large window into the garden. This way they were able to cut down on the costs of heating, but the bill for the rates had been staggering. Neither of them had anticipated it would be that high!

Sean left to make his pickup at 8.30, anticipating it would take him 20 minutes to get there, but after making his way back through the village, he rounded a sharp left hand bend to find there'd been an accident ahead.

There was a motorbike lying on its side, and two motorcyclists sprawled in the road a few metres further on. One looked to be unconscious, but the other was writhing around and groaning.

He quickly jumped out and went to their aid, but was surprised to find their motorcycle leathers completely intact. He would have thought that being thrown some distance on the tarmac surface, it might have sustained more damage than it had.

As he bent over them, he suddenly felt a heavy thump across his back, and unable to stop himself, he sprawled forward onto the road, where he felt another blow land across his shoulders.

Trying to scramble to his feet, he realised that the two motorcyclists were also up on their feet and standing over him, with another two men standing alongside, holding heavy baseball bats.

'What is this?' he shouted, as a heavy motorcycle boot landed in his chest and knocked him to the ground once more.

Winded, it took him some moments to regain his breath. He tried to remember the training he'd received as a soldier, but it was many years ago now, and he wasn't as fit as he'd once been – or as young! Besides which, the odds were stacked against him – four against one!

The motorcycle rider was now standing over him, but far enough away so that he couldn't easily reach him. He'd discarded his helmet but his face was still mainly hidden by a balaclava.

'Do you remember shooting someone – another motorcycle rider, outside a hotel some time ago?'

Sean didn't know what to say as he looked up at him, but the man started to speak again before he could muster his senses. He remembered only too well!

Now the man had come closer and was bending towards him.

'I see you do remember,' he spat, 'and so do I! He was my brother, and the other man was my cousin. Have you anything to say for yourself?'

Sean couldn't think of any answer, he was too busy trying to think of a way out of this situation.

Suddenly he made a wild grab for the man's legs. He'd come closer while he was talking, and he now seemed within reach. Two of the others were standing behind him – if he could catch him off balance, he'd crash backwards into them and they might all go down together, giving him a chance to get to his feet, where he might stand a better chance. The man, however, had noticed his sudden movement and sidestepped quickly, just as another blow from the baseball bat hit him across the shoulders from behind. He hadn't realised the fourth man was there.

'Not so big a man now are you, without your gun?' the first man said, standing just out of reach once more, and fumbling a motorcycle chain out of his pocket, which he proceeded to wrap around his gloved knuckles.

It was like a sudden unspoken signal as they all lunged towards him, raining blows on him from all sides.

The first few were agony, but as they continued, he began to feel himself losing all hold on reality, and finally his sensibilities grew numb as he lost consciousness.

Finally, the first man, breathing heavily from his exertions, drew back and called for them all to stop; listening as the familiar sound of a tractor could be heard trundling towards them in the distance.

So near to home, the tractor could easily be his father returning after a late night in the fields, or one of the neighbours who knew him and his bike well.

'Let's get out of here before we get caught,' he said. 'We'll take the minibus up onto the moors and burn it.'

They picked up the keys from where Sean had dropped them and one of the men climbed into the vehicle; the other retrieving his motorbike from a farm gateway further on, before moving off down the lane to wait for Alan and his companion.

'Let's toss him over the hedge for now. Somebody's bound to find him soon, but we gotta' get out of here now.'

The two of them lifted the still unconscious man over the hedge and heard the heavy thud as he landed on the other side; but what they hadn't realised was that there was a sloping bank on the other side, and once he'd landed he rolled down the slope and into a thick tangle of bushes.

Hearing the tractor coming nearer, they both mounted the bike and roared off after the minibus.

Next morning Jess woke just after eight o'clock, surprised to find Sean hadn't returned. She'd expected to find him sleeping soundly alongside her after his late night.

Perhaps he'd slept in the kitchen so that he didn't wake her, but when she donned her dressing gown and went through, he wasn't there either. Her next thought was that he may have got up early and gone straight to work, but then he would surely have left a note.

That thought was confirmed when she didn't find the minibus in the garage either, and she thought if that was the case, he'd ring her shortly; but as the morning dragged on, there was still no word from him.

By twelve o'clock, he still hadn't 'phoned and she decided to ring the office herself.

'I'm sorry Mrs. Martello,' the receptionist said. 'Your husband hasn't been into work this morning, and he hasn't left word as to where he'll be. Do you want me to get him to 'phone you when he does come in?'

The staff in his office had all been told they'd married, and now they all thought of her as Sean's wife.

'Yes please,' she answered as she put the 'phone down.

But still the day dragged on with no word from him, and it was shortly after 6p.m. that a police car pulled up to the house and a man and a woman constable stepped out.

'Mrs. Martello?' the man queried when she answered the door. 'Can we come in for a moment?'

She ushered them into the kitchen before explaining that she lived with Sean but they weren't married. She didn't know why she'd felt it necessary to tell them that, but something told her that perhaps she ought to.

'Has something happened to him?' she asked agitatedly.

'We don't know,' he answered. 'We've found a minibus on the Denbigh Moors, but there was nobody with it. We traced it to your hus' . . . Mr. Martello's business, but he hasn't been into work today. Would you have any idea where he is?'

She explained what Sean had been doing last night and where he'd been going, admitting she had no idea where he was now, and that he hadn't been home since.

'Could the minibus have broken down and he's still trying to get home?' she asked.

That didn't sound feasible to her even as she said it. He always carried his mobile with him, and she'd found no sign of it in the house that morning. His usual habit when at home was to leave it on the end of the kitchen island, where it was accessible from either the kitchen or the living space, and he always switched it off and left it there when they went to bed.

She was clutching at straws! Sean shouldn't have been anywhere near the Denbigh Moors, and she had no idea why the minibus should have been found there either.

They looked at each other before the woman answered her query.

'It seems unlikely. The vehicle was found at the bottom of a rocky ravine, and there are signs at the top that it was driven across a grassy area before plunging over the edge. There was no one inside, and if he'd been in the vehicle when it went over, it seems likely he'd have been seriously injured.'

She omitted to say that the vehicle had cart wheeled several times before it reached the bottom, and over numerous large boulders, before coming to rest on its roof; but there were no signs of blood inside the driver or passenger compartments.

Everyone, including the police, where baffled as to how the minibus had got there, and where Sean might be. It was miles away from where it should have been.

After twenty four hours and with still no sign of his whereabouts, the police where becoming concerned; and tried to retrace his movements, starting with the area around where the vehicle had been found, but they drew a complete blank there.

Then they turned their attention to the time and the route he'd have taken after leaving his home. There was only one way to reach the main road from there, and knowing where his ultimate destination had been, they realised he'd probably have been going in that direction.

The call Sean had taken for the last minute booking was traced to an unregistered pay as you go mobile, and the call had been made from somewhere near his office. The address he'd been given had been scribbled on a piece of paper on his desk, but when they checked it out, the address didn't exist. Although the road did, the house number given was 146, and the houses ended at 140.

This had definitely been some sort of setup, and they needed to scrutinise his background to see why somebody should have wanted to do him harm. Jess told them they'd only been living in their present home for a short time, so it was unlikely there'd be any connection here, but they made a thorough search through the house and his belongings before abandoning the search. They'd found nothing out of the ordinary!

The next place they needed to search was his office, and after that, the premises where he operated from, questioning all the employees.

Jess had been worried that they'd find the gun, but it hadn't come to light, and she wondered if it might still be back at the farmhouse. As far as she knew, he'd made no move towards selling it, and she wondered if he intended keeping it on as a bolthole.

The police obviously weren't aware of the farm, and nor did they ask where they'd been living previously. She went back there as soon as she was sure they'd finished with the house, finding the gun in a locked metal box at the bottom of the old wardrobe that had once belonged to his parents.

She thought of throwing it in the lake near the farmhouse, but knew that would be one of the places they'd search if they became aware of his ownership of the farm. Besides that, it was also very shallow, and might dry up almost entirely if they had a hot summer. That was far too close for comfort!

In the end, she motored out to Llyn Celyn, near the town of Bala. It was situated on a quiet moorland road, and although it was busy in the summer, as autumn was fast approaching, the road was quiet. No other car passed while she was there. She threw the gun out as far out into the lake as she could manage. It sank from sight immediately! Now, she hoped, there was no other way of linking him to the shooting outside the hotel.

It was a further twelve hours before Sean was found!

A young woman out riding her horse heard what she thought was a groan from the other side of the hedge. Her horse too had heard something, as he rolled his eyes towards the sound and pricked up his ears, before turning his head in the same direction.

He was only a young animal and could be quite skittish when strange things beyond his comprehension happened, but she managed to calm him with a few quiet words and stroking his neck gently.

When he seemed calm enough, she dismounted and tied him to a farm gate before leaning over and looking back towards where the sound had come from. There was a deep depression in the ground at that point filled with nettles and Rose Bay Willow herb, as well as some rather stunted hawthorn bushes.

She heard the sound again, and so did the horse. Gentling him once more, she climbed over the gate and went towards the hollow. Hearing further noises from within its confines, she scrambled down into the dip, where she found the battered and bruised body of Sean. He was barely alive after the beating he'd received, and taking out her mobile, she called for an ambulance immediately.

The paramedics too were amazed when they found him and bundled him into the ambulance as quickly as possible. Time was of the essence and they needed to get him help as quickly as possible.

The doctors hummed and hawed over his condition when he was wheeled into A & E, and there was a lot of heavy sighing and head shaking as they ministered to him as best they could.

It was immediately apparent that all his cheeks, eye and jaw bones were broken, as were most of his ribs; and both lungs appeared to have been punctured.

Sean died just over an hour later without ever regaining consciousness!

CHAPTER 29

Jess was perturbed and upset when she heard about Sean's death, but couldn't help feeling more concerned about how it would affect her.

She'd always known she didn't love him; at least, not as much as she should have done. She looked on him as more of a friend with benefits, and in some way, as her benefactor.

She had nothing of her own – all she had was what she'd shared with Sean, and she soon realised that with them never having married; that would all come to an end with his death. She'd have no entitlement to anything he'd owned and none of the money in his bank account would come to her. There'd be no life insurance either – if he'd ever taken any out.

But he did still have a wife somewhere, and although he'd had no idea where she was now, the legal eagles would soon track her down, and she'd descend like wildfire when she realised how much Havergill was worth.

Jess's tenure here would be short lived once she arrived to claim her bounty, and she herself had nothing, save the few hundred pounds she had left in her own bank account.

Searching through the house after his death, all she found was £360 in twenties stashed in a suit pocket. The bank account was held solely in his name, and he'd already told her he'd never made a Will. It was one of the things he'd always meant to get around to.

Everything he owned would now go into probate, and even if something had been coming her way, she'd never be able to afford the upkeep of this large house, and nor did she want to. It was far too big for just the two of them, and she had no idea why he'd wanted to buy it in the first place, except to fulfil his dream of turning it into an upmarket brothel.

Very soon, the situation began to escalate out of her control.

Firstly were the 'final demand' letters that began to arrive. They were all addressed to him, and she opened the first few, but once she began to recognise who they were from, she stopped opening them altogether. They weren't her responsibility after all.

The next thing was when the debt collectors began knocking at the door!

Nobody had told her to leave the house as yet, but the time was fast approaching when she'd have no alternative – but where could she go? What little money she had she spent on buying food and petrol, although she tried to be frugal with that, using the car only for visits to the supermarket. She'd soon learned on which days and what time of the day it was best to go to pick up things that were reduced in price, but the money was still dwindling fast, and once that was gone, she had no job and no other form of income to replace it.

It was on one wet and miserable afternoon, when she seemed to have been sitting for hours pondering her plight, and wondering where she could find a job, that there was a thunderous knocking on the door.

Opening it with trepidation, she found bailiffs standing on the doorstep.

'We're here to repossess this house on behalf of your mortgage company,' he said, in a soft but determined voice. 'Can you gather together your things and leave as quickly as possible. We can give you two hours.'

She wasn't aware until recently that Sean had taken out a mortgage on the house – naively enough, she thought he'd bought it outright. She should have realised he wouldn't have that sort of money floating around.

Nothing in the house belonged to her, so she had very little of her own to remove, and as they waited, she gathered together her things and loaded them into her car. Luckily, she'd still kept it; getting old but still working well. Sean had offered to buy her a new one, but she was glad she hadn't taken him up on that offer now, as she would probably have lost that as well.

She saw Martin's pickup drive past on the road as she made her way down the drive, and it occurred to her to prevail on him to help her out, but then she realised it wasn't in any way possible. He'd made it very clear at their last meeting that he didn't want to see her again.

Then a brainwave hit her! There was still the farm! As far as she knew, Sean had been sentimental about it as it had once belonged to his parents and he'd done nothing about selling it as yet. She didn't even know if he'd ever intended to. She could make that her bolthole for the time being. Then another inspiration came to her! The ring she'd been given by the old gent was still in the chest of drawers at the farm, where she'd taped it to the bottom of a drawer. She could sell that, and that would give her enough to live on until she could find a job, and leave her some left over in the bank for her future. Perhaps if nobody else knew about his ownership of the farm, she could make that her permanent home as well.

When she reached it, it had started to rain heavily and the stone farmhouse looked cold and indomitable in the greyness of the day that had settled around it. The surrounding branches of the trees hung listless as they dripped heavy drops of water down to the ground and the far reaching views from the front windows were hidden by the mist rising from the low lying ground beyond. She felt cold shivers running up and down her spine as she looked at it. It was very forbidding in this murky gloom.

Retrieving the key from where it was always left; in a hole in the dry stone wall surrounding the property, she let herself in.

It was cold when she stepped inside and the electric didn't work when she tried the lights. She couldn't tell whether he'd had it switched off or whether the bills hadn't been paid here either.

Apart from that, everything was just as they'd left it previously, and there was plenty of fuel in the outhouse to light the multi fuel stoves; one in the kitchen, and one in the living room. Without electric, she couldn't light the oil fired range, but it was still quite warm as yet, and the stoves would suffice for the time being; but what she'd do if she was still here in the winter she didn't like to dwell on.

As well as a table, the kitchen was also large enough to accommodate two armchairs and she could spend most of her time in here until she had enough money to reconnect the electric.

She found a tin of Irish stew in the walk-in pantry, and another of peaches. At least she had some food, and there were plenty of other tinned and dry goods as well; things like pasta and rice – but she had no means of cooking them. The tin of stew she opened, and once the stove was warming up, she left it on top to heat through while she checked the rest of the house.

The bed was still made, and she took the sheets, duvet and pillows down to the kitchen, draping them across the armchairs to air in front of the stove in case they were damp.

Returning to the bedroom, she extricated the envelope from its hiding place beneath the drawer and emptied it onto the bed, where the tissue paper package fell out. Even as she picked it up, it didn't feel right. She couldn't feel the ring inside the wrapping.

Once it was opened, and the tissue paper was spread out, there was no sign of the ring. It was gone! And the only other person who'd known it was there was Sean!

Martin was already aware that Sean had died, but he wasn't aware of the details and what had happened to him, or why, but news soon reached him that there were bailiffs removing everything from the house. He rang Riley to tell him.

'They've only been there a few months!' he said incredulously when he heard the news. 'Will it have any repercussions on us?'

'None whatsoever,' Martin replied. 'We made a deal and all the documents were legally signed. The money's been paid over and there's no comeback on us. The property belongs entirely to Sean now, or it did, and nothing whatsoever to do with us any more.'

'What about his wife?' Riley continued.

'I've no idea!' Martin replied. 'I haven't seen any sign of her since the bailiffs arrived. I've no idea where she's gone, but I don't think she's at the house any more.'

He knew full well she wasn't there. When he'd heard the news, he'd gone straight round to see if he could be of any help. He felt he owed her something after their previous relationship, even if it was only a few pounds to tide her over. He had no idea of how much trouble Sean's death had left her in, or that they hadn't ever been married.

Riley broke the news to Connie when he put the 'phone down, and she too asked the same question as to whether it would have any impact on them, but he reassured her that they had no responsibility for it whatsoever.

Lying in bed that night, Riley broached the subject of the cottage being for sale, and asked if she might be interested in taking a look while they were there.

She knew straight away what he was angling at, but decided that she'd go along with it for the time being. It would save an argument when she was really tired and needed some sleep.

She'd made a lot of new friends at work, and really didn't want to move away from the home she loved. It would be a big upheaval, and living in the country was something she'd never experienced before. It would be a lonely existence from his description of where it was, and she'd have to give up her job, as well as him having to find new clients once more for his own business. It had taken him months to get it up and running properly again after his accident, and money had been really tight during that period. She didn't want to face having to go through that again.

Next day they set off into Wales. They'd decided to stay overnight, and were in luck when they 'phoned the hotel they'd previously stayed at and were told they had a room free.

They spent the day looking round the two houses which were now almost completed. Martin told them that both had now been sold, Naomi's sister and her husband having paid the deposit on Plot 3.

They also had a quick look at Havergill as well, but it looked no different from the last time he'd seen it, save for the new garage built at the side. It now had a 'For Sale' sign displayed prominently at the roadside.

They'd left the car at the entrance and walked up to look at the house, but as they were about to get in and drive round to the cottage, a woman drew up in front of them and got out. She smiled as she came over to the passenger side of the car, and Connie wound down her window, a quizzical look on her face. She knew nobody round here, and wondered why she wanted to speak to them, as she bent down and leaned in. Riley didn't at first recognise her, until she introduced herself.

'Remember me?' she smiled brightly towards him, after giving Connie a brief nod of acknowledgment.

He shook his head. She was vaguely familiar but he just couldn't place her.

'No . . . sorry,' he said.

'Nell Radcliffe,' she said by way of explanation. 'My father-in-law owns the farm next door – Rosehill.'

'Oh, I'm so sorry,' he blustered. 'I should have remembered. What can we do for you?'

'It's my father-in-law! He's in his 80's now and he's going downhill fast. He may not have much longer to live. He'd like to speak to you about your family. He needs to tell you something about the past – something he's kept secret for years, and not even my boys know. He wants me to arrange a get-together if possible so he can tell you all together.'

'Of course,' Riley said, 'We're going home tomorrow, but perhaps we could see him before we leave if that's convenient.'

'I don't see why it shouldn't be,' she answered. 'It's Sunday and my boys will be free then as well. They work hard all week, so they always like to try and keep Sunday free for some relaxation, although they still have the animals to see to. Would twelve o'clock be all right, and I'll make us all some sandwiches. I have a nice fruit cake that I baked yesterday. I'm sure we'd all enjoy a slice of that.'

They were both intrigued by what the old man might have to tell them; Riley already having realised that there were many questions still to be answered.

They carried on to visit the cottage after that, finding the only way for vehicular access was by a narrow unmade lane leading to a farm; the rooftops of which were just visible in the distance.

Since Charles had given up driving and sold his car, the only person who visited him now was his son, and the track down to the cottage had become rather overgrown. They left the car just inside the entrance, where the ground showed signs of his son's car having parked.

The track from here carried on slightly downhill, and after they'd passed the first few bushes alongside, a small stream suddenly came into view on their left. It wasn't much more than two metres wide, but it cascaded over rocks where it created splashing and gurgling sounds as it continued on alongside the track until just before the cottage. Here it turned away towards their left, and was obviously making its way to join the river beyond.

Charles Farmer was outside when they arrived; sitting on a wooden bench alongside the front door; his pipe in his mouth and a newspaper held up in front of him.

Something alerted him to their presence and he dropped it down as they appeared.

'Come to view the house, have you?' he queried. 'The estate agents didn't say you were coming.'

'No,' Riley quickly put him right. 'I'm Riley Duncan, the owner of this land. Don't you remember me coming to see you some time ago?'

'Course I do! Didn't recognise you for a minute! Come on in!'

He got up from the seat rather arthritically and pushed open the front door, where he showed them into the living room.

'I take it this is your good lady wife?' he queried, as Connie smiled back at him and nodded.

'Would you like some tea?' he said to her, and then turning to Riley he continued, 'I seem to remember you prefer beer!'

Riley grinned and nodded.

'Nothing wrong with your memory is there?'

'Yeh, nothing wrong with my memory; although I must admit I do often forget things for short periods these days – like going into a room to fetch something, and then not being able to remember what I went there for in the first place. I get so annoyed with myself at times!'

Connie laughed.

'You don't have to be old for that to happen! I do it all the time myself!'

Charles left them then to fetch the drinks and Connie looked around the room, taking in its size and the inglenook fireplace with the inset stove. It was big enough to house a three piece suite and a table under the window with four chairs around it, as well as a small sideboard against the far wall. From this, she deduced there were probably only that one room and the kitchen downstairs; the rest of the ground floor comprising just a hallway and the stairs.

'Not very big, is it?' she whispered to Riley.

'Big enough for two people though – and very warm and cosy in the winter, I should imagine,' he whispered back. She frowned. He was trying to persuade her into taking an interest now – she knew the signs only too well.

Just at that moment, Charles returned with the drinks and a plate of biscuits, where he set them down on the table. As he handed Connie the cup and saucer, his hand trembled and he slopped it into the saucer.

'Damn!' he said, 'That's the trouble with growing old! Can't control my body either – that's growing older much faster than my brain! I'll go and fetch a cloth.'

'No, you sit down,' Connie said immediately, 'I'll go and get it. Is it by the sink?'

He nodded and put Riley's beer onto the small table next to his chair, while he collapsed into his usual armchair by the fireplace.

In the kitchen, Connie found it was much bigger than she'd expected, and stretched right across the back of the house, with a table and chairs under another window at the far end. There was a good view too from the window over the sink, with far reaching views over the back garden, and out across the river to the fields beyond.

Returning with the cloth, she noted another door at the bottom of the stairs, previously hidden from their view by the open front door.

There must be another room backing onto the kitchen as well – probably one having previously been used for another purpose – possibly a dining room and probably now superseded by the tables in the kitchen and the living room.

She wiped up the tea and returned the cloth to the kitchen. The tea, being in a teacup, was tepid when she finally managed to drink it.

Charles obviously thought they had more than a passing interest in their visit, and offered to show them upstairs before they left, but Connie quickly declined. She wanted to quash any ideas Riley may have of moving here. It was a lovely house, and could be made much more of with some updating and some fresh paintwork. The views all around would be magnificent too when the rest of the building and landscaping work had been completed, but it wasn't for her! A holiday home – yes – a permanent home – no!

Charles was continuing with the sales pitch.

'There are three bedrooms upstairs, but I use the dining room as a bedroom now,' he said, indicating the door at the bottom of the stairs, but not offering to show them inside. 'I'm afraid the house was built without a bathroom. Nobody had one when this place was built, but I added one on when I moved in. It's just off the kitchen, and the main bedroom has a small toilet and washbasin installed in one corner of the room. I suppose you'd call it an en suite these days. It's not very big, but it serves its purpose when you have to go to the toilet as often as I do during the night.' Connie laughed. She was well used to the ways of the elderly, and the incontinence they often suffered at night!

Making their excuses, she declined his offer to see the bedrooms and told him they'd have to be going, making her feelings quite plain to Riley. There was no way he was going to talk her into buying this place, or of living here!

CHAPTER 30

Martin and Kate joined them for dinner that night at the hotel, where Riley added the cost to that of the hotel room, and Martin thought it was time to impart some good news to them both before they left.

'Seeing as how three houses have now been sold and I have some capital in the bank, I've decided to release some of your share to you.'

Riley looked at him.

Their agreement state that he'd get his share of the profits after each house was sold, but he'd waived that verbally in order that Martin would have enough money to keep on with the building work. He wasn't short of money, and he didn't want Martin running out of capital before he'd finished. He was only too glad to have the responsibility of the property taken out of his hands and he was quite prepared to wait.

'I've already spoken to the solicitor, and he's agreed to release £50,000 to you next week. He's sending the documents over to your solicitor next week, together with a statement of account, and once you've signed and returned them, the money will be transferred into your bank account.'

Riley was overjoyed with the news and they both thanked him profusely.

'Have yourselves a decent holiday as soon as you can,' Martin said. 'It's been a long hard slog for all of us getting this far, but I'm glad everything's beginning to turn out well. I don't mind telling you, I've had some sleepless nights myself wondering if I'd done the right thing in taking on such a big commitment, and I'm sure you have too. You'll be glad to get this place off your hands for good, I shouldn't wonder.'

He didn't know how right he was! He took Martin's hand and shook it in gratitude as he stood up from the table.

'Well, I think it's time we made a move,' Martin was now saying. 'Kate's still not entirely over her ordeal yet, so I'd like to get her home. Thank you once again for the meal, and also for believing in me. Only two more houses to build, then we're home and dry. Even if they take more time to sell, I'll have enough money in the bank to keep me going for a while yet, and I've already got my eye on another piece of land near Talacre in Flintshire. The farmer who owns it is anxious to get together some cash, and if I can obtain planning permission, it'll be the perfect place for another two detached houses. They'll both overlook the sea and be very close to the beach. I'm sure there'll be no problem selling them, and I'll be building them along similar lines to Havergill, and with a similar price tag.'

Reaching their room that night, Connie could see that Riley had something on his mind, but she was tired and decided not to pursue it for the time being. They could probably talk in the morning before they left, or even on the drive home, but Riley was intent on speaking to her now.

As they lay in bed, he brought the conversation round to the cottage again.

'Do I take you're not interested in buying the cottage then?'

It was just an exploratory question, but she jumped in straight away, anxious to nip the idea in the bud.

'No, definitely not! I'm happy where I am, and I have loads of friends and acquaintances at work. I'd have to give all that up if we moved to the cottage, and I don't think I could live in such an isolated spot for very long either.'

'Then I've had another thought,' he persisted, trying to pacify her. 'How about we use the money Martin's giving me to put a deposit on the cottage and use it as a holiday home. We could let it out when we're not there and keep it for our own use when we're able to get away; that way it'd bring in enough income to pay a small mortgage until I have the money from the sale of the other houses to pay it off.'

There was silence between them while she thought about it.

He was intent on keeping a hold on the land his ancestors had worked so hard for, and she couldn't condemn him for that. The idea was certainly appealing, and it would make a nice little bolthole for holidays – but could they really afford it?

There wasn't just the purchase to consider. They'd have to pay an agent to market the holiday lettings, and then there was the consideration of it being so far away. It would mean regular trips to make sure everything was in order – and they'd need to find somebody reliable to clean it between tenancies. She couldn't contemplate travelling there every weekend to do the job herself. She worked hard enough at her own job without having to spend every weekend cleaning the cottage as well.

'I don't know, I'll have to think about it, but I'm too tired now. Let me give it some thought and we'll talk about it tomorrow,' she answered.

She knew he was excited and anxious to hear what Aled was going to tell them tomorrow – perhaps the problem of the cottage would go out of his head altogether by then.

Soon she fell asleep. Riley heard her breathing change as she drifted off, but he couldn't sleep himself. His mind was too full of all the possibilities tomorrow could bring, and it was well after 2a.m. before he finally fell asleep.

Noises in the corridor outside awoke Connie just before eight o'clock, as the hustle and bustle of a busy hotel came to life at the beginning of another day. Riley was still sleeping soundly, but she had to wake him – they finished serving breakfast at nine, and they didn't want to miss it.

He didn't mention the topic from last night as he showered and shaved before they made their way down to breakfast, but he was quiet and seemed thoughtful while they were eating.

They had to vacate the room by midday, so afterwards they went straight upstairs and packed their case, taking it down to the car and paying their bill.

It was still too early to leave for Rosehill Farm, and so they took a quiet stroll through the grounds, sitting on a convenient bench and looking out across the gardens. There was a fountain playing over an ornamental lily pond in the middle of the lawn, and she knew something was on his mind as they sat in silence watching the myriad of colours created by the sunlight dancing off the plumes of spray.

Suddenly he spoke, his voice sounding loud in the almost deserted garden.

'Have you thought over what we talked about last night?'

'Yes, I've thought about it, but I haven't made a decision yet. There's a lot to think about,' she answered, instinctively knowing this was what was on his mind.

'Like what?' He was still looking straight ahead, but his tone was slightly aggressive.

She started to pour out all the problems they could encounter by taking on a holiday cottage, as she realised he'd been looking at the whole prospect through rose tinted glasses. He obviously hadn't considered the problems they could encounter, and what was involved in taking on such a commitment.

He was quiet when she'd finished, and they sat in silence before he finally said, 'It's time we were making tracks to Rosehill. We don't want to be late after Nell going to all the trouble of making us some lunch.'

They'd only eaten poached eggs on toast for breakfast, and she was beginning to feel peckish again.

She hoped he'd taken in all she'd said about the drawbacks of running a holiday let, and she hoped this would be the last she'd hear of it.

CHAPTER 31

The back door to Rosehill Farm was open when they parked in the yard, and Nell, having seen them arrive through the kitchen window, came out to greet them.

'Come in,' she said, going straight to Connie and hugging her like a long lost friend. 'I'm so glad you could make it. This has been a weight on Aled's shoulders for so many years. He'll die a happy man if he can ease the burden today.'

Both of them were anxious to know what family secrets were about to be revealed, but Nell turned on her heel and walked back to the kitchen without saying another word.

She showed them straight into Aled's room where he was sitting up in bed, wearing a warm dressing gown over his pyjamas, and with several pillows heaped up behind him.

He looked very much more aged than the last time they'd seen him, and the contours of his face seemed to have shrunken, leaving them cadaver like, but his eyes were still bright and his smile was genuine.

'Glad to see you, lad,' he said, lifting his hand from the bed to shake Riley's, 'and you too, cariad,' to Connie.

His skin was now paper thin, and all the bones and veins stood out in stark relief.

She bent down and gave him a wary hug. She wasn't sure how weak he was, and whether it was just the pillows that were holding him upright.

'Lads'll be in soon,' Nell called from the kitchen where she was making tea for them all. 'They're just finishing up in the yard.'

They made small talk as they all sat around waiting for them, during which time Aled informed them that Nell knew what he had to say, but that the boys had no idea as yet. Nell would help him if he got stuck over anything. Her memory was much fresher than his, although what she knew was only second hand.

The boys arrived back soon afterwards, and they still had to wait while they showered and changed, by which time Riley was on tenterhooks, eager to hear what the old man had to say.

Once they were all settled, Nell brought in the sandwiches and cake and made them all a fresh mug of tea before Aled was ready to begin.

'Is everybody ready?' he asked.

They all nodded or made noises of assent, while Nell moved round to sit on the edge of the bed alongside the old man. She looked more as if she were helping to prop him up, rather than helping with his story.

'Firstly, you're all aware of Samuel Havers and who he was, but I want to go back a generation to his father, Jacob Havers. He was the one who bought Havergill in the first place, and at that time this farm formed part of the estate. My grandfather was one of his tenant farmers, and he bought it from Jacob just before his death in 1928, at the untimely age of just 58.

Samuel, as the eldest and only son, inherited the estate after he died. He was already married to Mary by then, who, it may surprise you to know, was my fathers' cousin. So, in a very tentative way, you are also part of my family as well as Samuel's,' he said, looking directly at Riley before continuing.

Riley knew that one was going to take some thinking about, but that could wait, for the time being he wanted to hear more of Aled's story.

'Samuel was always a cantankerous old bugger – pardon my expression – but it comes from the heart after knowing the man for so many years.

As you already know, their first two children, both boys, died in infancy, and their third child, Bernard, died when he was only 15.

Word around the village at the time was that Samuel had had some kind of altercation with the young teenager, and was angry that he'd stood up to him over something. We heard that there'd been a tussle and Bernard had been pushed into the river, but Samuel strode off and left him to get out by himself. He returned home alone, saying the lad had gone off in a strop.

Bernard's body was found washed up on the riverbank further downstream two days later!

After that, Mary had an affair with a local landowner, the only person who'd shown her any affection over the last few years, and the result was another child. She was terrified Samuel would find out that the child wasn't his, but whether he did or not, he brought her up as part of his family. He wasn't happy that the baby was a girl, and he treated her pretty badly, bundling her off to boarding school as soon as he was able. We always thought he knew she wasn't his.

Another girl was born three years later - that was your grandmother, Emily, but although he was disappointed once again in having another girl child, he treated her a lot better than Emma.

By this time, the man was growing more and more frustrated that Mary wasn't giving him a son. Their relationship was only just bearable by this time, and my father kept trying to get her to leave him, but she was too terrified of what Samuel would do if he found her, and she wouldn't leave her children. He treated her more as his property than his wife.

Finally, when she was almost at the end of her childbearing age, she presented him with a son – your great uncle Isaac – the man you've inherited the property from.

Samuel idolised the son he'd waited so long for, treating Mary more as a nanny for the child rather than as a wife. Their relationship had almost completely broken down by this time, and Mary's mental state was beginning to deteriorate rapidly, but she loved her child and took care of him with the aid of a young woman from the village.

After that there were no more children, and Samuel moved Mary out of his bed, and into the room next to the nursery.'

Here Aled seemed to run out of steam, and Nell looked concerned.

'Are you all right?' she said, leaning over him.

'I'm fine woman – don't fuss!' he said, 'but a little sip of whisky to whet the whistle wouldn't go amiss.'

She smiled indulgently and went to fetch it for him, offering to make more tea if anybody wanted it. They'd all drunk what they had while they were listening, but the food had hardly been touched, so fascinated had they been in listening to his story.

His grandsons Jack and Toby had heard tales about Samuel and Mary over the years, but now they were just beginning to come alive for them.

As for Riley, he was anxious to hear the rest of the story as well. He'd brought a small recorder with him, and had recorded everything the old man had said so far.

When they'd all had another drink and something to eat, Nell turned to Aled.

'Are you ready to go on?'

He nodded.

'I need to finish the story now. I may not be able to get you all together again before I join my beloved Amy. We were together for so long, and I'm anxious to see her again.'

None of the assembled party was big on religion; and Riley and Connie had never believed in being reunited after death, but if the old man believed in it, then who were they to contradict him as he began to speak again.

'I know you've heard the story of Emma being shut in the attic, so I'll begin there.

When she finished school, she didn't have any sort of occupation to go to, and she was at home all the time, but Samuel couldn't stand being around her. Sensing his hatred of her, she spent a lot of time outdoors. Sometimes she came here and helped around the farm, or she could often be found with the estate manager, who taught her a lot about wildlife, and she loved helping him with his job. She was particularly friendly with his daughters as well and spent a lot of her time with them.

One day she was on the riverbank with the man when Samuel caught them together. What they were doing I don't know, but she was 17 by then. They both protested they'd just been having a break and eating their lunch.

Samuel, however, was furious and laid into them both with a walking stick. When the man tried to stop him hitting Emma, Samuel pushed him violently backwards and he stumbled into the river. By the time he managed to scramble out, they were almost out of sight.

Samuel locked Emma in the attic and sacked the man immediately.

It was many months later that Mary approached my father and told him what had happened, and that Emma was still locked in the attic. Samuel seemed to have made it an excuse to keep her out of his sight, and he refused to let her out.

The only people she saw were her mother, and the maids who brought her food and took her to the bathroom.

My father was incensed when he heard that. He went straight up to the house and broke the attic door open. Luckily Samuel wasn't there or he might have killed him.

He waited while Emma got her things together and brought her here, where me and my brother moved into the same room together and she took over my room.

Samuel took it out on Mary when he heard Emma had gone, but luckily for him, he didn't touch her physically, or my father would probably have beaten him to a pulp. He was a big strong man in those days, and Samuel wouldn't have stood a chance against him.

Just after that, Emily decided to run off with a young man she'd met, and Samuel went after them, but he didn't find them. Word spread round the village that he was out to bring Emily back, and they'd both gone by the time he found out where they were living. You know the rest of the story about Emily, seeing as she was your grandmother.'

Here he stopped speaking for a moment and looked pointedly at Riley, who nodded in response. He didn't really know much about her as she'd died before he was born, but he was anxious for Aled to continue with the story. As she'd left the village, there probably wasn't anything he could tell him about where she went and who with anyway.

'As Isaac grew up,' Aled continued, 'he found his father growing more and more possessive of him, but Samuel's relationship with Mary was at an end, and they could barely stand to be in the same room together. Isaac hated the way he treated her, but there was little he could do about it, and his mother was in no fit state to live on her own anywhere. Her mental state was deteriorating rapidly, and whilst he was living at home, at least he was able to keep her under his own watchful eye.

Isaac was very fond of animals, and after sacking the estate manager, Samuel had brought in another man to oversee the estate and look after the deer. The man lived locally, and didn't need the use of the cottage, so it was left to become derelict, and Isaac took to using it as a bolthole when life at home began to get him down.

Samuel had also sold off, or rented out, a lot of the land belonging to the estate over the years, and Isaac talked him into letting him use 20 acres on the far side of the river to raise a small flock of sheep.

Knowing his son was growing restless, Samuel agreed, and he and the new man began breeding their own flock, often taking Mary with him when the weather was fine.

She was good with the animals and soon became adept at helping during lambing, but Samuel had noticed a change coming over Isaac. He seemed to be spending more and more time with their new man. Stefan was his name, and he was the son of a Polish immigrant.

Once he realised that they were forming an association, Samuel tried to get rid of the man, but there was an unholy row, and it ended with Isaac saying that if Stefan went, then he'd go too.

He was a grown man now, and he had no intention of letting Samuel dictate what he could, or couldn't do, with his life any more. Samuel, although unhappy about the situation, wasn't willing to let him go, and so let things ride for the time being, hoping that it would all come to nothing.

When Isaac was in his mid thirties, and realising Mary wasn't getting any better, he tried to persuade her to move into the cottage and live with him, but she refused, saying Samuel would never let her go, and would keep on harassing them both while she was there. She was his property and would never relinquish his hold over her, even though he didn't treat her as his wife any more.

Realising he was getting nowhere with her and that she'd never leave his father, he eventually decided it was time to leave. He had a life to lead, and that life was with Stefan, and no longer with his cantankerous father and piteous mother.

One day, when Samuel returned from work, he'd gone. Taken all his things and didn't even leave a note.

Samuel never ever did know where they'd gone, but he blamed Mary for colluding with him, and for letting his precious son leave home without a word. In a fit of anger, he had her admitted to a care home, where he paid for her keep, but never ever visited her.

She'd been there almost two years before my father found out, and, in a fit of anger he marched up to the house to have it out with Samuel.

Seeing how angry he was, I decided to follow him. He was a big strong man, and I didn't want him doing anything stupid.

Samuel was upstairs in his bedroom when we arrived, and my father bounded up the stairs to have it out with him.

An angry outburst broke out between them, and Samuel marched out of the room, where I was standing at the bottom of the stairs. He turned and confronted my father who was following him, bellowing like an enraged bull.

Angry words were exchanged between them, and as Samuel turned to walk away again, my father grabbed him by the back of his shirt and threw him against the wall.

It was Samuel who threw the first punch, and soon they were rolling around; punching and kicking each other. Samuel was getting the worst of it and his face was bloodied and battered from my father's big fists. He may have been an elderly man, but he still had plenty of fight left in him and he wasn't ready to give up.

As he managed to stand up, he aimed a vicious kick at my father, which caught him in the shin and angered him even more. He regained his balance and grabbed Samuel by the back of his shirt and the seat of his pants, and threw him bodily down the stairs.

He fell from top to bottom, and didn't move again!

I was in the hallway, and ran over to check the man; but it was obvious that he was already dead. His head was at an odd angle and he wasn't breathing. He'd obviously broken his neck in the fall.

My father was so shocked by the outcome of what he'd done that he just stood staring, not knowing what to do.

At the time, Samuel employed three servants in the house; a cook who prepared his meals when he returned from work and left as soon as she'd washed up; an ex-army manservant who looked after his clothes and anything else a manservant does for his master, and a lady who cleaned during the day while he was out. Luckily all three had gone home before that, and Samuel was alone in the house.

Apart from me and my father, nobody else knew what had happened.

There was no central heating in the house, and all the rooms were heated by coal fires, but a gas heater stood in the hallway alongside the staircase. It did little to heat such a big area, but at least it kept the chill off.

Not far from it was the doorway to the drawing room, and alongside that was a heavy curtain they drew across in the winter to keep out the draughts.

It seemed the answer to a prayer!

It was on casters, and so I pushed it towards the curtain, as if Samuel had knocked it there during his fall. It wasn't long before it began to smoulder and finally burst into flames. Shortly afterwards, the wood panelling began to blister and catch light. It seemed to be ages before it caught properly, but once it had, the flames began to spread along the hallway and up towards the ceiling. They were soon licking against the sides of the staircase and it wouldn't be long before that caught alight too.

My father had now come out of his daze and joined me, being careful to step around Samuel's body as he reached the bottom. He was very scared when he saw he'd killed the man, but I explained that if his body burned in the wreckage, nobody would know he hadn't fallen down the stairs by accident and knocked the heater when he landed. After the fire, there'd be nothing left of his flesh to indicate the cuts and bruises.

As the fire was now burning intensely, we both got outside as quickly as possible, closing the door behind us so as not to indicate anybody else had been in the house with him.

We waited for almost an hour, watching the flames grow and finally start to engulf the roof, before we went back to the farm and rang the fire brigade. We said we'd smelled smoke and when it began to drift towards the farm, we'd gone to investigate, finding Havergill well alight.

We told them Samuel was living alone and was the only one likely to be there at that time of night.'

Aled's voice was becoming weaker, and he finally stopped speaking as silence followed his last words. He seemed to be slipping into a doze, but they were full of questions; one that Riley was particularly anxious to have an answer to, but as he opened his mouth to speak, Nell raised her eyes and shook her head.

'Let's leave him to sleep for a bit. We'll give him a couple of hours if you've time. He probably has more to say.'

It wasn't yet three o'clock, so Riley and Connie both agreed they had the time to wait. It would only take around an hour to get home, and they had no plans for the rest of the day.

Going out into the afternoon sunshine, Nell opened a couple of bottles of her homemade elderflower wine, and brought out some more fruit cake, where they all sat round the wooden picnic table to enjoy the refreshments.

'Good job I decided to make two wasn't it?' she said, as they all tucked in again.

She answered some of the questions they asked of her, but the more probing ones she wanted to leave for Aled, saying he'd be refreshed and ready to begin again after his nap. He usually took an afternoon nap at this time anyway.

Toby and Jack left to milk the cows at four o'clock, and Nell decided to leave waking Aled until their return, to which Riley and Connie agreed.

She walked them round the farm, and they stood watching the boys milking for a while, having another mug of tea while Toby and Jack washed and changed again.

When they joined them, Nell went back into the house to check on Aled, finding he was awake and ready to finish the story. He was anxious to get it told before everybody had to leave.

They found him drinking a mug of tea, holding it in his claw-like hands while Nell sat next to him in case he couldn't manage to hold it properly.

He smiled when they trooped in, and Connie noticed that his face was drooping slightly on one side. He must have had a small stroke recently as well, and she realised there was every possibility of him having another in the near future.

'Sorry about that,' he said, his voice firmer and louder now. 'The perils of growing old I'm afraid! Haven't got the stamina I once had!'

The boys soon joined them, and Aled took up where he'd left off.

'After the fire was put out, the police were called to the scene, but they were happy that Samuel's death had been an accident, and as I'd hoped, they concluded that the heater had caused the fire.

Once it was all over and done with, and we had a Death Certificate for Samuel, my father went to the nursing home and brought Mary home. They weren't willing to keep her there anyway, seeing as nobody was paying the bills any more.

She was glad to be back, and she improved no end when she was with familiar and friendly faces once again, but she never ever asked about Samuel after she was told he was dead. I think she was rather glad he was gone, and she wasn't living in his shadow anymore.'

Here he paused again, and Nell took up the thread for a while.

'I got on well with Mary, even though she was older than me, and she lived here for another two years before she died.'

Riley had a pressing question burning in his mind, and he was bursting to ask it.

'But what happened to Emma. You said she was locked in the attic for months, and then she came to live here. What happened to her after that? I've searched for a death record for her, but I can't find one. Is she still alive?'

Nell looked to Aled and he nodded to her before taking up the thread again. This was his part of the story to tell.

'Sadly, she's not still alive, she died three years ago, and her name wasn't Emma then – it was Amy! You'll find the record of her death under Amy Jackson!'

Riley and Connie exchanged looks, just as Jack broke in.

'You mean Grandma Amy was actually Emma Havers?'

Aled nodded.

'Got it in one! When we managed to get her out of the attic room, we knew, even though Samuel had never wanted her, she was one of his possessions and he'd never give her up without a fight.

When she came to live here, we changed everything about her. She always wore her hair in a long plait that fell below her shoulder blades, so we cut it very short and dyed it a different colour. Then we set about keeping her well away from the boundaries with Samuel's land so that if he did see her, it would only be from a distance, and we changed her usual skirts and blouses for jeans and sloppy sweaters.

He may have suspected she was here, but if he did see her, she wouldn't look anything like the Emma he'd once known.

We grew very fond of each other while she was living here, and she changed her name by Deed Poll. After my father died, I took over the farm and we lived here as man and wife, but we never did marry. It just never seemed necessary, and we only ever had the one child.'

Looking pointedly at Jack and Toby he said, 'That was your father!'

Now he was growing tired again, and Nell shooed them all out before going back and settling the old man more comfortably.

There were still questions Riley wanted to ask – one in particular that was niggling at him, and just before they left, he asked Nell to see if she could answer it.

'Several people seem to have heard a violin playing around the grounds of Havergill. Some of them seem to think there's a ghost attached to the house. Do you know anything about it?'

She laughed.

'Well, I've heard it called some things, but never a ghost before.'

He looked at her, puzzled, prompting her to explain.

'Mary was the great violin player. She'd learned as a child and she was good at it. She taught Emma to play it while she was locked in the attic, and when she came here to live with us, Aled bought her another. I took an interest as well, and she taught me to play in my spare time, but I'm afraid I never mastered it as well as Amy. Aled and the boys hated the sound of it, so I started going out into the woods to practise. They're behind the old house and it's quiet and peaceful out there. I can play to my hearts' content without disturbing anyone, but I'm still not very good at it. It was probably me they've heard.'

Riley accepted the explanation, but he wasn't so sure it was right. From what he'd heard, everybody who'd heard it said it was a quiet ghostly sound drifting in the air and stopping immediately they'd tried to listen for it, however, he didn't try to contradict her and they left for home shortly afterwards.

Two weeks later, Nell rang to tell them that Aled had slipped away in his sleep, and when she'd found him in the morning, he looked totally at peace with the world.

He would have finally closed his eyes on the world thinking that he was about to join his beloved Amy once more!

CHAPTER 32

It was several months later before Martin completed the last of the five houses he'd been allowed planning permission for. The sales of Plots 2 and 3 had been completed and they were now being occupied; but Havergill still remained unsold. The mortgage company who'd repossessed the property had put it up for sale at a much reduced price from that which it had originally been sold for, but so far there'd been no takers.

'It's jinxed that place, I reckon,' Martin remarked to Riley on one of his rare visits. 'I'm only glad we managed to find a buyer so quickly and it's not our responsibility any more. I put all the expertise and knowledge I had into the building of that place, but perhaps I was fulfilling my own ambitions instead of building an ordinary family home. It's far too large for most people, and those with families big enough to fill it haven't got that sort of money to spend on a home in the first place, never mind paying for its upkeep.'

Riley had to agree with him. He was probably right, although the reduced price might, and probably would, attract somebody in the end. They'd probably never know what a bargain they were getting!

The last house to be completed was at the very far side of the land, and had been built between the woods and the lane which ran towards the cottage where Charles Farmer had lived. It was also the smallest of all the houses, with only three bedrooms, but it still had an acre of land attached to it, and its driveway led straight out onto the road. It was already attracting quite a bit of interest.

Charles had already moved out and was now living with his son and daughter-in-law, but the cottage remained unsold. It would make a warm and cosy home for someone, with plenty of open ground for the kids to run around in – but perhaps it was just that that was precluding its sale. It was quite a way from the road, and as there was no bus service to speak of, it would mean every school journey, and also that to the shops, would have to be undertaken by car.

Riley had brought the subject up with Connie several times about buying it, but as she still kept saying she needed more time to think, he'd now come to the conclusion that her answer was ultimately going to be no. If she'd wanted to live there, she'd have been only too keen to snap it up immediately. It wasn't that she didn't like the cottage; just that she didn't want to live in such a remote spot, and she didn't want the responsibility of owning a holiday cottage either.

Eventually he'd dropped the subject, realising that they were comfortable enough where they were; and it would mean starting all over again with her having to find a new job, and him having to find new clients. They were both approaching their forties, and perhaps they would be happier just staying put – after all, he'd soon have the rest of the money from his agreement with Martin, and then they'd be able to afford holidays to more exotic and exciting places in the future. Perhaps they'd even be able to move to a bigger house – somewhere detached and with more privacy, but did they really need somewhere bigger? They were both happy where they were. He wondered whether a move and all the upheaval it would cause was really necessary? Perhaps Connie was right. Perhaps they were better off staying in the warm and cosy little home they'd created together.

Jess was still living in the farmhouse, and still trying to eke out the small amount of money she had left. She didn't know how much it would cost to have the electric switched back on, but if she made any inquiries, it might bring to light a large unpaid bill. Once they knew somebody was living in the house, they'd probably pursue her for it. It would mean a cold hard winter for her, but she'd have to tough it out. At least she had a roof over her head and there were plenty of candles and matches in the pantry! Who knows, she might be able to find a job to keep her head above water, but she'd had no luck so far, and prostitution wasn't a qualification for any job she knew of.

She'd been into Denbigh that afternoon for some essentials. She'd visited all the shops she knew displayed postcards for jobs in their windows, but there were none she was qualified for, except for two that were asking for part-time shop workers. She'd never done shop work before, but decided she'd apply anyway. How hard could it be? She'd always been a quick learner, and with that in mind, she put £5 of credit on her mobile 'phone, intending to ring when she arrived home.

It was quiet when she got back and she'd bought a reduced price sandwich for her evening meal. She'd have to make do with that and a tin of soup from the pantry. It seemed a long time since she'd eaten a proper meal, and she longed for even one single portion of fish and chips. When browsing the supermarket for bargains one evening, she'd passed the chip shop on the way back to her car. It smelt delicious, and her stomach rumbled at the prospect, but she only had 20p left in her purse.

As she passed the alley alongside the shop, there was a man rummaging in the bins. She watched as he brought out a plastic bag full of scraps, and wondered how long it'd be before she was forced to stoop to that level. Please God she'd find a job before she was forced to those lengths.

There was still a good amount of coal in the shed, which she hadn't used much of so far, using up the logs that were already there and well dried.

Most of her days she spent walking the woods and picking up sticks and larger logs to dry out for the winter. There was a metal wheelbarrow in the shed, and that had done duty for transporting them back, where she had a large pile already drying out.

She opened the front door and took her shopping through to the kitchen before going out to the shed to bring in more logs. Once she got the stove going, she could heat a kettle of water on top of it and make herself a drink.

It was as she was collecting the logs together that she got a prickly feeling down her spine. It was the strange feeling that she wasn't alone!

Turning to look at the door, it stood wide open and there was nobody there. She could see sunlight spilling across the grass behind her and lighting up the fields beyond, but the feeling still persisted.

Trying to shrug it off, she continued filling the wood basket she'd brought with her to carry them back, but as she went towards the door, the feeling returned.

It was as she walked out into the sunlight that a burly figure stepped into her line of vision.

'Mrs. Martello?' his deep voice queried. His words sounded more like a statement than a question.

She dropped the basket of logs and stared, seeing two uniformed police officers standing behind him.

She nodded, unable to find any words. They seemed stuck like a lump in her throat and she felt herself trembling.

'Jess Martello, I'm arresting you for conspiracy in the murder of Tim Kirkbride and Tony Warren . . .' the rest of what he said was lost in a blur.

She'd never had any idea of the lads' names who'd tried to rob her, but she knew immediately what this was all about. She'd had no idea what Sean was capable of, but by then, it was too late to try and evade the issue. She'd made her bed and now she'd have to lie on it – come rain or shine. The deed was done!

How could they have known who she was, and how had they found her in this remote spot. She'd thought she was safe and in the clear.

They took her to the police station and questioned her where she decided to confess everything. Something must have led them to her, and they probably had enough proof to convict her as well. If she confessed now, she could plead that she didn't even know Sean had a gun; didn't know what he was capable of. It might mean her getting off altogether if she could convince a jury of that, and ultimately her story was true. She **hadn't** known Sean had a gun!

It seemed that after Sean's death, a small motorbike pannier had been found at the side of the road. It contained evidence which took them to Alan Kirkbride, and also on the outside of the pannier were blood and fragments of bone belonging to Sean Martello.

After questioning, the lad had finally came clean and admitted his part in the robbery in which his brother and cousin had been killed, as well as the subsequent attack on Sean. He seemed to think that the reason for the attack was somehow mitigated by Sean's having shot two members of his family, and the old maxim of an eye for an eye was a good enough reason for his actions, but was shocked when he learned that Sean had ultimately died from his injuries. That hadn't been their intention – it had only been to give him a good pasting.

He'd also told them of following Sean to his home, the location of which they were already aware.

There was only one company in the area supplying both mini buses and limos, and it had been easy enough to tie Sean to that company. When they'd questioned the staff, they said there was no booking for either of the vehicles on the two nights in question, so Sean must have taken them out himself.

The mini-bus wasn't in the company's garage when they checked, but the limo was. It hadn't been used since Sean's death, and they impounded it immediately; handing it over to forensics. They found powder burns on the side of the rear door from where he'd fired from, and also traces of gun oil on the front passenger seat where he'd thrown it down as they made a hasty getaway.

They also knew a woman had been involved, but the description given by the porter didn't match that of Jess. When the staff were questioned, an eagle eyed waiter delivering late night sandwiches and coffee to a guest on the same floor, remembered seeing her arrive and knew which room she'd gone into.

Hotel records soon showed the occupant of the room on that night, and when questioned, he found he still had her number in his 'phone. He eagerly handed it over to police. He didn't know what it was all about, but was anxious to disassociate himself with any dealings the police might have with her.

They traced the number back to Jess, and found out that she was living in the same house as Sean, but the house had been repossessed after his death and she wasn't there anymore.

Police records soon brought to light another address for Sean – a remote farmhouse on the side of Halkyn Mountain. He'd been arrested and charged some years ago after a drunken pub brawl in which another man had sustained serious injuries, and that was the address he'd been using at the time.

They didn't know if he still owned the farm, but decided to check it out anyway – and with more success than they'd expected!

It had taken some time to fit all the pieces into the jigsaw, but with Jess and Alan Kirkbride's confessions, they had pretty watertight cases against them both.

In court, Alan was jailed for 10 years on a charge of manslaughter, but Jess's tearful rendition of her evidence, and the confession of her presence on the night, with absolutely no knowledge that Sean was carrying a gun, or that he even owned one, won the judge round. He ultimately believed her story and she didn't receive a custodial sentence. She was given a suspended one, and returned to her meagre existence in the farmhouse once more – but at least she had a roof over her head and no creditors knocking at her door!

Printed in Great Britain
by Amazon